Seriously Pucked

CHICAGO RACKETEERS
BOOK THREE

EMMA FOXX

Copyright © 2024 by Blake Wilder Books, LLC

All rights reserved.

No part of this book may be reproduced in any form or by any electronic or mechanical means, including information storage and retrieval systems, without written permission from the author, except for the use of brief quotations in a book review.

Cover Design from Qamber Designs

About The Book

Dating and falling in love is fun.

Getting serious is…well, serious.

It means real-life situations, like fathers getting sick, people you love getting injured, and…maybe worst of all…work parties with your significant others. *Shudder*.

But this is what it's like when you're in a relationship. Things aren't always rainbows and unicorns. Even if you're living and laughing with, and having hot sex every night, with three men who worship the ground you walk on. Trust me, that's *amazing*. Really amazing. I'd-probably-give-up-cookies-for-this amazing. And best of all…my men would never make me give up cookies.

But I'm having to hang on a lot tighter for this ride than I expected. Because I'm not just figuring things out with one guy. I've got *three*. And if we're seriously going to do this, then we have to figure out if we're really all in for better or worse.

Seriously Pucked

By
Emma Foxx

CHAPTER 1
Nathan

"DOES she have any idea how much you love her?" Val asks.

I look away from the spectacle of Crew proving how strong he is by carrying Danielle over one shoulder and a box of her books on the other up the front steps of our new house.

I look at Valerie instead. "Because I let her sleep with that jackass too?" I ask.

Val shakes her head. "Even more than that, this house that you bought her."

I sigh. I've been trying not to let on that I *really* do not like the new Cookie & Co. residence. But Val knows me well. And when Danielle isn't looking, I probably let my frowns show.

"Hughes and McNeill helped buy it."

Val shakes her head. "You know what I mean. The only reason *you're* here is that girl."

I watch Crew carry her through the imposing black wooden front door. Her laughter reaches me and it makes my heart squeeze the way it always does.

Val is so damn right.

Danielle Larkin is the only person on the planet that could get me to give up my penthouse apartment near the lake to live in a brownstone in Lincoln Park.

The house is nice. Very nice. The remodel we did on it took forever–or so it seemed–and cost a fortune. But it turned out… very nice.

If a little skinny. Lacking in light. With an absurd number of stairs.

It's no light-filled penthouse with floor-to-ceiling windows with a killer view of the Chicago skyline on the south side and Lake Michigan to the north.

Where I lived alone.

I already miss my doorman and concierge services and we haven't even spent a single night here.

"Danielle and Michael wanted a more homey feeling home," I tell Val. "They wanted a neighborhood and an actual house."

She nods. "They are definitely home and neighborhood types."

Yeah, they are. There had been talk about how fun it will be to have kids trick-or-treating at Halloween, and decorating at Christmas, and meeting the neighbors.

Michael and Danielle have a lot of things in common like that. It doesn't bother me. Exactly. But there are definitely moments, like when we're picking out furniture, choosing which rooms are going to be whose 'alone space' (yes, we absolutely all need our own alone space), and shopping for new dishes and towels, that I'm reminded of the ways that Michael is the perfect man for Danielle.

If she was a one-man woman, anyway.

Thank God, she's not. Thank God she loves, needs, and wants me too.

Even though she knows that the idea of meeting the neighbors gives me heartburn. Home should be a sanctuary from the outside world, not a place where I get accosted by conversation just trying to get in the damn front door.

"Val! Get in here! You gotta see the game room and the theater room!" Crew calls from the doorway. "It's fucking amazing!

Val looks up at me. She's grinning. Fucking *grinning*. Crew McNeill can make Val grin.

"He said you bought a popcorn machine. Like the ones they have at concession stands. He's told me all about the theater room with the recliners. And I believe there's a pool table, ping-pong table, and two arcade video games?"

I roll my eyes. "Three. There are three arcade video games. And I did *not* buy any of that for him. McNeill is a fucking millionaire. He bought his own toys."

"Come on, Val!" Danielle calls, poking her head under the arm Crew has braced on the doorjamb. "The recliners have *massagers* in them!"

Yeah, she also loves, wants, and needs Crew.

She's definitely not a one-man woman.

I'm thrilled she's happy. But damn, my hockey team star makes my girlfriend act like a little kid sometimes and they drive me a little nuts.

"We're not done unpacking!" I call to them. "No playing until we're done!"

Crew pulls Danielle up beside him and says something in her ear. She grins and calls out to me, "Please, Nathan? Just for a little bit? I *promise* we'll be good later."

Crew says something else to her and she laughs.

"Okay, *I'll* be good later," she says flirtatiously.

Right. She's trying to use the I'll-be-your-good-girl-Nathan to get away with something. And Crew thinks that will help *him* get away with something.

And...they're probably right.

Because I do really fucking like it when Danielle is my good girl. And I like it even more when she *owes* me for something.

Val laughs, watching my face as I grit my teeth and narrow my eyes.

"Where's Michael?" I ask.

He's a lot better at making them both behave. Because I just get frustrated. And I'm easily led around by my dick with our woman.

Michael is the more reasonable one.

"He's unpacking the kitchen," Crew says, his arm around Danielle, who he's finally allowed to stand on her own feet.

"Does he know you're fucking around and not working?" I ask.

"I mean...he probably assumes, right?" Crew asks.

I take a step closer to the brick front steps. "Let me put it this way," I finally say. "If all your shit isn't put away by bedtime tonight...you're sleeping on the couch."

Do I sound like I'm trying to lay down rules with a child? I do. And it's not entirely inaccurate.

Does it sound stupid that I'm telling a grown man where he has to sleep?

Yes. But he's assuming he's going to sleep in *my* bed...which I'll have to make, which I also hate.

I blow out a breath.

I guess it's *our* bed.

We have a big, huge-assed bed—custom made and also fucking expensive—that we're all intending to share in the biggest bedroom in the house.

We all have our own spaces when we need alone time, but now that we're sharing a house, the sleeping arrangements are...together.

All together.

Every night.

I'll admit that I've had a couple of second-thoughts.

But I can absolutely fuck Danielle in the shower, on the couch, in the kitchen...or in that damned bed by ourselves any time I want without the loneliness that comes when she stays over at Crew's or Michael's ...so it will be fine.

And it can definitely work to threaten Crew.

"Does that go for Dani too?" Crew asks. "Because she hasn't unpacked her boxes either."

"Tattle-tale," she says, poking him in the side.

He laughs and hugs her close. "You and I can cuddle up on the couch together tonight, sweet girl. Have you seen that couch?"

"I guess that's true," she says, grinning up at him as his hand goes to her ass.

Or it could *not* work to threaten Crew because everything always works out for the Golden Boy.

And I'm not sleeping in the big family bed with just Hughes.

Fucking McNeill.

The couch he bought is as absurd as the number of steps in this house. It's a giant sectional with ottomans that can move in or out to form one massive square of fabric that's roughly the size of a hockey rink. In a house that is narrow. It's like parking a jumbo jet on a helicopter pad. The math doesn't work for the space.

But Crew insisted it was the only way we could all be on the couch together comfortably and he isn't wrong. It just looks… dumb. I prefer streamlined furniture with a low profile. Sculptural. Not an oversized bean bag for four.

Ascending the many stairs, I go through the front door with a sigh. Love is hard.

"Compromise is absolutely killing you, isn't it?" Val asks.

"Slowly and surely," I tell her. "But I'll get used to it."

Danielle is worth it. Her happiness makes me happy.

Most of the time.

The living room is crammed with boxes. The movers have already left and half of these boxes should have been taken upstairs. I knew I couldn't trust Crew and his youthful knees to act as the enforcer with the movers, but I had a very important meeting I couldn't miss this morning.

I half-heartedly shift a couple of boxes around, looking for the ones labeled with my name. I spot one labeled Michael, which Crew has crossed off and written "Doc" below. Then there is one right on top that Danielle has labeled with a Sharpie, "Nathan's Bachelor Box."

"What's in here?" I ask.

Danielle, who is on the first step ready to descend into the game room, pauses and gives me an adorable smile. Her red hair is in a twisted braid that I want to tug. Just pull until she's over here in my arms, reminding me why I'm changing everything in my life for her. Okay, not *everything*, but a lot.

"Just some things I wasn't sure you'd want to keep or not. I found them in your bathroom when I was helping you pack."

I give her a little smile. "Thanks."

"And, Nathan, I *do* understand that all of this mess is making you crazy and I promise to make Crew unpack at least a few boxes tonight, okay?" she asks.

She's serious now and I remind myself that she knows all three of us well and even when she's goofing around with Crew, she respects me and Michael, and knows our limits.

"Thank you, sweet girl."

She blows me a kiss and disappears down the stairs.

Val follows her, giving me a look. "Smile, Nathan. Life is good."

Yeah, it is. I wouldn't exactly say that I'm having a blast, certainly not like my girlfriend and her other boyfriend downstairs exploring their personal arcade, but it is good. Though I can't help but shake my head when I hear a shriek of laughter drift up the stairs from Danielle.

Using my keys, I rip open the box and peer inside. There's a box of condoms, which I do *not* use with Danielle. I have the delicious freedom of going bare with her, given the exclusivity of our relationship. Don't need the condoms anymore. I set them on another box and continue digging in my so-called bachelor box.

There's a pair of panties that aren't Danielle's. I know all her underwear and this purple satin thong thing isn't her style at all. They must have been left behind by a former friend-with-benefits. Don't need those either.

Under the panties is what I've always referred to as a hospitality kit. In the past, I never wanted women touching my personal stuff, so I had unopened toothbrushes, makeup wipes, deodorant, and sleep T-shirts for 'guests'.

Unneeded and unwanted now.

Danielle can touch whatever she wants of mine.

I put everything back in the box and head through the open concept main floor into the kitchen, past Michael, who is unpacking his spices, and out the back door. I toss the entire box into the garbage can, feeling a whole lot better about this living arrangement.

"You good, Boss?" Michael says when I come back in and look around the kitchen.

The bar isn't unpacked yet, but I spot my bourbon sitting on the built-in buffet. I unstop it, lift the whole bottle to my lips, and take a full finger of rye right down the gullet.

It burns, but I shake my head a little and tell Hughes, "Never been better."

"We probably should have hired someone to make up the bed and unpack for Crew," Michael says.

"I'm texting my assistant to do that right now." My fingers are flying over my phone.

"Good plan." Michael sets his olive oil by the stove. "It is a nice house. I love this kitchen. The copper hood is a piece of art, man."

"It is." It was Michael's one personal request, that he have a custom hood designed. Crew gets his hot tub and a game room.

I hear Danielle's laughter drift up from the basement and I feel my lips curl in spite of myself.

Danielle. That's what I got. Plus, two new best friends.

That's all I really need.

CHAPTER 2
Crew

"WE'RE LEAVING!" Michael calls down the steps.

"That means you have two hours to get your stuff unpacked!" Nathan yells.

I grin. Michael and Nathan have to head up to the arena for meetings. Val has to go, too, since she's Nathan's assistant.

That leaves me and Dani here at home alone.

And I know Hughes and Armstrong are both smarter than to think I'm going to spend that time unpacking any stupid boxes.

"Don't hurry home!" I yell back.

"Don't spend the entire time naked!" Michael replies.

I just grin. Dani looks over at me, eyebrows up, but also grinning.

We're in our gaming recliners, screwing around with our new video game system. It's amazing. The biggest screen I've ever had.

I'm teaching Dani the rules of the racing game and enjoying how frustrated she gets with how fucking bad she is at it. I'm giving her one more lesson and then I'm turning this into strip racing. Every time I pass her on the course, she has to take off a piece of clothing.

Of course, she's only in pants and a T-shirt and since we're at home and she's very obedient about the no-panties-at-home rule, it won't take long to get her naked. And once she's naked, I won't give a fuck about my big screen anymore.

No, I don't have to play games to get her naked, but it *is* a really fun way to do it. I love playing around with her. She's the best sex I've ever had, but she's also the most fun I've ever had. She's my best friend. The one I love to be silly with, the one I love to cuddle with, the one I love to make laugh, the one I love to share all my dreams and fears with. Because even though I can be goofier with her than any other girl ever, she always makes me feel loved. I can never be too ridiculous, or too sappy, or too messy, or too vulnerable with her. She always loves me no matter what.

"Crew!" Nathan yells down the stairs. "Do we need to bring Danielle with us? Or will you actually get something done if she stays here with you?"

"Oh, I'm going to get something done," I promise, looking over at my girl and waggling my eyebrows.

Dani giggles.

God, I fucking love her giggles. Maybe we'll play some hide-and-seek. Or tag. I love to chase her.

It's not like I have to wait for Michael and Nathan to leave to get Dani naked. But it's definitely fun to feel like we're getting away with something.

"Crew!" Nathan barks.

"What? You're messing up my concentration, Boss!" I yell back, playing the part of the petulant child that I know makes Nathan nuts.

"Danielle," Nathan says. "Make sure he unpacks!"

She laughs again. "I'll do my best!" she calls back to him.

"You're kidding right?" I hear Michael ask Nathan.

They must both be standing at the top of the stairs.

"He'll tie her up, and stuff panties in her mouth if she tries to boss him around."

Oh, I really like that idea. I look over at Dani. Her cheeks are pink. She likes the idea too.

"Damn it, he's never going to unpack, is he?" Nathan asks.

Michael laughs. "No. You just need to close the door to his room and ignore it. Come on, we're going to be late."

I listen to their footsteps across the first floor, then the sound of the door opening and shutting.

I look over at Dani. "You wanna try to boss me around, Dani girl?" I ask, setting my game controller on the table between our recliners.

She lifts her shoulder and gives me a cute, sexy as fuck look. "Maybe."

"Try it," I say.

"Crew, you need to go upstairs right now and unpack your boxes," she says. With zero force behind her words.

"Michael unpacked more than half of *your* boxes," I point out. "You shouldn't get to tell me what to do."

"Nathan wants me to make you do it."

"And you always do everything Nathan tells you to."

The pink in her cheeks gets darker. Because she does, actually, do everything Nathan tells her to. Because she loves when he calls her a good girl and rewards her. He's very good with the rewards.

"Nathan is very…persuasive," she says.

Uh, huh. I've witnessed Nathan's type of persuasion. "Okay." I get to my feet. "Tell you what. You be persuasive with me. I bet we can get a few things unboxed."

She looks at the TV screen, then up at me. "We're done playing?"

I hold out my hand to her. "Oh, no, pretty girl. We're just getting started."

She grins and puts her game controller down. "This is going to work out really well for me." She takes my hand and I pull her out of the chair.

"How so?"

"I'm going to get you now and then when Nathan and Michael get home, they'll be so pleased with all the work I got you to do that they'll be *very* happy with me."

I reach up and cup her face. "You're fucking perfect, you know that?"

I would have never imagined falling for a woman who wanted two other men at the same time, but now I can't imagine being with anyone else in any other situation.

She beams. She absolutely soaks up our praise like a little flower in the sun.

"I love you so damned much," I tell her.

"I love you too." She gives me that sweet smile that's all mine.

She has a different smile for each of us. I'm not sure she's aware of it. I'm pretty sure the other guys have noticed too, though.

"And I'm going to do my damnedest to be sure you're really fucking tired and sore before those guys get home and get all *happy* with you," I tell her.

She starts to reply but I sweep her up into my arms and she gives a little shriek before she wraps her arm around my neck and I start up the steps.

CHAPTER 3

CREW CARRIES me up to his room and sets me on top of one of the many boxes still littering the space.

I laugh. "You have a lot to do here."

His eyes rake over me. "I wouldn't say you're *a lot*. You're just right, Dani girl."

I cross my arms and shake my head. Even though I know it's fairly ineffective with this man. "You're supposed to *work*. Don't start that sexy sweet talk with me."

"It's just stuff. It doesn't really need to be unpacked."

"What about your clothes? Shouldn't those go in your dresser and closet at least? That's such a great dresser."

He looks at me thoughtfully for a moment. Then crosses to one of the boxes labeled with his name, rips open the top, and dumps the contents on the floor. It's a collection of T-shirts, shorts and socks. There doesn't seem to be any specific organization to what he threw in the box, though.

He scoops up an armful of T-shirts, turns and walks to his dresser, pulls open a drawer, and dumps them in.

He closes it and turns to look at me. "There. What do I get for doing that?"

I lift a brow, trying to look stern. I know it fails. I'm not really the stern type anyway, and this is Crew. No way can I be stern with him. He's my…sexy playmate. He's fun, and he can make me laugh no matter what's going on. Nathan makes me feel protected. Michael makes me feel adored. Crew makes me feel *comforted*.

They're all home to me in different ways. Crew is like putting on my softest, favorite pajamas, and vegging out in front of my favorite movie with my favorite snacks. I can't imagine ever actually being angry at him. Annoyed, maybe sometimes. But even then, I find him adorable.

Which is a problem because he knows it.

I give him a tiny frown and shake my head. "That's hardly anything. You don't get a reward for that. How about *all* the boxes of clothes?"

He sighs as if he's very put upon, goes over and scoops up the rest of the clothes then dumps them unceremoniously into another drawer.

Then he turns. "Lose the shirt."

I think about arguing with him, but then wonder why. I want to be naked with him. And he did at least unpack one box. I can tell Nathan that I was successful in getting one of Crew's boxes emptied. So I strip my T-shirt over my head.

He gives me a little smirk. "I like how this is going so far."

"Do another box."

He crosses to another box, rips the strip of tape off the top and tosses it aside. He looks inside. Then he dumps it out. It's a bunch of miscellaneous knickknacks. There are some framed photos, some hockey pucks—of course—a baseball, and a couple of books.

He picks up as many things as he can carry, steps into his closet, and deposits them on the top shelf.

"Crew," I laugh. "Don't you at least want your photos out where you can see them?"

He gives a very dramatic, teenage-girl-my-life-is-so-hard sigh, grabs the four framed photographs and sets them on top of his dresser. He turns, and says, "Bra."

I'm not surprised he chose my bra instead of my pants. We both know there's nothing under these pants and once those are gone, there will be no more play unpacking.

I reach back and unhook my bra and drop it onto the floor.

He takes a little longer drinking me in now. It amazes me how my men always react to my naked body. They've all seen me naked so many times, and in so many positions, in so many dirty situations, but they all act as if every time is the first time.

My nipples bead and goosebumps break out over my body.

"One more box, Dani girl," he says.

He goes to one of the smaller ones, opens it, carries the whole box to his dresser and dumps underwear and socks into the top drawer.

"Lose them," he says, turning to me.

Obviously, he means my pants. I stand and slide them down my legs.

His eyes darken. He licks his lips as he steps toward me. Then hoists me over his shoulder.

"Crew? Where are we going?"

It doesn't matter to me. I intend to have sex with my men in every single room of this house. On any surface that will support us.

"Our bedroom," he said simply.

And I know exactly what he means. The room that we're going to share with Nathan and Michael. Michael, Crew, and I each have our private spaces. I have a cute reading room with a cozy loveseat, tall lamp, and tons of bookcases, along with my own bathroom with a huge bathtub and a walk-in closet.

But when it comes to *bedtime,* we're going to all be together in the gigantic master bedroom in the custom-made bed.

"Nathan will not be happy if we christen the bed without him," I say.

Crew chuckles. "Exactly."

He tosses me onto the bed and goes to the bedside table. I watch him, curious. That normally holds a few toys for me and lube.

He turns to face me, running a bright pink silk tie back and forth between his hands.

"What's going on?" I ask, my breathing getting faster.

"You were bossy."

Michael's words come back to me—*he'll tie her up, and stuff her panties in her mouth if she tries to boss him around.*

I'm not wearing any panties. Of course, there might be some mixed in with Nathan's things in his dresser. They'd be easy enough to find if Crew wanted to muffle my sounds.

But sure enough, he kneels with one knee on the mattress, reaches for my wrists and pulls them up over my head. He loops the silk tie around my wrists and then fastens them to the headboard.

I know that the guys ordered a headboard like this specifically for this purpose.

He does it all before it even occurs to me to fight him, or argue.

After I'm restrained I tug on the ties. "Crew?"

He grins down at me and brushes my hair back away from my face. "I know I'm the easiest one for you, pretty girl. But you also know that sometimes I like taking control."

Yes he does. They all do. They just do it in different ways.

"So right now, right here, you're all mine."

I love when we're all together, but I also love my one-on-one time with each of my guys.

I pretend to fight, tugging on the ties. "Crew, let me touch you."

"Nope. I'm going to make you squirm. And beg."

He sheds his clothes, which is totally unfair now that I can't touch him. I whimper. I love Crew's body. He's a professional hockey player, for fuck's sake. His body is perfection.

"I want to touch you," I pout.

"I know. That's going to make it so fun to tease you." He

crawls up onto the bed and braces his hands on either side of my head but holding his body over mine.

He leans in and kisses me deeply. His tongue strokes mine slowly and firmly. When he lifts his head he stares down at me for a long moment.

"My favorite problem every day is deciding where to start touching and tasting this body," he says gruffly. "Especially when it's just me. I don't want these pretty nipples–" He takes one between his finger and thumb, squeezing, then tugging with exactly the pressure he knows I love. "–to be aching while I have my tongue buried deep in your needy pussy." He skates a hand down my body, uses one big hand to pull my thighs wider, then runs a thick middle finger through my wetness before slipping it into me slowly. "And when my finger or tongue is here–" He thrusts in and out and I try to arch closer. "–I can't give enough attention to you here–" He turns his hand and presses his thumb against my ass.

I moan. "*Crew.*"

"You're so fucking needy, sweet girl." He lowers his head, sucking on my nipple hard.

"Yes." God, I want to grab his head.

"You really do need all three of us to fill you up enough. And we–" He pumps his finger deep, adding a second. "Fucking–" His thumb slips past my tight circle of muscles. "Love it."

I cry out. "God, Crew! More!"

He takes my mouth in a deep kiss, thrusting his fingers into me

But then he pulls back. "But I'm gonna do what I can here."

I whimper at the loss of his touch. "Crew, I need–"

"Don't make me get the panties to stuff in your mouth, Dani," he warns, reaching for the bedside table drawer again. "I want to hear you calling my name and I want to kiss you while I fuck you. But you need to stop telling me what to do. I know how to fill my girl up even without Doc and Nate here."

He holds up one of the slimmer vibrators. The look on his face is cocky. And wicked. He pushes back to kneel between my legs and slides it into his mouth, getting it wet.

I squirm, pulling on the restraints, wanting to move my hands to touch him out of habit. Or touch myself. My body is on fire and I'm aching everywhere.

I have a huge, hot, dirty talking hockey player who I'm madly in love with between my thighs and I can't touch him. I'm going crazy.

He licks up and down the vibrator, his eyes on me, roaming over my body.

I lift a foot, deciding at least I can try to push him with what I've got to work with. I try to move around his hips to drag even a toe over his hard, thick cock, but he catches my ankle.

"Ah, ah, ah. No. You just lay there and take this," he scolds.

"I want you," I say, panting. "Please, fuck me, Crew."

"Oh, no worries," he promises. "I intend to put some marks in this bedroom wall from this headboard."

I try to think of what I can say to get him to stop teasing and just do this.

Competition with Nathan used to do it but that's been less and less effective as we've all gotten closer and their relationship has deepened.

Still, I try. "Nathan would definitely want my first orgasm in our new bed to be on his cock."

Crew doesn't take the bait. He grins knowingly. "Dani?" he asks, taking the vibrator out of his mouth and slipping it into my wet pussy.

It feels good but it's too small.

"What?" I groan.

"Shut up and take my cock like a good girl." Then he takes the vibrator and slips it into my ass.

I gasp in surprise and pleasure. "Oh, yes."

He turns it on as he thrusts his huge cock into my pussy.

The double penetration is amazing. The fullness isn't as much as when I have two of my guys at once, but the vibrations lick along different nerve endings and I immediately feel an orgasm start to twist low and hot.

"Crew!"

"I told you I've got you." He gives me that cocky smirk again as he thrusts deep.

I can see his ab muscles ripple as he moves inside me, his arms flex as he holds my thighs wide, one hand under my ass, holding the vibrator in place. Then he reaches up with his other hand and pinches one of my nipples.

"Look at you," he says, his voice rough. "Spread out, tied up, filled up. You look like I'm using you, like I'm totally in charge, dominating you. But we both know that you have all of me in the palm of your hand, don't we, Dani? We both know, we *all* know, that I'm stupid in love with you. All I want is for you to be happy and completely fulfilled."

The words are sweet and seem at odds with the way he's fucking me, deep and hard. But they're perfect. We're in a bed built for four, getting some alone time before the two other men who live with us get home. We're in this entire situation because these men all love me and want me so much that they're willing to do this very non-traditional relationship because it's what *I* need.

"I love you," I gasp as he plunges deeper.

"I know you do," he says. "And that's why–" He moves the vibrator in and out as he fucks me faster. "You're going to scream out *my* name first in this huge-assed, amazing bedroom in *our* awesome new house."

He leans over, taking my mouth in a kiss, shifting his hips to hit a spot that I've *never* been able to hit on my own. Not that I've tried at all since meeting my guys.

"Come for me, pretty girl," he says against my mouth. "Squeeze my cock with all you've got. Pull it all out of me."

And I do. My orgasm slams into me, all of my muscles tightening, and then unwinding as heat and intense pleasure flood through me.

"Crew! Oh, yes Crew! God, yes!"

He roars my name as he comes, his body tensing as he fills me.

He sags forward, bracing his hand on the mattress, and pulls the vibrator out as he withdraws. He tosses the vibrator onto the mattress beside me, then leans in and kisses me deeply.

Then he pushes back to kneeling and grins down at me.

That smile always makes me smile back, but it also makes me suspicious. "Wha–"

Then I hear it.

The front door just opened.

My gaze flies to the clock on the bedside table.

"They're home early," I say, eyes going wide.

I don't know why but I feel a rush of adrenaline. It's not like they're going to be angry. Probably not even surprised. Still, I feel like Crew and I have been naughty. And for just a moment, my primal brain tells me that I need to not get caught.

But Crew grins down at me, not moving.

"I don't think they're early, pretty girl. I think they lied to you."

"You mean they didn't intend to be gone for two hours?"

"Or they cut it short after they realized they were leaving us alone."

I narrow my eyes slightly. "They lied to *me*? What about you?"

"I think you underestimate how well I know those guys."

"Crew!" I narrow my eyes. "You knew they'd be home early and catch us like this?"

He runs a hand up and down my inner thigh, his gaze hot as it travels over me, completely open, and very dirty from what we were just doing.

"Yeah, I had a pretty good idea. Or at least I was hoping."

"You planned this," I say as I realize it. "You tied me up and played long enough for them to get home to catch us."

He grins. "You don't have to thank me." He starts to move off the bed.

"You have to untie me, at least."

He grins wickedly. "No. I like you all way too much for that."

I hear footsteps on the stairs and Nathan calling out to me. "Danielle? Are you up here?"

Crew chuckles. "He's not a great actor."

Again, for some reason, I squirm against my restraints. I know I'm not getting loose until one of them unties me. Still, my instinct is to try.

My heart is pounding, and I have goosebumps all over my body.

"Doesn't look like they got a lot done, Boss," Michael says, obviously outside of the door to Crew's room.

"Surprise, surprise," Nathan says dryly.

Their footsteps are coming closer.

I squirm on the bed, pulling on the restraints. "Crew! Come on!"

He's watching me squirm, his grin growing. He's also getting hard again. But he pulls his shorts on and runs a hand through his hair.

"Nope."

Then Nathan's in the doorway. "Well, what do we have here?"

He really isn't a good actor. But I feel my entire body flush and it's hard to take a deep breath.

Michael is right behind him. "I don't think bossing Crew around worked very well."

Crew chuckles. He's still watching me. "You didn't think them standing at the top of the stairs and mentioning things like you bossing me into unpacking and tying you up was a coincidence, did you?"

My eyes go from him to the two men standing in the doorway, already shedding their clothes.

So this is all their suggestion. It looks like Crew can follow directions after all.

"*This* wasn't exactly what I had in mind," Nathan says, his eyes locked on me, but his words clearly for Crew.

"Oh?" Crew asks, feigning innocence. "I thought for sure you wanted me to fuck her in our bed the first time."

"Don't you have a big-assed sofa *and* a pool table in the game room?" Nathan asks.

"I do," Crew says. "And now that you mention it, those would have totally worked, wouldn't they?"

I fight a smile. Crew loves to poke Nathan every chance he gets. Nathan really should have expected this.

"Naughty girl, starting all of this without us," Nathan says to me.

"It was all Crew! He carried me up here."

"Oh, and you fought him *really* hard, I'm sure," Michael says, coming toward the bed and unbuckling his belt.

"I tried to get him to work," I say, my tone pleading. "He unpacked three boxes."

"Three boxes out of about twenty?" Nathan says. "That's not a very good percentage, Danielle." He stops right next to the bed, his shirt unbuttoned and pants unzipped.

"I tried to incentivize him."

If I didn't know Nathan as well as I do, I would've missed the tiny hint of a twitch at the corner of his mouth. "I think we all know that Crew is incapable of being disciplined unless there's a hockey stick in his hand. And even then, it's questionable how much he actually *learns*."

I start wiggling harder as he drops his pants and shrugs out of his shirt.

"I was hoping to come home and reward you for being a good girl," he says. "But I guess it's punishment for a naughty girl instead."

My eyes go to Crew. "You have to help me. This is your fault."

He pulls his T-shirt on. "I think I'm going to go down and set a new high score on Alien Hunters."

My eyes go wide. "Crew!" That's the only one of our video games that I've actually beat him at. I currently hold the high score.

He smirks. "Play with you later, naughty girl." And he leaves.

He doesn't even want to watch.

Oh, he's in so much trouble later.

"I am so glad that you're naughty sometimes," Nathan says gruffly.

Then he flips me over to my stomach, my hands still tied to the headboard, pulls my ass up, and gives me a sharp smack.

And I forget all about video games, high scores, and revenge plots.

At least for now.

CHAPTER 4
Michael

"ARE YOU COLD?" I ask Dani, pulling her tighter against my chest and rubbing her forearms. I have a blanket wrapped around us but it's still spring in Chicago, so there's a definite bite in the night air.

She turns to smile up at me, her green eyes shining in the soft glow of our deck lights. "A little, but it's fine. I'm enjoying the view. Michael, we have a *yard*. In the city. And this beautiful house."

We're out on the back deck, snuggled up under a blanket in a chaise lounge chair that was delivered a few days ago before we moved in. We're up to our ears in boxes that Crew still hasn't touched—Dani either, for that matter, since we spent half of the afternoon breaking in our new bed—but the chaos isn't bothering me. Not right now. Not when I have this moment of calm with the girl I love.

Her hair is tickling my nose, her ass tucked up against my dick and thighs, and the neighbors' houses are all crowded around ours, lights going on and off as people shift around inside, going about their nightly routines. The domestic vibe is almost as comforting as having Dani leaning on me.

I'm so fucking *content* in this moment, I almost can't believe it.

"I haven't had a yard since I left Decatur," I tell her. "It's amazing, isn't it? Even if it is the size of a postage stamp." It's mostly consumed by the deck and the garage but there's a tiny patch of grass that is giving me life. I'm going to add some raised garden beds as soon as the weather breaks.

"It is amazing. So is the house." Dani raises her lips, questing a kiss.

I brush my mouth over hers.

"Thank you for giving me this," she says softly. "All of this. I'm so happy."

"Me too," I say gruffly, emotion getting the best of me. Sometimes I'm almost overwhelmed by how I fucking love and need this woman. "I'll give you anything you want, sweetheart. Anything."

"I already have everything."

Except my ring on her finger. Which I've been thinking about more and more these last couple of months.

I know it's fast but my feelings are real. With Dani, everything has clicked into place and I want to just keep moving forward.

As I'm reaching for my wine glass on the table next to us, the French door to the back of the house opens and Nathan steps outside.

"Fuck, it's cold out here," he says, grimacing. "We need to add heaters."

That's Nathan. Any immediate discomfort of any sort, and he's already coming up with ways to eliminate it.

"Or you could put shoes on," I say. "And a coat." He's barefoot and wearing nothing but loose lounge pants and a T-shirt.

"I could." But he doesn't, instead bending over us to kiss Dani before dropping into another chair and taking in the view.

"Wine?" Dani asks him, holding out her glass for him.

"Thanks." He takes it and swallows a huge sip. "God, this is downright suburban, isn't it? I've seen at least seventeen dogs being walked on our block in the last thirty minutes. We're not getting a dog, are we? It seems like a requirement to live here."

"I have no interest in a dog," I assure him.

Dani shoots me an amused look. We both know Nathan is here under duress. But he loves Dani enough to give up his penthouse and doorman and be forced to interact with other human beings. This house is mine and Dani's dream, not his, and I appreciate that he's compromising, though I worry a little his grumbling is more serious than just general Nathan grumpiness and that he'll grow to resent this.

Though I do trust Nathan is mature enough to let us know if that's ever a real issue. Would I move back to a penthouse downtown? I don't know. If that's what the other three in our foursome wanted, I would. But then again, it wouldn't be as good for raising kids.

And yes, I'm thinking about our future kids already.

The back door to the house next door opens, and a man walks out onto his deck with a dog, which means he's all of five feet away from us, given how narrow these lots are.

Nathan swears under his breath, his shoulders tensing. "Oh God, it's the neighbor."

Dani reaches out and laces her fingers through his to calm him down.

"I've got this," I tell him, when it's obvious the neighbor is waiting for his pug to do its business down in the yard. I shift Dani a little and peel myself out of the lounge chair.

"Hey, how's it going?" I say, waving to the man as I stand up and move toward the end of our deck.

"Hey, neighbor, great to meet you," he says, waving in return. "Glad to see the moving trucks were here today. We've been wondering when you would be done with renovations."

Below us, there's a short iron fence marking the property line, but both decks are off the first floor, not street level, so we're elevated above the fencing. I can actually reach out and shake the man's hand, which I do. "Michael Hughes. Pleasure. Yes, we're finally moved in. Well, our stuff is here, anyway. We should be unpacking, but clearly we're not. I hope the remodeling wasn't too much of a disturbance for you."

"Not at all. Glad to see the property getting spruced up. Mark Acker. Great to meet you."

"This is Dani," I say, gesturing behind me. "And Nathan."

Mark is around forty, with an easy-going smile, a lean but fit build, and a thinning hairline. Like Nathan, he's in lounge pants and a T-shirt, but he's also wearing a puffer coat and slides and has a dab pen in his hand, which he takes a hit off of. I smell marijuana. He glances back at the house suddenly, like he's afraid he's going to get busted.

"Sorry. I thought I heard my daughter," he explains. "She has turned bedtime into an hour-long process that I call the Stall Games." Then he peers over at us again, clearly curious. "Danielle, Nathan, nice to meet you both."

Dani starts to get up, but Mark waves her off. "Don't get up. You look comfortable. Moving sucks."

"It hasn't been too bad," she says, the corner of her mouth turning up. "The guys have been doing most of the work."

I know exactly what our dirty girl is thinking about. How she tried to force Crew into unpacking and ended up tied to our bed, getting her ass spanked hard by Nathan as my dick eased in and out of her mouth. The memory has me clearing my throat.

Mark is clearly too polite to ask about our dynamic. Or maybe he thinks Nathan is her brother. Or uncle. Or maybe he doesn't give a shit. But at any rate, I'm grateful not to have to explain. It's not so much that I care what other people think about our relationship, but sometimes it's a pain in the ass when I want to just have an easy conversation. People are always curious and have lots of questions that we wouldn't have to deal with if it were just me and Dani in a traditional male-female relationship.

I also hate having to introduce her as my girlfriend. The word feels weak for what we share and for a man my age. I want to be able to say she's my *wife*.

The thought isn't surprising to me. This isn't the first time I've had it. I know I want to marry Dani and spend the rest of my life with her. But the ferocity with which the desire washes over me right now catches me a little off guard.

Damn, I want everyone in the world to understand that Dani is my everything, my it girl, the endgame. I want to be able to introduce her as my forever person. I want *her* to know that, to me, she's perfect, and I want to settle into this house, make babies, buy a lakefront property and grow old together. The whole damn thing.

Nathan is shaking Mark's hand now, goosebumps on his arm, polite smile in place. A lifetime of training has made Nathan capable of appropriate social behavior, whether he enjoys it or not.

"What do you do, Mark?" Nathan asks him now.

"Oh, I'm semi-retired. I had a bit of luck developing some tech and sold the business a year ago. I'm on the lookout for my next project."

The back door to his house opens and a woman with dark hair steps out. She looks younger than Mark, but is probably in her thirties.

"This is my wife, Marissa, who was my first employee." He gives us a grin. "She had a thing for the boss since day one."

Marissa rolls her eyes. "What a charming way to introduce me, honey." Her gaze sweeps over me and Nathan. "Hi, so you're the new neighbors. Are you...married?"

I realize she can't see Dani behind us and she thinks me and Nathan are a couple. "No, not married." I shift so Dani is visible. "I'm Michael, this is Nathan, and this is our girlfriend, Dani."

Two simple words–*our* and *girlfriend*. But put together they make everything instantly complicated.

Her mouth forms an "o" of surprise. She's clearly about to ask for clarification when Mark sucks on his dab pen and the smoke drifts toward her face. She grimaces and waves her hand vigorously. "Really, Mark?"

"What?" He does an admirable job of playing stupid. I almost believe he has no idea why she's irritated. "You should all come over for dinner some night. Or at least for a drink after our daughter goes to bed."

"We'd love that." I mean it. It reassures me Mark has no judgment and I appreciate it. I'd also love to be able to shoot the shit with my neighbor while we drink a beer at the grill. That's my idea of having a home in a family-friendly neighborhood and it's why we moved here.

"Do you have children?" Marissa asks.

Dani has stood up now, the blanket wrapped around her, and she shakes her head. "No kids."

"We have Crew," Nathan says dryly.

Dani laughs. "Nathan."

"Crew?" Marissa asks. "Do you have a dog? Our pug, Gracie, would absolutely love a playmate."

"Gracie is our daughter, babe," Mark says. "The dog's name is Hannah, remember?"

"I did it again?" Marissa exclaims, looking dismayed. "Oh, my God, pregnancy brain is so real."

"It's not your fault," Mark reassures her. "We shouldn't have let Gracie name the dog." He looks at us. "She wanted the dog to sound like she could be her sister. Mission accomplished, right?"

"You're expecting?" Dani asks. "Congratulations! That's wonderful."

"Yes, congratulations," I say, excited at the idea of having multiple kids next door.

This is absolutely what I wanted. A connection with other couples, young families. Except we're not just a couple, we're a couple within a larger relationship, but the same principle applies.

Mark and Marissa have what I want with Dani. Marriage. Kids. The house and the dog. Okay, I lied to Nathan when I said I have *no* interest in a dog. A dog is on my 'someday' list.

"Thank you." Marissa smiles before tossing another pointed glare at Mark's vape. He gets the hint and slips it in his pocket with a sheepish shrug. "So who is Crew? Your cat?"

"Or your pet pot-bellied pig? Chicken? Goat?" Mark asks, oblivious to his wife's sudden alarm.

"I don't think we're allowed to have farm animals on this block," Marissa says.

"What's the difference between having a dog and a pig?" Mark asks. "They both crap in the yard."

Nathan laughs.

"We don't have any pets, farm animals or otherwise," I assure Marissa.

"Crew is my other boyfriend," Dani says softly, her chin coming up slightly, as if she's expecting subtle or not-so-subtle slut shaming to be tossed in her direction.

Protective instincts kick in. I reach my arm out and she steps into my embrace. Nathan kisses her temple. We're a united front, and no one is going to be rude to our girl on our watch.

But Mark nods like it all makes sense to him, and Marissa just blinks. She's officially speechless.

Nathan is done with the small talk. I can read his body language. I also know he's contemplating why he didn't install privacy decking before we moved in because now we have to pal around with the neighbors.

"Dinner sounds fantastic," I tell Mark. "We're looking forward to it."

"I'm freezing," Nathan says. "I'm going to head inside. It was a pleasure, Mark and Marissa. Danielle?"

"I'll be there in a minute," she tells him with a smile. She turns her lips up to receive a kiss. "I love you."

"I love you, too." He gives her a soft smile, one that he reserves just for her.

Nathan is putty when it comes to Dani.

The back door swings open, hard, Crew style. He never does anything halfway. "Hey, what's the Wi-Fi password?"

"That's Crew," I tell Mark and Marissa. To him I call out, "Come meet the new neighbors."

"The password is "listen to me when I tell you important shit," Nathan says dryly, shifting past him.

"Is it really that or is that your idea of a joke, Boss? Because that's a really fucking long password and I will change it to "Nate is old," which is easy to remember." Crew bounds out onto the deck in his socks, jeans, and a hoodie. "Holy shit, it's cold out here! We need heaters once my hot tub arrives."

Crew doesn't like discomforts either. He's also always willing to throw money at anything that will make him more comfortable or make things more fun. He and Nathan actually have more in common than either of them realize.

But Crew does like people. And recognition. Which he instantly gets from Mark.

"Aren't you Crew McNeill?" Mark asks, lifting his vape halfway to his mouth before he realizes he's not supposed to smoke in front of his wife. He slips it back into his pocket again and sticks out his hand. "Mark Ackers. Huge Racketeers fan."

A grin splits Crew's face. "I am. It's great to meet you."

"He's having a great season," Dani gushes.

Which doesn't bother me. She should gush about Crew. He's an amazing player, and she's proud of him. But I can feel Marissa's eyes on me, studying my reaction.

"Do they not get along?" she asks me, clearly curious. "Nathan and Crew?"

Crew and Mark are discussing the playoffs and the Racketeers prospects.

"They do. They just like to give each other a hard time."

"Ah," Marissa says.

There are a thousand questions behind that one word.

I get it. I understand everyone's curiosity about how our relationship works.

Sometimes I even wonder how it works myself.

And what it would be like to have Dani solo.

Easier. It would be easier. I know that.

But it wouldn't be the same. And I like what we have.

So I content myself with the fact that Cookie & Co. is what makes Dani happy, and that's what matters to me.

But I want to marry her.

Tonight I'm more sure than ever.

And Nathan and Crew and I need to have a talk.

CHAPTER 5
Michael

AFTER ANOTHER TEN minutes of chatting, Dani shivers and I use it as an excuse to say goodnight to Mark and Marissa. "I should get her inside."

"Of course. Nice to meet you," Mark says.

"We'll see you," I say. And I mean it. I hope to further this potential friendship.

"They're so nice," Dani says as we step inside and head downstairs.

"They are. Dinner or drinks with them sounds good. What do you think?"

She laughs. "I'd love to. But that's not really Nathan's thing."

"No. But…" I pause. "We could go without him. Just you and me."

She looks up at me. "Yes, I guess we could. He'd probably appreciate that."

"I'm sure he would." I steer her toward the primary bathroom where the enormous soaker tub is. "You should take a hot bath and warm up."

"Are you coming in with me?" she asks with a little smile.

I reach up into the cupboard and withdraw her favorite bubble bath. "I'll come up and scrub your back later. But you just relax for a while."

She sighs a happy sigh. "That sounds nice."

I grin. The three of us guys keep her "busy." Especially when she's naked. She deserves some down time to herself too.

I go to the tub and start running the water. I know exactly the temperature she likes best. She undresses as I pour in the bubble bath. She puts her hair up and I study her body unabashedly.

Yes, I get hard. I will never not want her. But I can leave her alone when she needs some time to herself.

I also need to have an important conversation and it's better if I broach this subject with Nathan and Crew without Dani. No, we shouldn't have big discussions that affect all of us without her, but I honestly don't know how the guys will feel about what I'm going to say and in this case, they probably need to hear what I'm thinking about first.

I hold out my hand to Dani and she takes it, letting me help her into the tub. She sighs as she sinks into the bubbles. "Thank you, Michael."

I kiss her forehead. "Love you."

"Love you, too." Her eyes slide shut as she leans her head back.

I leave her soaking and go find my other two roommates.

My friends.

For now, anyway.

No, don't think that way. They won't be surprised by what you're going to say.

No, not surprised. But they might not like it.

I find them both in the kitchen.

Nathan is on one of the stools at the counter, scrolling through his emails on his phone. Crew is, of course, rummaging in the fridge.

"Hey, I need to talk to you guys about something," I say, trying to sound casual.

"Where's Danielle?" Nathan asks.

"Taking a bath."

"Are we drawing straws for who gets to go up and make sure she washes behind her ears?" Crew asks with a teasing tone.

"No, this is something kind of serious."

Crew turns, a jug of milk, a container of takeout food, and a bowl of grapes in his arms. "I take bath time with Dani very seriously."

I blow out a breath. "I need to talk to you about one of those things that is only an issue because there are four of us. Typically, I'd know exactly what to do, but in our situation, I need to run it past you guys."

Nathan frowns. "What do you mean?"

I feel a surge of frustration. "I mean that if I was just dating her on my own, I'd know exactly what to do and I'd just do it. But there are two other people now and…I thought I should include you."

Crew sets his food down and leans back against the counter, crossing his arms. Nathan puts his phone down.

"Is she alright?" Crew asks, obvious worry in his voice. "Is she sick or something?"

Okay, that's a fair guess since I'm a doctor and I'm frowning as if I'm about to deliver bad news. I shake my head. "No. She's not sick. She's…perfect."

"We're listening," Nathan says. But he sounds suspicious.

I'm just going to put it out there. "I want to marry Dani."

They both look at me for a moment as if expecting me to go on. But that is the bottom line, and I need to see their reaction to that first.

Nathan is the first one to respond. "That's not really huge news, Hughes."

"Aren't we already kind of married?" Crew asks. "We're living together. No one is seeing anyone else. No one's planning to go anywhere anytime soon, right?"

I brace my hands on the marble countertop. "Marriage is more than that. You know that. It's a true commitment. It's an official statement, a vow to the world that you're in it together, forever."

Crew and Nathan exchange a glance, then Crew says, "Yeah. I guess I thought that's what we were doing here."

I take a breath. "Between the four of us, we're committed. I get that. I know we all feel it. But I want to make it official. I want everyone to know. I don't want to call her my girlfriend. She's so much more than that. And, if it was just Dani and me, I'd be down on one knee giving her a diamond ring. I want her to have my last name. I want to introduce her as my wife. That word carries a different weight. It carries a different responsibility and commitment. And I'm ready for that. I want a wife and children. I want to move forward with our lives. And I want to do that with Danielle."

Nathan and Crew are now staring at me.

It's several long heartbeats, and I honestly don't know what either one of them is going to say. I know they love her. I know they're committed to being with her and only her.

I do believe that Nathan doesn't expect to ever be with anyone else.

I don't really think Crew does either. But he's young.

I know Nathan has thought about his life and what the next ten and twenty years look like.

I'm not sure Crew has. He's maybe looked at the next five. And I'm guessing they've all been about hockey. Which is appropriate. That's what should be his primary focus. He has a different kind of career than most. His won't last for thirty more years so he has to put his all into now.

I'm sure he hasn't actually thought about marriage and children at this point. No matter how much Crew loves Dani, twenty-three is young to be thinking about any of this. Hell, he'd put no thought into home ownership and we'd had to teach him everything every step of the way.

Nathan finally nods. "I understand what you're saying. If this was a typical relationship, you'd just ask her to marry you, she would say yes, and you'd start planning a wedding. You'd plan when she's going to get pregnant, you'd pick out baby names. It'd be easy and straightforward. But it's all different when there are two other guys."

I nod. "Exactly."

"Well, I've given this some thought as well," Nathan says.

I'm not surprised.

However, Crew is it seems. "What? You've both been thinking about *proposing*? That's a very Hughes thing to do only a few months in, but you, Boss?"

"Of course," Nathan says, as if it's the most obvious thing. "What would I wait for?"

"Um…for it to make sense?" Crew says.

"Why doesn't this make sense?" Nathan asks. "I love her and want to be with her for the rest of my life. Why wouldn't I marry her?"

Crew looks back and forth between us. "We're not even unpacked from moving in together!"

"Some of us are unpacked," Nathan says dryly.

"You know what I mean!" Crew exclaims. "We just started dating."

"The three of us are not dating," Nathan snaps. "I'm dating Danielle. And I don't need longer than I've had to know that I love her and she's it for me."

"Are you insinuating that I don't love her?" Crew asks.

"I'm not insinuating anything," Nathan tells him. "I'm informing you of where I stand with Danielle. And I'm only doing it because we're all involved with her. Do whatever you want, McNeill. But if I want to marry Danielle, and Michael wants to have a baby with her, then we will."

Crew presses his lips together. He looks pissed off but he clearly doesn't have an argument he wants to share with us.

I frown though as I think over what Nathan just said. Something about it sounds off.

"Since you've been thinking about this too, share your thoughts," I say to Nathan.

He levels me with a direct look. "Okay. Fine. We can't all three legally marry her."

I nod.

"But one of us can. I figured I would marry her, and you and McNeill can be the fathers of her children."

My frown deepens. "Why would you be the one to legally marry her? You don't want to have children?"

He clenches his jaw, then says, "I can't get Danielle pregnant."

That wasn't what I was expecting. "Go on," I say.

"I was in a car accident when I was twelve. Some of the injuries left me infertile. I will never father Danielle's children biologically. Being a father was never something I even considered, because that was never an option. But since I've met Danielle and realized she wants to be a mother, I am absolutely dedicated to raising children with her. I would be open to adoption, but because you two have always been a part of this situation, I suppose I assumed our children would be yours biologically, but that we would all raise them together." He clears his throat.

I know that was difficult for him to share and I have to admit that hearing the gruff, sometimes closed off billionaire say he had assumed we'd all raise children together, children that would not be his biologically but that he was still open to being involved with, supporting, and loving makes my frustration fade.

"Does Dani know that you can't have children biologically?" I ask.

"She does."

Of course, that wouldn't change how that loving, sweet woman felt about a man she was in love with. I nod. "Have you talked about having children?"

"Not specifically, but she knows I'm open to being a father. I assume that she assumes the children will be yours and Crew's biologically."

I swallow. "Thank you for telling us, Nathan. And of course, when I think about having children with Dani, I assume you would be a part of any child's life. We would do all of that together. No matter which of us is the biological father. Obviously, there's the chance that both Crew and I could father a child. Or maybe more than one." I glance at Crew and then frown. "You okay, McNeill?"

The kid has gone white. He slumps down on a stool and covers his face with his hands. "And now we're talking about *kids*?"

"*I* am talking about kids," Nathan says to him. "I'm forty-one. As it is, a child would be graduating high school when I'm nearly sixty." He takes a second, then adds, "But it's up to you and Hughes and Danielle if there are children. That's not my call."

Crew just groans, obviously feeling some pressure from that now that he knows both Nathan and I want kids.

But I know that was hard for Nathan to say. To admit that there's something huge about his life and the life of the woman he loves that's out of his control.

Which is why he wants to legally marry her—at least one of the reasons. The possessive side of him wants her to have his last name, I'm sure, but being her husband legally also gives him more involvement. With medical decisions, financial situations, just in every way that a legal marriage binds two people together.

"This situation is different because we—us guys—are all in different places in our lives," I say. "But we were when we all got started. This can't really be a surprise, McNeill. When it comes to dating, we give Danielle very different things. In good ways. We complement each other. But when it comes to these real-life situations and the future, obviously we're on different pages."

"You think?" Crew asks. He shakes his head. "I had to get involved with a woman who fell in love with two old guys, didn't I? I should have introduced her to some young, hot hockey players who weren't thinking about marriage either and—"

He's cut off by a low growl from Nathan.

"McNeill," I warn. I don't like the whole idea of Danielle being shared by Crew and two other younger guys, either. At all. Yes, a lot of this current complication probably has to do with Nathan's and my ages, but it's our reality and she is with us, no matter how much easier it might be for any one of us if it was different.

"I'm just saying, this sharing thing seemed really straightforward at first," Crew says.

Yeah. It did.

"So, what do we do?" Nathan asks. "Should we ask her together? I'll be honest. I'd rather propose on my own."

I feel both my brows lift. "I wasn't inviting you to my proposal, Nathan."

He frowns, but nods. "Right. And I don't want you on our honeymoon."

"You'd take her on a honeymoon alone?" I ask. I hadn't even thought of that.

"Wouldn't you?" he asks.

I mean...I don't know. That seems right. It would be Dani and I getting married. I'd love to have time alone with her as my wife. Even if she married Nathan too. But that also seems...wrong.

I scrub a hand over my face. "I don't know. I guess? But it also feels like we should do all of it together."

"But we're not marrying each other," Nathan points out.

He's right. On one hand. "But we're essentially committing to a lifelong relationship together if we're both committing to that with her."

He sighs, but nods. "Okay. But if ours is legal, and yours is more of a commitment ceremony, then–"

I cut him off. "I didn't agree to that. You said you thought that would work but I didn't say I was okay with that."

He scowls. "She needs a legal husband."

"Does she?" I ask. "Why?"

"The children will have one of you on their birth certificates as their biological father," he says.

I'm starting to understand where he's coming from.

"But the kids won't need to feel that one of us is their father more than another," I say. "There's nothing at all wrong with children knowing they have four adults who love them equally."

He lifts a brow. "Not to point out the obvious Hughes, but everyone will know which children are yours and which are Crew's."

Crew snorts. "I can't believe you just said that."

Nathan glares at him. "Why? It's true. Clearly, it won't matter to us. We'll be there for them." He looks at me again. "I would be honored if your child considered me a second father. But yes, you both will have obvious claims in their lives."

"You'll feel like you need to have an obvious claim? A place in Dani's life?" I ask. "You have to know that you do already. Right now."

He runs an agitated hand through his hair. "I'm just saying that making her legally my wife gives me a specific place in the family."

There it is. It's not just about control or staking a claim. His last name means something to him because it means something to everyone else. It's his identity. Literally, but it also informs his place in society and the world. He is Nathan Armstrong and when someone hears that name, they instantly know several things about him. Things he's proud of. He's used to leaning on that. Of course, it makes sense that he would want to put his last name on the most important thing in his life—Danielle.

I think about having kids. The children will be mine. And Crew's if he decides he wants that. I suppose the kids could have Dani's last name, but…I do feel a pang in my chest thinking about it not being Hughes.

Yeah, I get where Nathan is coming from.

Fuck, this is so damned complicated.

What started out as sexy fun has turned into more than any of us expected.

And we're in over our heads.

I blow out a breath. "This is a lot," I finally say. "Maybe we need to table this discussion for now. Everyone needs to do some thinking."

"Are you willing to wait?" Nathan asks.

And that's a great question. Am I willing to wait for Danielle because Nathan and Crew have different ideas and needs from mine?

"I don't think any of us should have to give up our dreams because of the others, do you?" I ask. "That's not what we signed up for. We signed up for…Dani. To make her happy together. But we're still individuals with lives and things we want."

Nathan nods. "But we have a relationship with one another. There's no avoiding that. And this is what relationships are. Compromising. Everyone has to give up a little to make it work."

That seems like it should have been my line.

But I don't want to give anything up.

Which sounds more like a Nathan line.

Everything feels like it's getting mixed up.

Fuck.

CHAPTER 6
Dani

"MY GOD, YOU LOOK GORGEOUS."

My stomach flips at the words and the husky tone in Michael's voice. The way he's looking at me makes my heart rate pick up. "Thank you. It fits perfectly."

He crosses the hotel room to me and smooths a hand over the midnight blue lace clinging to my hip. "I knew it would. You take my breath away."

He'd bought the dress for me earlier today. When we'd been packing at home to come to the medical conference in Vegas, he'd mentioned this formal cocktail party and dinner and I'd started digging through my closet, but he'd told me not to worry. That he'd buy me something appropriate once we got here.

Shopping in Las Vegas at the high-end boutique for this gorgeous dress with my handsome, romantic doctor boyfriend had been like a dream. I'd felt very Julia Roberts in Pretty Woman. Except all of the sales clerks had been *very* nice to me.

I'd modeled five dresses one by one for Michael. The hot looks he'd given me and all the compliments he'd showered on me had made me feel like a princess. Then, when I was hanging the emerald green dress I liked best back on the hanger and was preparing to pull my street clothes on, he'd come into the dressing room with me, carrying this gorgeous deep blue lacey thing. He'd helped me step into it, zipping it up slowly, while twisting my hair up with his hand as he stood behind me. We both took in my image in the mirror before locking eyes in our reflections.

"This one," he'd said simply.

I'd nodded. It's perfect. It has a halter-type bodice, leaving my shoulders and arms bare. The dress fits against my breasts, stomach and hips but the skirt flares a little, hitting me mid-thigh. It has a pretty lace overlay and I feel sophisticated and sexy in it.

I run my hand up the lapel of his perfectly fitted suit jacket that defines his biceps and his chest muscles. "You look so handsome, too."

He not only looks great in a suit, as usual, but he smells amazing. We've only been in Vegas for a few hours. We flew in earlier today, checked into a fabulous penthouse suite, had lunch, went shopping, then came back to get ready for tonight. We haven't even had sex yet. But I'm excited. I've spent time alone with all three of my guys from time to time, Nathan in particular because he's in Chicago more frequently than Crew and Michael. I've had to work to spend more time with them, but we do dinner dates, movies, shows, or even parties like tonight. I've accompanied both Nathan and Michael to charitable events and Crew to PR events where we've dressed up. But this is different.

This is a medical conference where Michael is an attendee as well as a speaker. He's doing two talks this week. I don't know about what specifically. Something about sports medicine, obviously. But it won't matter to me. I won't be there. I get to sleep in, hang out at the pool, shop some more, go to the spa...whatever I want while he's attending the conference during the first half of the day. Then in the afternoons and evenings, he's all mine.

I love being here with him. I love that he *wants* me here with him.

I've never had an entire week of one-on-one time alone with any of the guys, and it feels so strange to be a twosome when we're usually a foursome. But I know it will be fun. Michael's already made me feel like there's nowhere he'd rather be, and this trip is about spending time with me, while the conference is an afterthought.

We've held hands, laughed, hugged, kissed, talked, and it's so fun knowing that everyone looking at us knows we're a couple. I love being this man's girlfriend. He's so sophisticated and intelligent and charming and handsome. He could probably meet a woman on every block who would be delighted to have a drink, or more, with him. But he's with *me* and I know that people can tell just by watching us together that we're in love.

I can also admit that even though we rarely have any problems when we all go out together in Chicago, when we're a foursome it's just…more complicated. Even the people who support us make it into a thing. We're semi-famous as "Cookie and Co.", the most well-known hockey family in the league, so when we're out and about, our supporters want to voice their approval, they want to shake hands, sometimes they want photos with us. Here, with just Michael and me, it feels easier. Not better, but definitely easier.

"Stand by the window," Michael tells me, taking out his phone.

I move to the floor-to-ceiling windows that look down on the Strip. "Okay." I grin at him over my shoulder. "Why?"

"The guys will be so jealous that they can't see you like this in person, but they deserve a photo of our girl looking so fucking beautiful."

My heart squeezes. He means it. Michael is very free with his compliments and I know the guys all love me no matter how I look or what I'm wearing, but this is…sweet. That he wants to share this with them.

"It feels weird without them, doesn't it?" I ask.

He nods. "It does. I feel guilty, to be honest."

"Guilty?"

"Having you all to myself is amazing, Cookie," he says, giving me a smile. "And I know they'd take the same opportunity if they could. But we just moved into the house. We're not really settled. I don't know, it just feels like I whisked you off to fuck and have fun for a week in Vegas while they're back home without you, dealing with the post move-in shit."

I laugh. "You're *working*. It's not *only* fucking and fun." I also suspect Crew isn't dealing with anything and Nathan has hired out whatever is left to do.

He grins. "Well, I *could* have come alone. I could have left you in Chicago with them."

I smile. "I'm really glad you didn't. We're going to have fun. And Nathan and Crew will be fine."

Michael grimaces. "They're now *living together*. Without us there."

I think about that. Yeah, okay, he has a point. "Hopefully they're both still there when we get back."

He chuckles. "Give me a smile, beautiful," he says, lifting his phone.

I do, posing for my guys. Before I met them, I wouldn't have considered myself a seductress, but it feels safe and freeing to show off my sexy side for these men.

Michael sends the photo to our group chat and my phone dings. I pick it up just because I want to see the shot too.

Crew responds almost immediately.

> Jesus Christ. You look amazing, Dani

> I can be in Vegas in four hours.

That's Nathan, of course.

Michael just shakes his head. "That was maybe a mistake now that I think about it." He types quickly.

> Only need one date, thanks, Boss.

Nathan responds.

> I'll bring Crew. You take him to the party and Danielle and I will stay in.

Michael nods. "Definitely a mistake."
I laugh. I reply to them all.

> I love you all.

"You ready to go?" Michael asks.
"Yes. We're going down early?"
"I need to get you out of this room and lost in the crowd, just in case Nathan does actually get on a plane."

I don't say anything like 'he wouldn't do that' because…this *is* Nathan Armstrong.

I smile widely and let Michael escort me to the elevator. Being loved by these three men is amazing.

I am *their* princess.

"Dr. Samson, I'd like to introduce you to my girlfriend, Danielle Larkin."

Michael's hand is on my lower back as he introduces me to another colleague and friend. Or at least colleague. I assume he's friends with most of these people. Michael makes friends so easily and everyone he's introduced me to has seemed very happy to see him.

"Hi, Dr. Samson."

The man looks about Nathan's age. He's in a very nice suit and has perfectly manicured hands. He takes my hand. "It's a pleasure, Danielle." He turns to the woman next to him. "This is my wife, Tara."

Tara is beautiful. Also in her early to mid-forties. She gives me a small smile. Then she very obviously looks me up and down.

"Goodness, Michael, where did you two meet? Did you do a presentation at a local high school?"

My eyebrows rise and I feel Michael tense beside me. Okay, that was catty as hell, but it's obvious to me that Tara is covering up some roots and has had some Botox between her eyebrows, so I decide to take it as a compliment.

I laugh as if completely unbothered…or like I missed her dig at my age. "A hockey game, actually." I pause and add, "A professional game, not a high school game."

Tara glances at me, clearly not amused by my answer, but she's mostly focused on Michael. "We've never seen you here with a date before."

"I never had a serious girlfriend during one of these conferences before," Michael says. He draws me closer to his side, resting his hand possessively on my hip. "But now, you won't see me without a date again. Danielle will be a regular as well."

My heart does a little flip in my chest. I love any time one of the guys makes a reference to our future. I smile up at him and he returns it. Then I smile at Dr. and Mrs. Samson. "I look forward to it."

Again, Tara doesn't address me. "I thought you'd just started seeing each other. We, of course, follow the Racketeers. We know about…your situation. And that it's relatively new."

Well, I suppose that was inevitable. It's not as if people in Chicago are the only ones who follow the hockey team. And if Michael is renowned enough to be presenting at their annual conference about sports medicine topics, it makes sense that at least a few of the people in the field would follow him and his career.

It also makes her comment about us meeting at a high school even bitchier.

Her husband coughs. "Tara."

She glances at him. "What? They are quite open about their relationship in Chicago. He can't expect that people here won't know."

"Of course I don't expect that," Michael says. "I have several friends in the room who are privy to what's going on in my personal life."

I almost cough at that. The implication that Dr. Samson and Tara are not included on that friend list is clear.

"We've been together for about five months," I offer, because I feel like I need to say *something*.

I know there are people who don't believe a woman can actually, truly love three men. I know because I see those comments online and have received messages telling me as much. But after the first few that I can admit shocked me, I've realized that it doesn't matter what other people think.

The people that *really* matter are me, Michael, Nathan, and Crew. Those are the only people that need to believe this is real and that I can, and do, love all three of them.

It's nice that most of our family members and friends also believe it, but I realized at Christmas, when we went home to meet each other's families and got a mix of reactions, that yes, it makes things easier if they're all on board, but it doesn't make what the four of us have any less real if they're not.

And I certainly don't need to care about a doctor and his wife that I'll see maybe once a year at some big convention.

The only thing that keeps me from telling Tara Samson just that is not knowing for sure what role, if any, Dr. Samson has in Michael's professional life.

"Five months," Tara says, now looking directly at me. "That's not even two months per man."

"Excuse us," Michael says, his hand pressing into my lower back. "I need to say hello to Dr. Caswell."

He steers me away from the Samsons and through the crowd in the hotel ballroom. But we don't go talk to anyone new. He pulls me around a corner.

"Michael, what–" I look up at him and see that his jaw is tight and his eyes are glittering with anger.

"I'm so fucking sorry, Cookie. She was way out of line." He

pulls in a breath. "I should have known better than to introduce you to them."

I frown. "You couldn't have known how she'd act."

"Oh, yes, I could. Tara Samson has always been a bitch."

I give a soft laugh. "Oh."

"She *always* comments on my single status. And…" He trails off, studying my face, as if he's not sure he should tell me more.

"And what?"

"Since I turned her down three years ago, she approaches me at every conference and makes some comment about how lonely I must be or how a man like me shouldn't be alone and…" He runs a hand over his face. "Fuck. I introduced you because I wanted her to see that I was no longer single and that I have an amazing woman in my life and that I'm very serious about her." He shakes his head. "I should have known it would backfire."

I narrow my eyes. "Are you telling me that she propositioned you for sex?"

"Yes."

"She's *married*."

"Yes."

"And she thought that wouldn't matter to you?" I ask. "She doesn't know you at all."

He laughs and reaches up to cup my cheek. "That's not the only reason I said no. But thank you for knowing that was part of it."

I smile. "What were the other reasons?"

"I like sweet, loving, big-hearted women who love to snuggle." He takes a little step forward so one of his feet is between mine. "And who smile, laugh, cry, and gasp out loud while they read." His thumb strokes over my jaw. "Who like whipped cream on top of their coffee and think no one notices that they lick the first dollop off and always have to add a second." He leans in. "Who think that having their bath towel warmed up for them before they step out of the shower is the height of romance. Who tear up when someone brings them flowers just because. Who leave little sticky notes around the house that say things like *your smile this morning made my whole day wonderful."* He puts his mouth against my ear. "And whose pussy is my favorite place on the entire planet to be."

I'm melting by the time he's done and he captures my mouth in a deep, hot, yet sweet kiss. In my heels, I don't have to stretch as far as I usually do to kiss him back. I loop my arms around his neck and lean into him.

When we pull apart, I look at him and say, "I don't deserve you."

"Yes, you do. And I'm all yours."

"Well good, because even though I don't, I'm not giving you up," I tell him. This man is so, so good and I know it. I'm not ever letting him go.

He kisses me again. "I'm sorry about Tara. We're only going to talk to nice people for the rest of the night. Hell, for the rest of the week."

I nod. "Okay." But I pull my bottom lip between my teeth.

Michael frees it with his thumb. "What are you thinking?"

"I just...how many people know about the four of us?"

"I have three very good friends here, with their wives. They're also in sports medicine and we've known each other for years. They all know. I don't know who else. It's possible there are several people who know. But those three are the only ones that we'll likely have any ongoing interactions with. We'll be sitting with them at dinner."

"And they're fine with it?"

"Two are. The other just doesn't really mention it."

I nod. "Maybe we should just...not mention it too? I mean, should I not talk about Nathan and Crew? I don't know that they'll come up but sometimes when I'm telling a story, it's just natural to talk about them."

"Of course it is," Michael says in that easy way of his. "And I don't want you feeling awkward or like you have to watch every word you say. Be yourself. Nathan and Crew are a part of our life. There's no reason to hide that."

"You're sure?"

"Of course."

As always, Michael is the calming force. I'm not ashamed of Nathan or Crew. In fact, I feel amazed almost daily that all of these men fell in love with me and not only want to be with me but are willing to face what our unconventional relationship brings into our lives.

But I just really hadn't thought through the idea that people *here* would know. I guess I'd thought maybe I'd just be one man's girlfriend this week and it would be...easy.

Michael kisses me again, then takes my hand and leads me back into the ballroom. We cross the room, winding through clusters of people. He smiles and greets several, but we don't stop to talk to anyone. He takes me to the bar and gets us each a glass of champagne.

Then he takes me to meet two of the couples who we'll be sitting with at dinner. They are friendly and say it's a pleasure to meet me. Both men are sports medicine physicians, so the men start talking about some new technique for thumb sprains that they've all tried with varying levels of success.

I see the curiosity in the women's eyes when they look at me, but they stick to asking about my bookstore and the amazing season the Racketeers are having. They do mention Crew's name —it's impossible to talk about the Racketeers season without mentioning Crew McNeill—and I feel a surge of pride, but none of us say anything about him being one of my boyfriends.

Not even me.

And I feel weird about it.

Very weird. And guilty. And awkward. Because I want to say how much I love him and how proud I am, but that also doesn't really fit in the conversation.

The whole thing just gives me a sick feeling.

After about thirty minutes, we all move into another huge ballroom that's been set up for dinner. We're seated with these four, as Michael said, along with another couple.

Conversation continues to be pleasant and superficial.

About half-way through the meal, I reach into my clutch for an ibuprofen tablet and glance at my phone, wondering if I can quickly, surreptitiously check the score of Crew's game going on at this very moment.

I nearly weep with relief and joy to find that I have new text messages. Something to focus on other than the conversation going on around the table.

All three couples have kids that they're telling stories about. All three couples have been skiing together recently. All three couples have some hilarious story to share—a disastrous DIY home project, a new puppy, or their kindergartner telling the teacher about mommy and daddy having sex in the laundry room.

I've been watching Michael. He's the same age as these people. Would he like to go skiing with these friends? If we did, would Nathan and Crew come? Would they be okay with us going without them? A vacation is a little different than a medical conference where Michael is a presenter. Does Michael wish he had kids by now? Would he like a dog? Nathan wouldn't. I know for a fact Crew would, even without asking. But does Crew want kids? Because it doesn't matter if only Michael wants kids. There are *three* men in my life who have to want the same thing.

And if we do have kids, the stories those children might tell their kindergarten teacher could be doozies. Just having four of us sitting down at parent-teacher conferences will likely be an adjustment for everyone.

I take two ibuprofens and wash them down with champagne.

Michael notices. He leans over. "You okay?" he asks, quietly.

I give him a smile and nod. I don't want him to know I'm spiraling when he's trying so hard to make me comfortable. There's no way to go into kids, dogs, and skiing right now anyway.

He settles his hand on my thigh under the table, but he tunes back into the conversation about an article he contributed to a sports medicine journal three months ago about hip injuries in hockey goalies.

I listen with curiosity and a sense of bewilderment. I didn't know he wrote papers like that or that he was published in medical journals. And we were together three months ago. I know he sits on the couch with me while I read and write my romances. I guess I haven't paid as much attention to what he's doing as he does to what I'm doing.

That makes me feel bad, too.

Feeling like less than an A+ girlfriend and all mixed up about things like vacations, couple friends, and parent-teacher conferences, I pull my phone out and see messages from Nathan.

> Miss you.

That's all the first one says, but it still makes my heart flip in my chest.

It's just between him and me, rather than in our group chat that includes Crew and Michael.

God, I miss him too. I always miss my guys when we're apart. When they're out of town for games and such, I enjoy time with Luna or even just on my own, but I'm always ready to see them. This feels different, though. Tonight I'm feeling...off, I guess. This isn't going the way I expected and I'm not comfortable. Whether it's the other people's reactions to me or mine to them, I'm feeling flustered. Or maybe it just really is so weird for there to be only two of us here.

> I miss you too. So much.

> Are you alright?

It was the 'so much' that got his attention, I'm sure. I can picture the frown on his face. He's so protective, and I know he isn't thrilled that I'm here in Vegas with Michael for the entire week. But he didn't say a thing about us leaving. However, if he thinks for a moment that I'm not happy or safe, he will throw a fit.

He really might actually get on a plane.

I'd love that.

> I wish you were here

I stop before I send the text.

I can't tell Nathan I wish he was here. Especially not if he's worried about me.

That's not fair to him or Michael.

Nathan really might come to Vegas, and that would piss Michael off. It would also be unfair for me to make Nathan come comfort me when really I'm fine.

I'm better than fine.

Do I prefer my happy, sexy little bubble in Chicago where I have all three guys who dote on me and have basically convinced me that I can do no wrong? Of course.

Could I get my big, grumpy, in-charge, protective billionaire boyfriend here to save me in just a few hours? To make me feel better? To sweep me away from *anything* that makes me even the slightest bit uncomfortable? Yes. Easily. One text is all it would take.

It wouldn't take much more than that to get Crew here, too, and he'd definitely make sure I have fun and forget all of this discomfort.

But I can't do that.

I don't *need* to do that.

I'm just feeling insecure because I'm not sure what I bring to the conversation with Michael's colleagues. Plus, I don't like having some of these people give me the side-eye. But I'm not going to die from that. Even if they are Michael's friends. If he isn't bothered by their reactions, then I shouldn't be. We're going to face a whole variety of opinions and curiosity from people about our relationship forever.

I just don't want Michael to regret bringing me. This conference is about him and his professional achievements, not about standing up for our poly relationship.

I delete what I started to write to Nathan and tell him I'm fine. I know how to steer this. I can make Nathan and myself feel better. I text again.

> But my new thong is kind of itchy. If you were here, I know you'd let me put it in your pocket.

> I wouldn't have let you wear it in the first place.

I smile at the response that doesn't surprise me a bit. He texts again.

> That skirt is the perfect length to slide my hand up your thigh under the table and finger your sweet pussy during dinner.

I feel heat sweep through me.

Yeah, *this* will help. This is all I need. I just need a little reminder that this one dinner will pass, and everything outside of this is fine. I text him again.

> Can you keep talking to me?

> Of course. Where are you?

> At dinner. Where are you?

> My office. Is Doc with you?

> Yes. But he's got a lot of friends and colleagues here. They're talking medicine.

> It's difficult being in those professional situations when you're there beside him, looking so fucking gorgeous, all his, when all he wants is to take you out and make you laugh and make memories with you, before taking you to bed and making sure you never think of Vegas without thinking about the night he made you scream his name over and over.

I stare at the screen. Wow.

> How do you know that's what Michael's thinking?

> Because I know him. And because that's how I feel every time I'm with you and have to pay attention to something else at the same time.

> I'm that much of a distraction?

> Absolutely. In the best possible way. I've had at least six professional acquaintances comment on how much more pleasant I am to be around when you're there.

I laugh softly. Michael squeezes my thigh lightly. I look up, but he's still in conversation with the other men at the table, but I take that little squeeze as "love you."

I look back down at my phone and text Nathan.

> Michael's pretty caught up in his colleagues. Maybe he's got better self-control than you do. <winky emoji> <kissy face emoji>

> Oh, he definitely does. But I guarantee he's thinking about running his hand up your thigh right now.

> You don't even know that he can reach my thigh.

> He can. He might be socializing but he's got you right next to him.

I love that my guys know one another so well too. There's something about it that makes me feel as warm as I do when I realize how well one of them knows me.

> Okay, you're right. We're at the table, eating dinner, I'm next to him on one side.

> Where is he touching you?

> How do you know he's touching me at all?

> Where, Danielle?

He's so sure Michael's got a hand on me. I like that too. I love how my guys like watching each other with me. Especially when it comes to hands-on stuff.

I have an idea of how to make this *really* fun.

For all three of us.

CHAPTER 7
Dani

I TEXT NATHAN AGAIN.

> His hand is on my thigh.

> Under your skirt?

I study the back of Michael's big hand. I love his hands. Not only are they large and strong, with thick fingers, but they're so capable.

He takes care of patients with those hands, evaluating and treating injuries in seconds, his mind and hands working quickly to take care of the Racketeers.

I love watching him cook. When he's cutting, stirring, whipping, chopping he's completely in control as he creates the most amazing, delicious things for all of us. Cooking is definitely one of his love languages.

When he holds my hand in one of his, he always makes me feel cared for and safe. When he cups my cheek or brushes my hair back from my face, I feel loved and cherished. And those hands can give me pleasure beyond anything even my romance-writing-dirty-mind could dream up.

But that hand is now just resting right above my knee. Definitely not under my skirt.

I want to see what Nathan says.

> What would you do right now if it was your hand?

> I'd run my hand up until I could feel how wet your panties are.

I swallow and shift on the chair, moving a little closer to Michael. He would. Nathan would never be shy about touching me in public. Even indecently.

> I'd keep my conversation going as you wiggled on your chair, my little dirty slut.

I freeze for a second. It's almost like Nathan can *see* me. He knows me that well.

> But I'd lean over and whisper to you to stay still. And you're such a good girl that you would. You'd spread your knees wider under the table for me, but to everyone else you'd smile and nod and sip your wine and act like nothing was happening.

I sit up a little straighter, reaching for my wine glass. The movement brings me closer to the edge of my chair and Michael's hand moves up my leg an inch, though not on purpose. I take a sip of chardonnay–I'd much prefer a Moscato, or even a sweet red–and smile even though I have no idea who's speaking or what they're talking about. Michael's hand is hot on my leg and I'm hearing "you're such a good girl" in my ear in Nathan's voice, then Michael's, then Crew's.

God, can anyone see my hard nipples through the bodice of this dress?

I look down to check. Nope, I'm good right now. But Nathan has sent another text.

> Then, since you're wearing that fucking thong, I'd run my finger up and down over your clit through the material, making sure you were very, very sorry you left that on and can't feel me right up against your sweetness.

I blow out a little breath and put my hand on Michael's. I run my thumb back and forth across his knuckles. He squeezes my leg again, but doesn't look at me or interrupt his conversation.

> I'd tease you like that until I know it's killing you to sit still. Then I'd slip my finger under the edge of that tiny scrap and slide my finger into your sweet, tight, wet, pussy, watching your face, knowing that you want to gasp and moan but that you can't.

Oh. God. I should have never started this.

I move Michael's hand up my leg a few inches.

I feel his arm tense. But he still doesn't look at me. Or do anything else.

> I'd lean over and whisper that you can't come, no matter what, not until I say so.

I take another long drink of wine and realize I've emptied my glass. I set the glass down and reach for my water, taking a huge gulp.

> But the second we're inside that elevator, I would back you up against the wall, rip that thong off of you, and finger fuck you until the elevator stopped on another floor. I'd pull my hand away just before the next people get on. But I'd hold that thong in my hand–if they looked closely they'd see, I wouldn't hide it– and I'd lift my fingers to my mouth and lick you off of them behind the backs of total strangers while your pussy drips and throbs for me all the way up to the penthouse. Where you would hike that skirt up, bend over, and beg me to fuck you without even stepping out of your heels, like my sweet, dirty, perfect little slut.

I'm nearly panting. This was such a terrible, but awesome idea.

I move Michael's hand higher, until he rests on the lacy hem of my skirt.

He doesn't move it, up or down, and he's not talking now. But he's looking across the table at the other doctors, listening to what they're saying.

So I slide his hand higher.

Then he moves.

He pulls his hand away from me.

I frown up at him, but he doesn't look at me.

I'm still breathing fast, but I cross my legs and type into my phone.

> Well, no, Michael's hand is not under my skirt.

Again, I almost add, *wish you were here*. But that makes my chest feel tight. I'm happy to be here with Michael. I love him and love having one-on-one time with him. He and Nathan are very different men. Just because Nathan would feel me up under the table and play dirty games with me, doesn't mean Michael has to.

But Michael pulling away makes me feel really strange. My

stomach twists. Michael has *never* rejected me. Not ever. He's never not touched me given the chance. I feel almost embarrassed. I type to Nathan.

> I tried to move his hand up but he pulled away.

My cheeks are actually burning. I need Nathan to say something sexy. Or sweet. Something to make me feel less ashamed.

> You need to get up and excuse yourself to the restroom.

> Why, Nathan?

> He'll follow. He wants to touch you, but something's holding him back.

I look up at Michael. He's still engrossed in conversation.

I lean over, putting my hand on Michael's thigh now. "I'm going to the ladies' room," I murmur.

Now he finally looks at me. "Can it wait so I can just give our goodbyes?" he murmurs. "I'm ready to head out in a few minutes once I make some excuse. I know you were probably ready fifteen minutes ago."

"Sure." I'm relieved. And a little embarrassed. I realize I was texting Nathan longer than I intended to. I've lost the thread of conversation going around the table.

My phone vibrates again, but I ignore it. Nathan will assume I've followed his suggestion and gone off to a dark corner with Michael.

I turn to the woman next to me and smile, trying to pull something conversational out of my muddled brain. "That's a lovely necklace," I tell her.

She smiles politely. "Thank you." Then she turns back to her husband.

Michael gives me a sympathetic shrug.

Finally, a few minutes later our dishes are cleared, my glass of wine has been refilled again, and Michael stands, buttons the front of his jacket and holds his hand out to me.

He takes my hand and tugs me up, then tucks me under his arm.

"We're heading over to the casino," one of the doctors says to Michael. "Will you join us?"

"I think we're going to call it a night," Michael says. "Maybe another time this week."

"Okay, sounds good."

Michael turns me from the table, and we start toward the doors of the ballroom.

His hand is resting heavily and possessively on my hip. I also feel a tension in him that I know is annoyance. He's been annoyed *around* me before. With Nathan. With Crew. With my parents. There were a couple of moments with our contractors on our new house. There have been moments after games where he's been annoyed with a player or one of the coaches.

But Michael has never been annoyed *with me* before.

That I know of anyway.

"Michael, I–"

"I know," he says quietly. He gives my hip a squeeze.

A little startled, I press my lips together and let him lead me across the large room where we'd had cocktails and where people now linger. I wasn't even sure what I was going to say, so how does he know? But as we step out into the hallway and turn toward the elevators, Michael stops, turns, and looks down at me.

"That wasn't an enjoyable evening for you. I know. I appreciate you trying."

Which instantly makes me feel terrible. I'm not sure how hard I was actually trying. I defaulted to texting Nathan when I started to get in my head and worry about not fitting in with a professional crowd.

"I didn't expect to feel so awkward," I confess. "I'm sorry I wasn't more of a hit with your friends. I just don't have much to contribute when the women are talking about things like going into labor during their MCATs or taking a family vacation to Stockholm because that's where the *au pair* is from and they want their toddler to experience her culture."

Michael actually chuckles softly. "I think they're lying when they claim their three-year-old liked pickled herring."

That makes me laugh too, in relief. "I thought you were upset with me."

He shakes his head. Then he takes my hand and starts in the opposite direction. He pushes a door open and we step outside. We're in front of the hotel and casino, but we're off to the side of the main drive so there are fewer people and the vehicles are pulling past us to pick up and drop off passengers.

Michael shrugs out of his suit jacket and puts it around my shoulders. It's huge on me and smells amazing. I lift my shoulder and take a breath. His scent calms me. When he takes my hand and leads me down the sidewalk to a space where we can stand alone, I follow readily.

When we're alone-ish, he faces me. "I wasn't upset with you. I was frustrated that the situation wasn't easier for you. For us. I was hoping we'd slide easily into this setting as a couple."

"A couple like all your friends are," I fill in.

He nods. "But that's not fair. This is new for you. For us. So I'm upset with myself for thrusting you into a social situation with total strangers. Also, for wishing that people could just mind their own damn business and not have an opinion about our relationship. And for being jealous when you were texting Nathan."

"How did you know it was Nathan?"

"I glanced down and saw your screen."

"I see. You're feeling jealous?" I ask, actually confused. My guys are never jealous.

He steps forward and takes a breath. "Yes."

My eyes go wide. I didn't expect him to feel it, but I *really* didn't expect him to admit it. "You are? That's...that doesn't happen."

He lifts a hand. "Of course it does. We don't get jealous about the physical stuff. We all love seeing you with the others because it makes you free and happy and satisfied in a way that *you* need. And that's so fucking hot and gorgeous. It gives *us* all something we can't get anywhere else. *We* all need you to be all of those things. Because we love you. And we're not jealous when we're all together emotionally. When we're at home together, or at Christmas, or for Crew's birthday. But when we're split up and one of us has your attention beyond the physical, it's very easy to be jealous of someone else having all your emotions and attention and energy."

"I…" I frown, thinking about all of that. "I didn't know that." I suppose it makes sense.

"I wanted your attention tonight. But I put you in a situation where you were uncomfortable and Nathan was the one to make you feel loved and secure. I'm jealous of that."

"I didn't want to be with him instead of with you," I quickly assure Michael. "I just felt…left out, I guess. I don't know those people and you were so tuned into them, but I had no way to contribute. Everyone is older than me, and everyone works in fields I know nothing about. I was feeling off-kilter. So yes, when Nathan checked in, it made me feel good. He's familiar and makes me feel special. And then you were touching me, but it seemed like it was just out of habit and…" I trail off as Michael's eyes flare with…something. Heat? Anger?

"Why was Nathan texting you?"

I wet my lips. "He misses me."

Michael nods. "Of course he does. They both do. You know that. What else?"

"He asked what we were doing."

Michael moves in closer. "What else, Dani?"

I lift my chin. I have a right to text the men I love, dammit. "He was telling me what he'd be doing if he was the one sitting next to me. And it wouldn't just be resting his hand on my knee."

Michael's eyes darken. "He was texting you about finger-fucking you under the table?"

My brows rise. I don't have to confirm it. "And then you pulled your hand away when I tried to move it up my leg."

"Danielle."

Crap. He almost never calls me Danielle. I feel like I'm in trouble. I meet his eyes.

"I love you. I respect you. I think you are beautiful, inside and out, and charming and delightful, and I want to have you with me all the time. I also love fucking you. I love making love to you. I love having my hands all over you any chance I get. The fact that I didn't have my hand up under your skirt at a professional dinner has nothing to do with how I feel about you or how much I want you." His jaw tightens for a moment. "No matter what *Nathan* texts to you, says to you, or even does to you."

I swallow. Then nod. He's right. "I know that. I'm sorry I got carried away with Nathan."

He studies my eyes for a long moment. Then he nods. "You're all mine tonight."

"Absolutely."

"All *mine*, Danielle. And I want everything."

"It's yours."

"Yes," he says, his voice low, firm, and gruff. "It is."

I give him a little smile. "We can even start in the elevator."

He cocks a brow. "Was that in Nathan's texts?"

Damn, these guys knowing me this well is a little unsettling. Or amazing. I nod. "Yes."

"Then no, we're not starting in the elevator," he says, slipping a hand to my lower back and escorting me back to the front of the hotel. "We're doing this purely *my* way."

CHAPTER 8
Michael

THE DOOR to the hotel room snicks shut softly behind us and I breathe a sigh of relief.

I'm alone with Dani.

Completely alone. I'm going to be *sure* I'm the only one on her mind.

She's standing there in that sexy as fuck cocktail dress, her wild red curls tumbling down over her shoulders, her cheeks pink, not from the heat, but from anticipation. I know she wants this as much as I do. An opportunity to reconnect away from the chaos of the move into the new house and the stress of meeting my colleagues.

I toss the room key on the table by the door and slide a hand into the thick halo of curls surrounding her high cheekbones. "My gorgeous, sweet girl. I really am so glad you're here with me. It means the world to me."

"I wouldn't miss it," she murmurs. "I'm happy to be here with you."

I can see it on her lips—she's going to apologize about not fitting in and the texting again.

I don't want that. I don't need that. I cut off any further words by covering her sweet mouth with my own. Dani sighs as I press my lips against hers in a tender kiss.

This woman. This mouth. What I wouldn't do for her. If she asked to leave tonight, I would bail on the conference and escort her back to Chicago, but I'm hoping I can distract her from missing Crew and Nathan and our safe space back home.

"I love your lips," I tell her, pulling back to smile at her, in danger of getting lost all over again in those green eyes that shine with love for me. "And I love *you*."

"I love you too, Michael. I love you more every single day."

The words warm me from the inside out. I knew that someday I'd fall for a woman, and it would be amazing and satisfying and deep, but I never knew how much I would actually *feel*. How every look she gives me, every word she speaks, every orgasm I coax from her is like the oxygen I need to breathe.

I can say it, but I want to show her as well. I want her to know that I'm here with her, here *for* her, because I can't imagine being anywhere else right at this moment.

And frankly, I need her to show me the same in return.

"May I?" I ask, gesturing to her cell phone she's clutching in both of her hands against her chest.

She nods and hands it to me. I set it to silent and place it on the table next to the room key. I do the same with mine.

"What if someone needs you?" she asks.

Kissing the delicate skin behind her ear, I murmur, "Do *you* need me?"

Dani's breath hitches ever so slightly, her head tilting to allow me better access to her neck. To her. "Yes, I need you," she says. "I need you so damn much."

"You're all that matters to me right now. I'm here to focus on you and how fucking good I can make you feel. I'm here to focus on *us*. Everyone else can wait. It's not about excluding Crew and Nathan. It's about being present in the moment, right here, right now, and this moment happens to just be the two of us."

"I like that," she says, and she gives me a shy smile, tucking her adorable little chin and glancing up at me from under her eyelashes. "I'm here with you. Fully open."

That Dani still can be coy with me in any way both amazes me and turns me on. "Oh, you're about to be fully open, trust me."

Dani's cheeks turn pink and the tip of her tongue darts out to dampen her lower lip. She giggles softly. "Show me what you mean," she says flirtatiously, drawing the back of her fingers across her chest, bringing my gaze to her cleavage.

"I'll definitely show you, my sweet, sexy girl," I say, dipping my head so that I can suck on the swell of her breast. "Show *and* tell."

Though we've done enough talking tonight, in my opinion.

Stripping off my jacket, I toss it on top of our phones on the table. It falls to the floor, and for once, I don't care. I just let it crumple onto the marble.

It's tempting to reach behind her neck and undo the tie of her dress, but I resist the urge. I want something different. I want to take my time, given that we have all night. So instead, I lift her thigh and settle her hip against mine so that she can feel the nudge of my swollen dick. "Feel how much I want you. Feel how fucking hard you make me, Cookie."

Dani grips my shoulders, arching her back as I follow the vein in her throat with my lips, trailing soft, worshipful kisses along her warm flesh. I love the way Dani tastes, and I love how she comes alive for me with the barest of touches. It's a tease, and she isn't known for her patience when it comes to sex.

Dani is already breathing hard. She bumps her hips forward against mine, gasping in pleasure when she makes greater contact with my dick. "I want you," she murmurs. "Please, Michael. Take me."

The fabric of her dress and my pants is an unwanted barrier for both of us, but I'm not going to take her hard and fast, not when I have her all to myself. Not when I can thoroughly love every inch of her. I want her quivering and dripping with desire for me before tonight is over.

"Don't worry, baby, you're going to get me. I'm going to spend *hours* pleasuring you and fucking that sweet little pussy."

"Hours?" she asks breathlessly.

"Hours," I promise.

Raising my head, I gather her even closer against my chest and devour her lips with mine, enjoying the taste of her mouth, the remnants of the sweet wine she drank only adding to her natural essence. It was a long day of travel and shopping and socializing with colleagues. A complicated, frustrating, and up and down long-ass day. I've been waiting for this—the moment when she sighs into my kiss, her hands reaching out, needing me to hold her steady.

She gives herself to me so completely that I'm in awe of her. That she's *mine*.

Desire is pumping through me, and I turn us, pushing her back against the wall of the hotel suite. She makes contact with a soft thump, a gasp escaping her lips. Sometimes I don't even know if she fully understands what she does to me. How completely she owns me.

Holding her against the wall, I take the kiss deeper, nipping at her bottom lip, then sweeping my tongue over it to soothe where I've bitten her.

She hasn't relaxed fully. She's in her head, about our conversation earlier, about Nathan and Crew.

I pull back completely, earning a tiny cry of disappointment from her. She watches me, yearning in her eyes. "Michael?" she asks, voice a little wobbly from uncertainty. "What do you want me to do?"

"Open for me, baby," I command. "Fucking open for me."

I mean her mouth, of course, and I mean her legs, her body.

But I also mean more than that. I want her to open all of herself for me the way she does every day, but even *more*. I want all of her.

Dani pulls back slightly, leaning away so she can take in my expression. She gives me a look that is a little puzzled, even as I deny her the opportunity to study me as I nibble her soft earlobe. She's curious again about my tone, which as I play the words back in my head, sounds harsher than normal.

"Show me what you want. I'm yours," she says simply.

That implicit trust she has in me is a heady aphrodisiac.

"That's right. You're *mine*. And all I want right now is you."

Teasing up under her dress, I stroke greedy fingers over her inner thighs until I find the scrap of lace she's wearing and I tease it to the side. Beneath that little bit of nothing, she's smooth and wet and I allow myself to groan when I feel how ready she is for me already.

I drop down and rest my knees on my fallen suit jacket and take the hem of her dress and yank it up so that her pretty pussy is exposed, inches in front of me. My mouth is hot, throat constricted. My muscles are tense, dick throbbing with the need to sink deep inside all that welcoming wet heat. But first, I want to taste her.

Running my palms up the inside of her thighs, over the smooth plane of creamy pale flesh, I follow the trail with my gaze. I already know every inch of her, but it never ceases to amaze me how beautiful she is, how this woman makes me feel.

Awe.

That's how I feel whenever I'm with Dani.

She fell into my life, and she's hijacked my damn heart.

"So damn pretty," I tell her now, brushing my thumbs over her soft, swollen folds. I ease them apart, studying her intimately, gently blowing my warm breath onto her.

I'm rewarded with a low moan, her fingertips digging into my shoulders. I tease at her, barely here, barely there, wanting to soak in every sound, every scent, every single sensation.

"Michael, do something," she pleads.

Maybe I'm punishing her for texting Nathan during dinner. Maybe I'm punishing myself for loving her so damn much it makes me insane. Loving her so much that I'm willing to be in this complicated situation where I can't just marry her and make her mine.

"Shhh. I am, baby, I am."

I massage her flesh, up and down, skirting her clit over and over, until Dani is breathing hard and rocking her hips forward, trying to entice me into further action. I watch in fascinated satisfaction as a trickle of moisture floods from her pussy and down onto my finger as I stroke up and down, never sinking inside her, never making contact with that tight bud she so desperately wants me to touch.

"Oh, my God," she says. "*Please.*"

I blow again, before flicking my tongue ever so briefly over her swollen bud. Dani jerks, colliding hard with the wall. I want to taste her as badly as she wants me to, but I love that we have all the time in the world right now, that I can play with her.

"Is this what you want?" I plunge my tongue deep inside her, immediately coated with her arousal, before I pull back and stroke hard from the bottom of her slit, right to the top, sucking on her clit. I push my thumb inside her tight channel.

Dani shudders and to my honest surprise, she breaks apart, crying out in agonized pleasure. I probably owe Nathan a thank you for priming her for me with his dirty texts. I smile against her pussy, maintaining the pressure on her clit, thumb stroking in and out so that she can ride out the wave. I'll never get tired of having her soak me in her pleasure. When she quiets down, the trembling in her thighs easing, I ease my thumb out of her and flick my tongue over it.

"I fucking love the way you taste," I tell her. "Come here."

I stand up, and with one swift motion, I undo the tie on the back of her dress so that the front falls over onto her chest and upper abdomen. After removing my tie, I scoop her up under her ass and lift her into my arms.

Her cheeks are flushed. She's breathing heavily and her eyes are shiny as she entwines her arms around my neck for support. "Please tell me you're taking me to bed."

"I am definitely taking you to bed."

But I'm not done playing. Not even close.

Setting her down at the edge of the bed, I toe off my shoes and pick up the remote control to open the blinds. The Bellagio fountains are across Las Vegas Boulevard, the rest of the Strip sprawling out on either side in an explosion of flashing lights. They dance over the room, illuminating Dani as she puts one hand on the bed and bends over to use the other to take off her heels.

"Don't. The heels stay on."

Her mouth opens in surprise but she nods. "Whatever you say."

"That's right. It's whatever I say." I unbutton my shirt and yank it off impatiently. "Turn around. I want this dress off now."

She does silently, obediently, sweeping her hair to the side to give me access to the zipper. I take it down in one smooth motion and push her dress over her hips so that it falls to the floor.

Still behind her, I step in closer, wrapping my arms around her, so that I can cup her pussy with one hand and tease at her nipple with the other. She wasn't wearing a bra with the dress, and the panties are a mere suggestion, a concession to being in public, so she's mostly naked now, except for the silver strappy heels.

My dick is resting right against her ass, but I'm still wearing my pants. I trust my control, but I'm not ready to get undressed fully yet. Running my lips over her hair, I slip a finger inside her, giving a few teasing strokes as I roll her nipple into a hard peak.

Then I step back.

She gives a cry of disappointment.

"On the bed," I tell her. "On all fours."

Dani doesn't hesitate. She tosses her hair back over her shoulder, all flushed skin and fuck-me eyes before climbing onto the big bed, knees immediately sinking into the plush bedspread.

I remove my belt and unbuckle my pants, but I still don't remove them before shifting in behind her. My hand is large as I skim it over the pale curve of her ass, reminding me how delicate she is compared to me, how feminine. Dani is watching me over her shoulder, teeth sinking into her pink lower lip. So many pink spots on Dani's body, and I want to taste them all.

Lowering my head, I tease apart her cheeks and flick my tongue over the sensitive flesh there. Dani shivers.

"Michael, oh...what..."

I've had fingers in her ass, and my dick, but I've never tongued her here. Not for lack of want, but for lack of opportunity. There's always too much going on with the four of us to take the time to pleasure her in this particular way. But now, I ease my tongue inside the opening, and Dani gives a shaky moan.

"Are you..."

She can't seem to finish her sentence, so I'll take that as a good sign. Gripping her on either side, I bury my tongue in her hole, stroking in and out, finding a rhythm that has her legs trembling, her cries rolling into one another. My need for her ramps up, my dick throbbing painfully in my dress pants, but I'm not ready to plunge it inside her. I want Dani wrecked, sobbing, shattered. And it's all on me tonight. I usually have two other men helping me devastate her, but now every single gasp, moan, cry, every bit of her pleasure is all my responsibility.

And I fucking love that.

Tucking a hand around her hip, the first contact of my thumb on her tight aching clit has her bucking, hard.

"Steady, pretty girl," I tell her, murmuring against her tight little ass. "This is just the beginning. You need to hold on."

After swirling both my tongue and my thumb in teasing circles over and over again, missing the mark, but touching just enough to fire off her pleasure nerves, Dani is begging.

"Michael, please. *More.*"

She's started to roll her hips, and thrust her ass back into my face in a desperate, questing invitation.

"More what?"

"Touch me."

"You want my finger inside your tight, wet pussy?"

"Yes."

"Do you want my tongue in your ass?"

She drags a shaky breath. "*Yes.*"

Again she offers herself to me, giving a little wiggle that demands I bring the palm of my hand down onto that curvy little bottom and spank her, hard.

Dani jumps a little but makes a purring sound of approval.

I love seeing my brown skin make contact with the pale smoothness of hers, and with each slap, the pink in her flesh increases, blooming out from where I've smacked her. When I slip my finger into her slick pussy, she fucks it, pumping her hips frantically. I give her one final spank before plunging my tongue in her tight channel, and add a second finger.

It only takes a second for Dani to come apart. She's gripping the bedspread like the mane of a horse as she matches my rhythm, pushing back to force me deeper inside her, as she shatters. Moisture floods my fingers and a deep, primal satisfaction rolls over me.

She's chanting my name through her orgasm. "*Michael, oh, yes, oh, yes.*"

When her hips slow, I ease back out of her, yanking my pants down and kicking them off. On the bed as fast as possible, I grip her hips tightly and push my dick inside her wet, welcoming heat.

I said I wasn't going to go hard and fast, but that's exactly what I do. I thrust so damn hard that with each plunge inside her pussy, she shifts up on the bed.

"You like that?" I ask her. "You like getting fucked hard by your man?"

"I love it," she vows, voice low and husky with desire. "Never stop."

When her head is in danger of making contact with the headboard, I bury my fingers in those red curls I adore so damn much and tug her head back. "Look at me when I fuck you."

She obeys, peering at me over a slim shoulder, eyes glassy

with desire, cheeks flushed, lips pouty. "God, you're so fucking *big*," she says.

My girl knows just what to say. I feel the tightening in my balls, feel a surge of momentum, and then I'm losing myself inside her, pounding my way through a powerful explosion.

"It's you," I tell her, shaking my head just a little. "You make me so damn *feral*."

"I love the way you make me feel, Michael."

"Good. Because I'm not finished with you." Resting inside her, I unfurl my fingers from her hair and trace down her spine.

Goosebumps rise in the wake of my touch. "You're so soft, Cookie. So beautiful."

I'm feeling a myriad of emotions and I recognize there is a hint of jealousy again that I'm not comfortable with. It's not about sex. I like seeing Dani being satisfied by all three of us. It's that when I was supposed to be alone with her here in Vegas, Nathan was her support system instead of me.

But the worst thing I can do is let those feelings linger.

Pulling out of her, I help her relax down onto the bed, sliding in beside her. I want to support her, always, and I want the same.

Shoving aside the thoughts that have no business here, when we're naked and entwined together, I drop a kiss on her shoulder. Dani rolls onto her back and raises her hand to my jaw, rubbing her knuckles across my beard.

"You're very important to me," she whispers, like she senses my conflicting emotions.

"That's good to hear." It is. I needed it more than I realized. Maybe even more than an *'I love you'* right now. "You're important to me too."

"What should we do now?"

That makes me smile. "Do you want to go gambling?"

Dani looks momentarily confused. "Oh! I mean, sure, I guess…"

I laugh. "I'm kidding. I'm not letting you out of this bed until I have to be at that damn conference tomorrow." I nuzzle in her neck. "You're going to have to put up with more dick, I hate to tell you."

Her face clears and she giggles. "You read my mind."

My hand gravitates to her pussy, and I stroke lazily. "You want more?"

She sighs into my touch, back arching, breath hitching. "Always. I always want you."

I need to hear that more than I'm willing to admit in this moment.

I also have the urge to roll on top of her and sink into her, face-to-face, in this very vanilla position. I want that contact with her. I go with my gut, already hard again, just from lying close to her, from seeing the way she responds to my touch.

Hitching her legs up onto my hips, I do just that, loving that I can sink into her body, gaze locked on hers. The heels she's still wearing bang against me and it feels like the literal kick in the ass I need. I know Dani loves me, I know she wants this. She's still learning how to navigate our unconventional relationship. We both are.

We move together, a slow, wet joining, her body open for me, along with her heart. She's wearing a profoundly vulnerable expression on her face that makes me want to take everything I said back, even when I know that would be stupid. But damn, this girl, damn, this pussy…I love making love to her.

"Are we okay?" she asks softly, tenderly running her fingers down my arms as I stroke in and out of her.

"We're very okay," I tell her. "We're amazing, Cookie." I'm balls deep in her and I know my answer is too simple for what we're both really feeling.

It's going to take being open and honest and having these difficult conversations to navigate a relationship as complex and deep as what the four of us have created. But right now, we've said enough. Right now, we just need to feel each other.

Leaning down, I kiss her, nibbling at the corners of her mouth, and sweeping my tongue over hers. She sighs into me and I absorb it into me, needing her trust, her love.

She's close to coming. I can sense it in her hitched breath, the way her inner muscles are clamping down on me, gripping my dick with a tight, hot fist that has me on the edge. But she's holding back.

"Come for me, baby," I murmur against her throat, rubbing my beard over her nipples the way she loves.

I reach down between our heated bodies and tease at her clit, wanting her to peak. To let go of the tension that's been created.

She breaks, nails digging into my biceps, and when I look up at her, there are tears in her eyes.

"Oh, baby." I maintain my rhythm, but I brush my lips over a drop of moisture that has trickled down her cheek. "It's okay. Everything is okay."

My own release is right there, and instinct has me closing my eyes, but I force them open. She needs me to be present, just like I want of her, and so I lock my gaze on hers and pump hard into her, the tight explosion deep inside her bringing a smile to her lips.

I stay inside her, pulling her into the crook of my arm, dusting kisses on her temple. "Look," I say, gesturing to the window. "The Bellagio fountains are going off."

Dani glances out the window. The fountains are a colorful burst of water, shooting up high into the nighttime sky.

She smiles softly. "They're beautiful."

"You're beautiful."

"Thank you." She reaches up a shaky hand and swipes at her eyes. "I think I drank too much wine tonight."

"Let me get you some water."

"No, it's fi—"

But I'm up and out of the bed, immediately concerned. I don't want her to have a hangover tomorrow. Besides, she drank more than she normally would because she felt out of her element and I feel bad about that. Cocktail parties with total strangers aren't an easy social feat, and I should have been more sympathetic to that.

Padding to the kitchenette of the suite, I pull a bottle of water out of the mini-fridge. I bring it to the bed, untwisting the cap for her.

She gives me a small smile, propping herself up in bed and taking the water from me. "I can untwist a cap."

"I know." Even as I say it, I'm pulling the bedspread back so I can flip it over her, not wanting her to get cold, even if it means covering her tempting naked body. "I like taking care of you."

She takes a sip. "You're good at it."

Climbing back onto the bed, I slip under the covers so I can align my body with hers. "What else can I do for you?"

We both know I'm not asking a simple question.

"Just love me," she says, simply.

"Done."

So I carry Dani into the shower and make love to her under the rain head faucet, massaging the tension out of her shoulders with shower gel in my hands, and taking her against the wall with easy, relaxed strokes in and out. I towel her off, and order her a snack from room service, then coax her to drink more water while we wait, finding a romantic classic film on TV for us to watch. When the food arrives, I feed her strawberries and cheese, catching the juice that trickles down her chin with a flick of my tongue, before dribbling some on her nipple to taste.

By the time I'm done, she's relaxed and sleepy, and dozes off several times, before finally giving me a mumbled, "I love you."

Once she's fully asleep, I ease out of the bed and go to the couch, finishing off the water I opened for her. I open my phone to check texts and emails and see I have a text from my real estate agent.

My apartment has been for sale for three months, since Cookie & Co. decided to buy a house together, and I finally have an offer on it. The inspection was the week before and it's been radio silence, which James had assured me was fine.

Now I have a message.

> Buyers pulled out. They didn't like the water damage on the kitchen ceiling.

That makes me frown as I sit down.

> There's no water damage.

> They said the moisture meter indicated water.

> Can't we just give them a credit?

> No, they're done with the deal. There's no saving it. I've been trying for three days. Their minds are made up.

It makes me unreasonably irritated.

> I've been very reasonable with them.

They looked at the property three times before making an offer, which was way under list price. My gut had told me to tell them to go pound salt, but the agent had encouraged me to accept the deal. I should have listened to my gut.

> I know. But we'll just sit tight and wait for another offer.

Water bottle in hand, I glance over at Dani, asleep in bed, and at the flashing lights of the Strip beyond. I should have closed the blinds for her.

> Just remove the listing. I'll hold on to the place and re-list in a year when the market is more stable.

I didn't think the property would be so difficult to sell.

But I didn't think loving a woman would be hard, either. Or rather, not loving a woman. Having a relationship. With a woman I love and two other men.

I realize I don't want to re-list the apartment until I know where everything stands with me, Dani, and the guys. This is more complicated than any of us anticipated. Loving someone is the easy part. Blending four lives is a bigger challenge than any of us expected.

CHAPTER 9
Nathan

IT'S JUST after midnight when my phone rings.

It's Hughes. So it's just after ten for him and Danielle.

"You don't get to tell me to leave Danielle alone," I tell him without a greeting.

"I know."

I stop with my mouth open. I hadn't expected that answer. After Danielle stopped responding to my texts, I'd texted Michael simply *you'd better take good care of our girl. She needs you.* I'd meant it all ways and I knew he knew that. He'd sent back, *she's fine, leave her alone.*

I'd been stewing about that since.

Now he's calling and I'm prepared to tell him exactly what I think about him giving me orders about Danielle and about him ignoring her in favor of professional colleagues.

But he sounds like he needs to talk.

I frown. "What's going on? Is Danielle alright?"

"Yes. She's fine."

"Are you?"

He doesn't answer right away. But then he says, "Yes. I am. Mostly."

Goddammit, my chest is tight, and my temper is a little short.

Things were tense in the twenty-four hours after we talked about marriage and kids and then decided to table the discussion. Then Hughes and Danielle took off for Vegas.

I don't like that she's gone for this entire week, out of touch, away from me, but I'll admit that is not a mature, healthy attitude. She's not my possession. She's my girlfriend. And she's not just *my* girlfriend. God knows I'm happy to share her when she's here. In fact, sharing her with Hughes and Crew is getting easier and more comfortable all the time. Ever since Christmas, things have shifted in a great direction. We all feel more secure and appreciate each other in new ways.

Yes, buying the house, renovating, and moving has been stressful but that's over now. Yes, having Michael and Danielle leave before we're completely unpacked isn't perfect timing, but it will be fine.

It's fine that she spends a few days away from me. I don't have to like it to be okay with it. And honestly, even if I feel pricks of jealousy at times thinking about her seeing the fountains at the Bellagio or winning at the Black Jack table or seeing a fun show for the first time with Michael, I also feel great that she's with a man who loves her as much as I do. Someone who will take care of her and make sure she has an amazing time.

That's why her text tonight indicating that she was clearly not having a good time frustrated me.

"Tonight was complicated," he says.

"I got that impression."

"I'm glad you texted to check on her."

"I love her, Hughes. When I'm thinking of her, when she's away from me, I'm going to text her and tell her that."

"I know. But...you didn't have to *sext* with her."

"I texted that I missed her. Then she told me that she felt out of place and was bored and asked me to talk to her. She started the sexy stuff. I wanted to give her support. I wanted to let her know that she's special, even if she's in a huge, crowded ballroom full of strangers. And if she wants to be playful, if that will take her mind off of things and remind her that there's someone who wants her no matter what, I'm game."

I hear his heavy sigh. Then he surprises me again by saying, "You're right. I just wanted her with *me*. Happy and fitting in and having fun. I'm very proud to have her by my side. She's charming and delightful and beautiful. It didn't occur to me that she would feel so out of place."

I just sit quietly for a moment. Michael Hughes is an incredibly intelligent man. I understand that. He's just working all of this out. And I appreciate the fact that he called me about it. Not only are we both in love with Danielle and have her best interest at heart—something I'm very happy he recognizes—we're friends. We need to be able to do this thing we're doing.

And now, after the other night of talking about marriage and kids, we need to be *really* good friends. This is forever for us.

"If she is going to be our plus one, the woman on our arm at these events for the rest of our lives, then we have to help her get comfortable. Answer her questions. Make sure she's okay and ready."

Michael's quiet for a long moment. Strangely, I feel a tightness in my gut. This relationship is different than any of us were expecting for our lives. And, as bad as it feels to admit sometimes, I think we all wonder if we're in too deep.

But I wait for Hughes to say something. He's our rock. He's the rational one. He'll make sense of this.

"I need to ask her if she wants to stay," he finally says.

"Do you think she might not?" I ask.

Strangely, I'm not excited about the idea of Danielle coming home early. I'm actually concerned. She and Michael need to be able to spend a week alone together. Any two of us need to be able to do that. Has it been weird being here with just Crew? Sure, a little. But only because we've never done it before. Again, if we're going to do this long-term, in various combinations, we all need to get used to it.

"I don't want her to leave. But I want her to be comfortable."

I nod. "Then she needs to stay. Not everything is always going to be rainbows and roses. And I think she'll have fun after some time. It's the first night."

He gives a soft chuckle. "I would've been expecting you to be all on board with getting her home sooner."

"If she *needed* to come home sooner, of course, I'd be on board. And I miss her. But I'm happy she's there with you. You two need this time together. It's fine."

He's quiet for a moment. Then he says, "I'm glad she felt like she could talk to you tonight. I like knowing that Dani can lean on you. It's kind of a lot being the only guy here for her."

I actually laugh out loud at that. "Our girl is too much for just one guy. We know this."

He laughs and I'm relieved. "I always want her to feel safe and happy and if I can't be the one doing it, I know you two can."

"I know exactly what you mean." I pause. "You *both* are okay? I really can send the plane."

Michael laughs. "Oh, I know you can. I'll talk to her. I want to stay, though."

"You know what, Hughes? Surprisingly, I want you both to stay too."

"Is it okay to remind you that you said that in a couple more days?"

"I'll probably deny it."

"That's what I thought." But he sounds like he's smiling now.

CHAPTER 10
Crew

I FUCKING HATE JUSTIN TRAVERS.

I haven't scored this entire game. I shot twice and they were both blocked.

No more.

This whole week has been fucked up. Dani and Michael have been gone for four days and I'm playing my second game while they are in Vegas. I've hated this whole week. But at least I scored in our last game. Tonight, so far, the Dragons are shutting me out.

But no more. I'm not some dumb hormonal teenage kid who needs his girlfriend around so he can play well. I'm a professional fucking athlete, one of the best in the NHL. I'm paid big bucks to do my job and dammit, I can do it no matter what is going on around me.

I race down the ice, glancing to my right. Jack Hayes is neck and neck with me along the sideboards. He passes over to me and I take the puck, heading straight for the goal.

This time.

This is the one.

I can feel it.

I pull my stick back and start my forward motion.

But the next thing I feel is a fuck ton of pain.

I hear the whistle and then my field of vision is filled with Jack''s face.

"Fuck. Are you okay?"

I don't know exactly what happened, but I don't think I'm okay. I become aware that my helmet is off. Which would probably explain the throbbing in my head. Clearly, I hit the back of my head on the ice. That's not good. I'm also aware of pain in my groin. Fuck. I've had strains before and that's what that feels like. But what the hell happened?

Justin Travers probably knows something about it.

I'm going to kill that fucker.

One of our trainers, Eli, and our assistant coach, Owen Phillips, join Jack as other players gather around.

"McNeil. What's up?" Eli asks, crouching next to me.

"Did I score?"

Coach Phillips chuckles. "Nope."

I squeeze my eyes shut. Fuck. I'm not blaming how I've played this week on Dani being gone. I can play well even when she's not home. I know this. But I hate that people are thinking that's the problem. I think Nathan's thinking that's the problem.

Then I think about the fact that Dani might have seen this injury. My mom saw the injury. My sister.

Okay, Dani and my mom are going to be more concerned than my sister. But if I smacked my head on the ice, even Luna's gonna know that's not good.

"You know where you are?" Eli asks.

"Lying on my back in the middle of the arena, looking like a dumbass. With no goals."

That all makes my head hurt even worse. And not because it hurts to think. Because the truth hurts.

Eli chuckles. "Well, he's oriented to time and place."

"And reality," someone else says.

I don't bother thinking hard enough to try to place the voice.

"So, someone help me up," I say.

"We're heading to the training room," Eli says. "You're out."

I want to protest but I know better. I'm fucking hurt. I probably have a concussion.

So, I'm out of the game.

With no points.

I wish Doc was here. It's not that I don't trust the other people on our medical staff. I definitely do. But Michael would be concerned, but he wouldn't baby me. He'd tell me the truth. If he pulled me out of the game, it would be for real. He wouldn't worry about being extra careful. He wouldn't worry about Nathan yelling at him for benching his best player. He wouldn't worry about me yelling at him for benching his best player. He'd do what was best for me healthwise, first. He can handle me and Nathan.

But it's the fact that I'm also his roommate, his friend, that I'm dating his girlfriend, that makes me trust he'd be extra concerned.

"Yeah," I agree with Eli. I need to get to the training room. I'm not helping the team much out here tonight anyway.

Somehow, they get me back behind the scenes. I'm aware the crowd cheers when I get upright, but other than that, I'm not really paying attention to what's going on around me. They check me over. Confirm a groin strain. That's nothing new. Annoying. I'll have to treat it. This actually could keep me on the bench for a couple of games. But I'm not going to die.

They go through the concussion checks as well. And, no surprise, I have one.

So that's gonna definitely keep me down for the next twenty-four to forty-eight hours, if not longer.

"I need a second," I hear a voice say.

I know that voice. Nathan's here.

I'm sitting on the edge of the exam table, but I have my eyes closed. The lights hurt.

I hear the sound of shuffling feet as people leave the room, and the door shut.

"Crew."

I crack an eye open. Nathan never calls me Crew. He calls me McNeil. "Hey, Boss."

I can see the concern on his face. "Are you alright?"

"They didn't tell you?"

He walks further into the room, his hands tucked into the pockets of his dress pants. "Yeah, they gave me the official report. Groin strain, concussion. But that's not you telling me. Are you alright?"

I managed to pry both eyes open. Now I realize I'm looking at my friend. The guy I live with. The guy who shares the woman I'm in love with. Not the owner of my team. Not my boss.

"Not really," I tell him, honestly. "I hurt like hell. And with me down for a couple games, it might be rough. Sorry."

"Don't be. The hit was illegal as fuck. Not your fault."

"I'm actually thinking more than I'm sorry about not being able to unpack my bedroom, or finish putting that table together downstairs."

Nathan gives me a half grin and shakes his head. "Like I really thought you were going to unpack the rest of your room in the next six months, anyway."

See, this makes me feel better. "They're going to let me go home, right?"

Nathan nods. "I'll be sure of it."

"You're going to have to babysit me."

Nathan's eyebrows arch. "I'm aware."

"I'm not a very good listener."

Nathan rolls his eyes. "Also very aware of that."

"It's just you and me, Boss. That kind of does suck. Sorry."

He nods. "It's okay. I've got you."

I let my eyes slide shut again. "Thanks."

"But before you relax too much, your girlfriend is blowing up my phone."

My heart flips in my chest. "She okay?" I ask. Without opening my eyes.

"Not really. She saw you go down. And when she called me, I

couldn't tell her much. I think she needs to hear your voice. You up for that?"

I hold my hand out. "Always."

"You will tell her you're okay."

"But I could get some real sweet attention and lovin' out of this," I say.

"McNeill." Ah, there's his boss-voice. "You *will* tell her you're okay. She doesn't need to be freaking out when she's so far away. Especially because you're fine."

"Yeah. I'll make her feel better."

I just lie there and listen to nothing for a moment and then him say, "Hey, sweetheart, he's right here." He pauses for a moment. "Yes." Pause. "Yes, Danielle." He sighs. "Danielle." He uses that firm voice with her that he needs to sometimes to get her to calm down. I smile slightly. "He's going to be okay. I'm going to take care of him. Here. Talk to him." He puts the phone in my hand. "You know what to do."

I nod. "Yeah, I got this." I lift the phone to my ear. "Hey, pretty girl."

"Crew?"

I can tell her voice is tight, like she's fighting tears.

My eyes open and I meet Nathan's gaze. He shakes his head. I sigh.

"Dani, I'm okay."

"No, you're not! I was watching the game and saw the fall. No matter what it is, you're not okay. They took you out of the game!"

"Shhh, honey, sweetie. It's a concussion. And a strain. I've had these before."

"Oh my God, Crew," she says, sniffing. "I hated seeing that. I mean I've seen you get smacked in the face and fall before, but this was awful. And they were talking on TV about how hard you hit your head and how dangerous that can be."

"Jesus, Hughes didn't shut it off?" I'm surprised. Michael should've been there keeping her calm.

"I'm in the room alone. Michael is down at a work dinner. I was watching by myself."

I swear under my breath. "I'm sorry. You shouldn't have been. He could've told you I'd be okay."

"But he doesn't know that. He's not there to examine you." She takes a shaky breath. "Oh my God, Michael needs to be there with you. What the fuck are we doing in Vegas?"

That makes me smile slightly. "Well, we know you're not winning any money, but hopefully you're having a great time, seeing some cool stuff, and fucking your brains out."

That startles her into silence for a moment. "I miss you. I'm worried about you," she said softly.

She makes my heart melt. As always. "I miss you too, Cookie. You'll be home soon. And I'm okay." There is silence for a moment. I say, "Take a deep breath, pretty girl."

She does.

"I'm alive and well. And I can't wait to see you. But I am going to be honest and tell you that I have a fucking horrible headache. So, I'm going to let you talk to Nathan. And you know Nate's not gonna lie to you."

She's quiet.

"Dani," I say firmly. "Tell me you know I'm okay."

"You're okay," she says softly. "But I do want to talk to Nathan."

"Of course, you do. I love you."

"I love you too," her voice wobbles again. I hear her sniff.

I hand the phone over to Nathan. "Please tell her something that will make her feel better."

He nods. "I'll be back to get you in a minute."

As he walks out the door. I hear him say, "Danielle, I'm here with him. Yes, I promise I will take care of him."

I lay back on the table and close my eyes.

I love the idea that Michael is with Dani, taking care of her. And I gotta admit, knowing that I can lean on Nathan is pretty great.

I bet I can even get him to stop for ice cream on our way home.

CHAPTER 11
Dani

THE SECOND THE hotel room door opens and Michael walks through it, I take a deep breath. I'm both relieved and terrified.

His expression is serious. "Hi, baby," he says. "We need to fly back to Chicago tonight."

My stomach plummets. "It's that bad?" I whisper. "I just talked to him and he said he's okay. Nathan said he's okay. But I need you to say it."

"What?" Michael shakes his head, moving past me and pulling out his suitcase and setting it on the bed.

"Please tell me Crew is going to be okay," I say.

He frowns. "Crew is going to be fine. I talked to Dr. Hamilton and he said it's a mild concussion."

I stare at his back. "Oh. But…then why do we have to go to Chicago?"

It flashes through my mind that Michael is still concerned about Crew, because he's one of his best friends. He just wants to be there for Crew. My heart melts a little at that. I move toward him, ready to pack as well.

"I just got a call from my sister. My father had a heart attack. I need to get to Decatur."

It takes a second for those words to really register. I turn away from the closet. "A *heart attack*? Oh, my God, Michael." I cross to him and slip my arms around his waist, hugging him from behind. "I'm so sorry."

He puts his hands over mine and squeezes me in return. "He's okay. No permanent damage to his heart. But I would like to see him and my mother, reassure them both."

"Of course. Absolutely." I press a kiss onto his back. "We're leaving tonight?"

He's throwing clothes into his suitcase in a haphazard way that isn't his usual behavior. He is normally tidy and proficient at folding his clothes. I step away from him to again reach for my own suitcase.

"Yes, I changed our flights to Chicago for midnight tonight."

I'm stupidly relieved that we're flying back home tonight. I want, no need, to see Crew with my own eyes. I don't see how any concussion can be mild. I saw his head connect with the ice. That was a hard hit.

"Then you're going to Decatur tomorrow?" I pull my clothes out of the dresser drawers and stack them in my suitcase.

"No, I'm going to Decatur tonight."

I watch him strip off the suit he was wearing at dinner. He's down to his boxer briefs. "What? Oh." I frown. "Does Nathan know about your father?" I'm overwhelmed by a myriad of emotions.

Michael doesn't look worried about his father, but he does look determined to get en route back home. I'm not sure what he needs from me. He's always the rock in every situation and I'm not certain how I can help him navigate this. Nathan, on the other hand, has been dealing with medical issues with his grandfather for a long time. He would probably know what to say.

Michael shakes his head. "No, I haven't told Nathan yet. There hasn't been time."

"Are *you* okay?" I ask, trying to probe just a little. "You must be so worried about Clayton."

"I spoke to the cardiologist. I feel comfortable with the prognosis and the care he's receiving." Michael pulls on sweatpants. "I don't mean to rush you, but can you get dressed, please? We have to leave in ten minutes."

"Yes, of course." I dig through my pile of clothes, trying to find something comfortable to throw on. "Are you sure you're okay? This is your father." The reality of that hits me suddenly and I abandon my suitcase and reach out for him.

Michael opens his arms and pulls me in for a hug. I breathe in deeply, always soothed by his scent. He rubs my back gently.

"I'll be okay, Cookie. Did you eat? We can get you something at the airport if you're still hungry." He kisses the top of my head.

"I ate." Of course, even in the midst of the news about his father, he's worrying about me. That's Michael. He doesn't want to talk about how he's feeling or what he needs. He's focused on taking care of me, his mom, his dad…everyone else. "What can I do, Michael?" I press, definitely wanting to help take care of *him*.

He pulls away and gives me a smile, though it doesn't really reach his eyes. "You can get dressed."

"Do you want me to go to Decatur with you?"

I'm new to being someone's girlfriend. I haven't had a boyfriend since college and that was being in the bubble of campus life. I never even met his family. But now I'm an adult, with grown men as my boyfriends, and I need to be there for them emotionally when I can be. I know Lorraine and Clayton. I'm very worried about both of them as well. I could go, and help Michael even if the thought of going to Decatur feels like I'll be letting down Crew.

But I'm not sure how helpful I'll really be. Michael doesn't really need help. He's the guy who takes care of everything. I might actually be more of a distraction than anything. He'd be worried about if I'd eaten, if I was getting enough rest, if I was too worried about Crew.

But I can see Crew, then go to Decatur, right? I can support them both.

"You don't have to do that. Go home and be with Crew." Michael is swiping on his phone, not even looking at me.

"Are you sure?"

"Of course. There." He shows me his phone. "I just bought a ticket to Decatur from O'Hare. One ticket."

I barely glance at it, missing the details entirely, troubled by my mixed emotions. "Okay. If you're sure."

Michael is the guy who knows best about *everything*. He knows what he needs right now more than I do.

"I'm sure. Now *please* get dressed." He pats my ass lightly, but with enough force that I get moving.

Michael is the quietest of my three boyfriends on any given day, but he's quiet even for him on the flight back to Chicago. He holds my hand the entire way, absentmindedly stroking my knuckles with his thumb. I don't know what to say. I'm worried about Clayton. I know things will be better for everyone once Michael's there. He's the rock for his mom, dad, and siblings just like he is for us.

"Will you call when you get there?" I ask him quietly. "You know we'll all want to know how your dad is."

He looks over at me. "Yes, of course. My flight from Chicago is just a little over an hour and then it will take some time to get to the hospital and get all the information from everyone, but I'll check in when I can."

I nod and squeeze his hand. "Please give your dad and mom both a hug from me."

He nods. "I will." He lifts my hand to his lips and presses a kiss to the back of it. "I love you."

"I love you too." My throat tightens suddenly. "So much."

I hate that we're going in opposite directions. I want to be with him and Crew both. I know Michael doesn't really need me, but I still want to be there for him. I don't know what I could possibly do, though. I know nothing about heart attacks except that they're serious and scary. I know that if my dad had one, I'd be a wreck. I also know I would want my guys right by my side, holding my hand, hugging me, and helping me make decisions.

But Michael isn't the one who needs people to help him make decisions. He always knows what to do. He's a doctor. He doesn't need any of us to tell him that things will be alright. He knows better than any of us if that's true. Or not.

We're quiet again. I want to ask him more about what he knows about his dad's condition, how it all happened, where he was, and what he was doing, how Lorraine is, which of his sisters are there at the hospital, and how they're doing. But I don't. Michael needs time to process all of this his way.

Eventually, I fall asleep, resting my head on Michael's strong, always capable shoulder, grateful for his support and understanding.

We arrive at six in the morning, groggy and bleary-eyed. Michael is uncharacteristically grumpy, squinting at the bright lights and rising sun beating down on us from the atrium.

"It's so hot in here," he complains. "This is the dumbest design for an airport. Build a glass box then cram it with thousands of people." He strips off his sweatshirt.

"Do you want some coffee?" I ask, looking left and right and seeing no sign of any of the shops being open. I spot a coffee shop in the distance but there's a line of two dozen people in front of it.

"No, thanks, I'm too hot."

"I can get it iced."

But Michael shakes his head, staring at his phone. "My flight leaves in an hour and I have to go back out and through security."

I'm not sure what to say. My brain is still not fully functioning from dozing in and out of sleep. Talking to Crew was a relief, but I'm still worried about his concussion. Once we hit the tarmac, I turned my phone off airplane mode and had six texts pop up, but none were from Crew. Two were from Nathan assuring me again everything is fine and that Crew is sleeping it off, but anxiety is gnawing at the pit of my stomach.

We exit the gate area and once we reach the area where we

have to separate, me to pick up our luggage, Michael to catch his next flight, we pause.

"This feels weird," I tell him.

He reaches up and tucks my hair behind my ear. "I know. I hope it's just for a few days."

I grasp his wrist, pressing his hand against my face. "Me too. I hope everything is okay and you can come home soon. But I know you need to be there with them. I'll be thinking about you constantly."

He cups my face and leans in to kiss me. "Thank you for Vegas," he says against my lips.

"I had an amazing time," I promise, kissing him again before he straightens.

"Take good care of Crew," he tells me.

I smile, even though my heart squeezes remembering how Crew looked lying on the ice, not moving. "I will."

"And Nathan. He's not really the nurse-maid type." Michael finally gives me a half-smile.

I return it. "It's only been a few hours." Michael told me that he'd gotten a report from the team's medical staff and they didn't even take Crew to the hospital and that he'd been released home.

"A few hours of Nathan and Crew being home together with Crew needing medical supervision." Michael pauses. "From Nathan. His girlfriend's boyfriend. And his boss."

I actually feel myself giggle softly. "Yeah, maybe I'd better hurry."

"Are you sure you can get my bag too?" Michael asks, frowning a little. "I can go down with you."

"You don't have time. I can handle it." Michael is continuing his travel with only his carry-on. I'm taking his suitcase with his work clothes back to our new house with me. "Let me do this for you."

Michael doesn't let me do things for him very often. It feels like the least I can do.

He gives me a soft kiss. "Thank you."

I kiss him back, pouring my love into it. When I pull back, I squeeze his forearms.

"Text me as soon as you get there. Give your family a hug from me."

"I will."

Then he heads off in one direction, and I dash off in the other.

CHAPTER 12
Crew

"CAN you just put that on the top shelf in the closet?" I ask.

"I am only unpacking this one box, and it's only because it's in the fucking way," Nathan says. "Do not think I'm going to do anything more."

"Yeah, I feel really bad about not being able to help unpack anymore," I say in a sweet tone that is completely fake. And I know Nathan knows it. He probably kind of wants to punch me but he won't because of my concussion.

"I swear you got hurt on purpose just to avoid the rest of the unpacking," Nathan bitches.

"Hey," I say. "Don't joke about that. I would never fuck around with hockey." I'm not kidding about that and I need Nathan to know that. Yes, because he's the team owner, but also… fuck, I want the guy to respect me.

That's annoying.

But true.

Nathan turns to face me. He's frowning. "I know, McNeill. I never question your dedication to the game or the team."

"Okay." I blow out a breath. This injury is really pissing me off. I always want to be playing but this point in the season is crucial. "Good."

"You're a hell of a player and...I know people tell you that all the time. I know you've heard it since you were a kid. I know you know that, but—" Nathan clears his throat. "You're truly going to be one that people talk about when they talk about hockey history. You could have gone anywhere. I'm very glad you chose the Racketeers. Not just because of what you do on the ice, but because you're a great representative of the team. I know we've got a very unconventional situation between us, and I'm glad you're here for lots of reasons outside of hockey, but I don't forget for one day what you bring to hockey in Chicago. To my team."

I blink at him. I don't know what to say. That is exactly the kind of thing I've always wanted to hear from an owner. And honestly, getting it from Nathan is...huge. The guy doesn't share his feelings often or easily.

And he'd definitely deny saying this if I ever tell anyone.

"Thanks, Nathan," I say. I never call him Nathan. "I'm really pissed I'm on the sidelines now. I really want the Cup. I've always wanted it, of course. But now, this year, this team...I want it more. And yes, because you and I are friends now, it means even more. But I swear I'd be playing this hard even if Dani had never come along and we'd never started this...thing."

"I know that." There's a pause, and then he asks the question I've been dreading, "Is Dani being away a part of any of how things have gone this week?"

I blow out a breath. "That's a fair question. And I've asked myself the same thing. But no. I'm just having an off week. Honestly, I love that girl with everything in me," I add. "But when I'm on the ice, I'm on the ice. I've missed her like crazy, but she's with Hughes and they're having fun and that's great and...." I don't know exactly how Nathan feels about Michael and Dani being off alone. But I know how I feel. "That actually makes me feel happy and comfortable. She's with a guy who's going to take amazingly good care of her and make her happy and they're going to have fun and I have nothing to worry about. So no, my shit play this week is all about me."

He just nods. He doesn't share his own feelings about the Vegas trip but he says, "Everyone has off games. You'll be back."

"You sure?"

"You're Crew Fucking McNeill," Nathan says. "Of course I'm sure. And," he adds. "I've put my money where my mouth is. You have a fucking huge paycheck to earn."

I chuckle. "Yeah, my boss is kind of a dick sometimes and he'll eventually be on my ass if I don't get my shit together."

"Damn right."

Just then, a soft voice says, "I love you both with everything in me, too."

We both swing toward the door. I'm sitting on the front of the recliner I have in my room, so when my head gets a little dizzy, I don't worry about falling over.

Nathan is leaning against my dresser. He straightens so quickly, the thing wobbles, and my bobbleheads—yes, of course, there's a Crew McNeill bobblehead and, of course, I have six of them—start nodding.

"Danielle," Nathan says, obviously surprised to see her.

Dani's home.

Thank God.

Wait, why is Dani home?

Those are my first three thoughts.

"What are you doing here?" Nathan asks, striding toward her. He pulls her into his arms for a hug, but says, "You weren't supposed to be home until tomorrow."

She squeezes him back, but peeks around him to look at me. "Crew got hurt. Of course I came home early."

My girl is home. "I am really, really hurt, Dani girl. Come make me feel better."

She laughs and goes up on tiptoe to kiss Nathan, before extracting herself from his arms. She looks up at him. "You okay?"

He shakes himself. "Of course. I'm thrilled to see you. Just surprised."

She takes my outstretched hand and I tug her into my lap. I

immediately wrap my arms around her and nuzzle my face into her neck, breathing her in. Her arms go around my neck too and she presses close, her lips against my temple.

"Watch it," Nathan says. "He really is hurt. You have to take it easy."

Dani pulls back and looks into my eyes. "Tell me how you are. Seriously."

"I'm okay. And even better now."

She glances at Nathan. "Of course I'll take it easy on him. I'm not going to do anything to hurt him. But you can't expect me to stay away."

I give her hip a little squeeze. "I have a mild concussion and a muscle strain. As much as I hate to say it, I'm not up for being your usual hotshot."

She leans in and gives me a gentle kiss. "I don't need you to be anything specific. Except healthy. I definitely need you to be healthy."

I see tears well up in her eyes and I immediately lift my hand to cup her cheek. "Gonna live through it. It's happened before. And I'm so glad you're here, but I hate that you cut your trip short."

"Don't be silly. I had to be here."

"Bet Michael's pissed at me."

"He's concerned. He's not just your doctor, he's your friend."

I nod. "Yeah. I know. I'm bracing myself for his lecture, though."

"Where is he?" Nathan asks.

Dani looks over at him. "On his way to Decatur."

I frown and look at Nathan. Decatur? What have I missed while my brain has been mushy?

"Why the hell is he going to Decatur?" Nathan asks.

Okay, I'm not the only one then.

Dani stares at Nathan. "He still hasn't told you?"

Nathan comes toward us. "Told me what?"

"Clayton had a heart attack," Dani says. "He's in the hospital."

"*What*? Is Clayton okay?" Nathan asks, sounding as alarmed as I feel.

"Yes, the doctors said it was a minor heart attack. Michael got the call about the same time Crew got hurt. We split up at the airport. He's probably on the plane right now."

Neither of us reply for a long moment. I look to Nathan. He's frowning deeply and he looks at me as if I'm supposed to know what to say. My first reaction is *why the hell did you let him go to Decatur alone?* So I decide not to say anything.

Dani leans away from me, studying my face. "What?"

I look from her to Nathan. He gives me nothing.

I focus on her. "I'm just…surprised…that you're here with us instead of with Michael."

"I'm here because you're hurt. If Clayton wasn't in the hospital we both would have come home early."

"Um, no," I say. "Michael would not have come home early for this, Dani." I squeeze her. "This is nothing that hasn't happened before. And will again." It's just a reality of hockey. It's a rough, physical sport.

She frowns. "I thought you'd be happy to see me."

"I am, baby." I kiss her cheek. "I love that you were worried about me. But…"

"But what?" she demands, frowning.

"But Michael's father is in the hospital," Nathan says. "You didn't think you should go with him?"

"I did think about going. We talked about it and he said he wanted me to come home. Michael is a rock," Dani says, meeting Nathan's gaze. "He doesn't really need anyone. Especially…me." She says it quietly.

I squeeze her hand and then grasp her chin, making her look at me. "Hey. Dani." Finally, she meets my eyes. "What does that mean? Michael loves you. Very much."

She nods. "I know he loves me. But he doesn't *need* me." She gives me a little smile. "Come on, Crew. You know that's true. He's the caregiver. He takes care of us. We don't take care of him.

And if I'd gone with him, I would have just been one more person for him to worry about." She pauses and sighs. "I think he was glad I chose to come home where you two could deal with me."

I don't know what to say to all of that because...well, she's not wrong.

I don't think Michael considers Dani a burden or anything like that, but it's definitely true that Hughes takes care of us and there's not much we do for him.

Nathan pulls his phone out of his pocket. He dials, but a moment later he shakes his head. "He's not answering."

"I told you he's on the plane," Dani says.

"We should all go, right?" I ask. "If we're all three there, then Hughes knows we'll take care of one another and we'll just be there. If he needs us."

Nathan nods. "Yeah. I mean...kind of. But you can't. You have to stay here and rest. And someone probably does need to stay with you, at least this first twenty-four hours."

Fucking concussion protocol.

"I'm going to be fine," I groan. My head is pounding but a sick father is a lot more serious than a headache.

"Listen, you need to take care of yourself. Michael would say the same thing. If you got on an airplane right now, he would kick my ass," Nathan says.

Dani crosses her arms across her stomach and says, "Michael will tell us if something is more serious with Clayton. Then we can decide what to do."

Nathan finally nods. "You're right. Michael will let us know if he needs us."

I think about that. What would he need us for? I would hope like hell he'd want us there if something really bad happened. God forbid. But as long as Clayton is mostly stable, Michael knows a hell of a lot more about it than we do. What could we say or do to make him feel better?

I run a hand through my hair. Fuck. This is complicated.

Michael is with us because he wants to be, not because he needs to be.

The rest of us, on the other hand, definitely need him.

I hope he knows that. I hope that makes him feel good. And not like we're all a bunch of problems he has to constantly deal with.

CHAPTER 13
Dani

NATHAN SLIPS into bed behind me, naked.

I'm lying on my side, also naked, facing Crew. He's sleeping on the far side of the mattress. I wanted him in here with us so we could keep an eye on him, but I know Nathan will want to snuggle—he always wants to be touching me when we're in bed—so I left a lot of space so as not to disturb Crew.

He's been asleep for about twenty minutes. His breathing is nice and even. I love seeing him whole and healthy. When he went to bed, he said his headache was much improved. But I hate the idea that he had pain, that his groin is bothering him, and that not being able to play is bothering him.

Nathan's big hand splays across my stomach, and he pulls me back into his body. I shiver with pleasure as he wraps around me. I love the way he seems to engulf me. He makes me feel safe. All my guys do, but Nathan's protectiveness is above and beyond. There's a power about him, even when he's just sitting at the kitchen breakfast bar having a cup of coffee. Strength and confidence exudes from him, and whenever he's around, I feel like everything is going to be okay.

He'll take care of it. Whatever it is.

Michael treats me more like an equal than someone he needs

to take care of. He's a caregiver, making me coffee, unpacking my boxes, making sure I've eaten, and so on. But he doesn't boss me around in the protective, possessive way Nathan does. Michael asks me for my opinions, he pushes me to make decisions. With Nathan, I can just turn things over and know he'll take care of me.

Crew is easy, of course. He makes me laugh, I make him laugh, he lights up when I walk into a room. I know he also would protect me no matter what happened, but Crew would do it physically, with his fists if needed.

Nathan has this cool, composed confidence. He gets shit done. People don't second-guess him.

Sure, a lot of the time it's because he has money and influence. But he wields it carefully. He makes shrewd business decisions, he expects other people to step up and meet his expectations, and he uses his money for good.

The only thing he's ever even slightly irrational about is me.

I can unravel this powerful, seemingly cold, always composed man.

And I love that.

He would do anything for me and it makes me feel adored and safe.

I press my ass against his already hard length. I'm not sure I have ever been naked and not felt Nathan hard.

His face is in my hair and he says roughly, "Keep doing that and you're going to end up getting fucked right next to your sleeping boyfriend."

It's all kinds of wrong, probably, but lust washes through me.

"Am I really supposed to believe that you weren't going to fuck me tonight?" I whisper.

I don't want to wake Crew up. He needs his rest. Besides, he's not supposed to have sex, and I know waking up to me naked in bed would arouse him. Certainly, waking up next to me having sex with Nathan next to him would arouse him. And that's not fair.

Nathan's hand runs back and forth across my belly. "Oh,

there's no chance you're not getting fucked. I just wanted to be very sure to point out that this is your fault."

I smile. "You told me to come to bed naked."

"Course I did. But you're the one who just rubbed this sweet ass against my cock."

"Do you want me to move away? Leave six inches between us?"

He rubs his face against my cheek, abrading my skin with his stubble. "You know very well that six inches isn't far enough to get away from my cock."

I laugh lightly. But he's not wrong. He definitely reaches over more than six inches. "Should we go out to the living room? Or into my room?"

His hand slides down my belly and between my legs. His thick middle finger starts circling over my clit.

"You're already wet. Such a bad girl. Have you been lying here thinking about how much this pretty pussy needs to be filled up and hoping I'd do it?"

"Yes," I say, my breath already catching.

"Very good answer. I love when your dirty little slut comes out for me."

I give a soft whimper. I know there are women who would not get off on being called sluts, but when my guys use it, it's very much a term of endearment. They love how needy I am for them. They love that I'll do anything for them. They love that I'm greedy for their cocks, and their touches, and the orgasms they give me.

They also love that they are the only ones who could make me like this. And I have no shame or hesitation in admitting that.

"We can't do this next to Crew," I say softly.

"Yes, we can. This bed is huge."

"He might wake up."

"His drugs are potent. But you will have to be quiet." He moves the hand that was just playing with my clit up to my mouth. He slips his wet finger past my lips. I suck it clean, then he covers my mouth with his hand and puts his mouth against my ear. "No screaming my name, Danielle."

That will be difficult. I'm very vocal during sex and the things these men do to me make it very difficult to not say very graphic things and make a lot of noise.

I shake my head. He simply says firmly, "Yes."

I pull on his wrist, trying to move his hand, but he just tightens it.

"You're going to be a good girl. Crew needs his sleep. But I need your pussy. And you're going to give us both what we need."

We could very easily go to any of the other multitude of rooms in this house. Nathan is staying here on purpose. It's not so much that it's his competition with Crew driving him. That would only work if Crew was actually awake. But there is something very dirty, and fun, about the situation. It's like we're sneaking around. Which might seem a little unfair, but Crew won't know. And it's Nathan. He's my boyfriend. It's not like Crew doesn't know that we fuck.

"Do I need to put something in your mouth?"

I shake my head. I'll be good for him. He knows that.

I love sex with Nathan. I love sex with all the guys. I love sex when it's all three guys at once and I love my one-on-one time with each of them. Each of them gives me something different. It's almost like I get to be a different woman with each of them.

With Nathan, what I love the best is the bossiness. I don't have to think about what to do to please him. He will absolutely tell me. I don't even have to think about how to make it good for *me*. Nathan always knows. There's no thinking. It's all pleasure.

He holds me tight with my back against his front. It works perfectly so that he can keep his mouth against my ear, one hand over my mouth, the other moving along my body. He starts with my nipples.

"You're going to come apart for me, Danielle," he says, low

and firm. "I'm going to fuck you deep and hard. But you're not going to make a sound."

He's going to try to push me. He's going to tell me to be quiet, then do everything he can to make me loud.

This is going to be fun.

He pinches and rolls one of my nipples, and I immediately squirm, pressing my ass harder into his cock.

"Your body is every fantasy I have ever had. I love touching you. I love the way you respond to me."

His cock pulses against my ass and I whimper softly. The fact that I can affect this man, this powerful, seemingly untouchable man, never ceases to make me feel bold and sexy.

Nathan has let down his walls with me, emotionally, but also physically. There is no other scenario I can imagine where Nathan would let other men do what Michael and Crew do to me. I can't imagine Nathan ever letting anyone touch something that matters to him. Not to mention how close he has to get to them physically, letting them see him be vulnerable too.

But that's what makes it all so special and so hot.

"The way you feel in my arms. The way your body fits against mine, I'll never stop craving this." He tugs on my nipple, then squeezes just enough to give me a stab of pain. Just the way he knows I love.

I give a muffled cry into his hand.

Something I always notice when it's just Nathan and me is that he uses I and me very purposefully. My guys share me openly and eagerly and none of them hesitate to say 'we' and 'they' when we're all together. But when it's just me and Nathan, he very much likes to point out that it's just him making me feel this way.

He slides his hand from my breast to my hip. I whimper again, in protest.

His hand over my mouth tightens just slightly. "Shhh. Your pussy needs attention," he says gruffly. "You play with your nipples. Keep them hard. Make this pussy nice and wet for me."

I immediately lift my hand to my nipple and start playing with it. I love to have my nipples stimulated, and it definitely makes me wetter. He slides his hand back and forth across my belly, then slips down to just barely brush over my clit with his middle finger.

I arch, trying to get closer to his touch. He pinches my inner thigh and I give another gasp.

"I can't spank you. Crew would definitely hear the delicious sound of my hand hitting your sweet ass. You know how much we all love that."

I'm breathing harder and I know he can feel it against his hand. I love being spanked, but Nathan is almost the only one who does it. The other guys do love to watch, though. And they definitely love to fuck me afterwards because it makes me so wet and hot and on edge.

"But I can still make sure you behave. And punish you if you don't." He pinches my thigh again, then moves to pinch my ass.

The combination of the dark, his hand over my mouth, and the fact that I have to stay quiet all combine to make this feel especially taboo. I know as soon as he slides a finger into me, my orgasm is going to start building.

I wiggle against him, trying to encourage him.

"I'm in charge," he reminds me, knowing exactly what I'm doing. "We're going at my pace, Danielle."

We always go at his pace. I can drive him crazy, I can push him, I can get him to speed up—or spank me some more when I want that—but he rarely lets me totally take control.

One of my fantasies is actually to handcuff Nathan to the bed and have my way with him. One of these days I'm going to share that fantasy with him. Being out of control like that will make him nuts, though. Still, I think he'll do it for me.

"Please," I say from behind his hand. It's too muffled to hear though. Which is unfortunate, because Nathan loves to hear me beg.

I feel his chest move with a light chuckle, however. He knows.

His hand moves between my legs, and his middle finger

immediately finds my clit. He presses with exactly the right amount of pressure and starts to rub. I swear, when women talk about how guys can't find their clit or their G-spot, I almost feel bad for having three hot men who can find mine with no trouble.

I *almost* feel bad.

I moan softly.

"So wet. So fucking ready," Nathan praises. "And all mine."

I love that I have this side effect of having three men sharing me. The sex when it's all four of us is amazing, but the slight edge of competition they all bring to our one-on-one sessions is definitely a perk.

I nod my head since I can't speak.

"Oh yes, all mine." His fingers move lower and he dips one inside. He teases just my entrance though. I protest with a soft snarl.

He doesn't care. He just chuckles darkly. He lifts the hand to his mouth. In my opinion, he's very noisy about licking it clean. "So fucking good. Too bad I can't bury my head between your legs. But we both know that would make you far too loud."

He's right. There's no way I could stay quiet for that.

"I can give this sweet clit plenty of attention like this though," he promises, returning his hand between my legs and circling my clit in delicious, slow, tempting circles. Instinctively, I try to arch against him again. He lets me, this time slipping a finger inside me. Then another.

I moan. I need to be filled up. I lift my top leg up and back, so that it rests over his, spreading my thighs.

"Oh, my pretty slut doesn't even need her mouth to beg for what she wants. You're showing me just what you need. Look at you, spreading your legs, arching this gorgeous body, begging me to fill you up and make you come."

That makes my hips strain toward his hand, wanting to take him deeper.

He kisses my neck, then bites down slightly as he slides a third finger into me.

Heat washes over me. Then he presses his thumb against my clit. My orgasm starts to coil.

I press my ass against him, then arch forward. I try to get closer to his hand, to tempt his cock, bucking my hips back and forth.

"Yes, fuck my hand gorgeous," he says. "Don't let a little restraint get in your way of taking what you need. Use my fingers and come all over my hand."

I try to suck in a breath, but with his hand covering my mouth, I feel like I don't get enough air. My head feels a little dizzy and all I can focus on is the ache that he's created between my legs. The one that he's not quite reaching. I need him deeper. I need to be filled with more than his fingers.

"Your cock," I try to say.

Of course he can't hear me.

But he knows.

"I might need to move my hand to hear your sweet voice asking for my cock."

I nod my head quickly.

"Don't wake Crew. He'll be so fucking jealous."

I shake my head in a silent promise to be quiet.

He slides his hand from my mouth to the front of my throat where it rests hot and heavy, and I feel possessed and protected.

"Tell me what you need, Danielle. Beg me."

"Please fuck me, Nathan," I whisper hoarsely. "Please. I need to come."

He squeezes gently on my throat. "Tell me what you need."

"Your cock. God, fill me up. Please."

"Do you think you can take it? Do you think you can take me deep, milk my cock, take all my cum, and the whole time keep all your sweet cries and moans inside?"

I nod my head quickly. "Yes. Yes, please," I whisper.

"Let's find out, without my hand covering your mouth."

Oh, no. I'm actually a little worried that I can't stay that quiet.

Without his hand covering my mouth, what if I forget and cry out?

But I don't have time to really think about it because he takes his hand from my pussy, clamps it on my hip, pulls me back, and sinks his cock inside me.

It fills me and stretches me in that perfect, delicious way that I need so much.

I gasp and it is a little loud.

I clamp my own hand over my mouth.

I whimper as he starts moving.

He's not trying to be quiet. Our skin slaps, and the bed moves.

I reach back and grasp his hip, trying to slow his thrusts down. We can't shake Crew awake.

But Nathan isn't stopping.

"Nathan," I gasp, trying to get his attention.

I have it.

His mouth is against my ear as he says, "You told me to fuck you and I'll do anything for you, so hold on. And be quiet."

He thrusts hard and hits that perfect spot and I gasp his name. Almost too loud.

"Naughty girl," he says into my hair.

Then he rolls me onto my stomach and presses my face into the pillow. He's stretched along my back, his cock still deep.

"Scream into the pillow if you need to, but I'm not letting up."

He starts thrusting in short, hard thrusts and I do gather the pillow against my face and let myself gasp and moan out loud. It's a relief to let my pleasure out that way.

I hear his harsh breathing but he's making no other noises.

Then Nathan reaches around, puts his finger against my clit, and I'm done.

He circles my clit, thrusts deep and hard and says in my ear, "My very naughty, dirty, loud, good girl."

And I come apart.

Anytime Nathan praises me, it works that way.

Even when the words seem graphic and dirty, he always knows exactly what I want and need.

I cry out into the pillow, coming hard around his cock.

His body stiffens, his fingers tighten against my hips, and he fills me up. Without making a noise.

He stays on top of me, breathing hard in my ear for several long minutes. He strokes a hand up and down my side from breast to hip and back again.

Finally, he rolls off, bringing me with him so we are once again spooning with my back to his front.

He pushes my hair back from my face and says against my neck, "You gorgeous thing, you are so fucking amazing."

And I snuggle close with a smile, his praise covering me and soaking in the way his body heat does, and doing exactly what I need him to—making me feel like everything is going to be okay.

CHAPTER 14
Michael

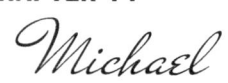

I HAND my mother a cup of tea and a sandwich, then move past her chair to sink onto the end of the couch closest to her.

I'm so relieved that she's finally sitting down. My dad is asleep in their bedroom, one of my sisters has gone home to check on her kids, and my other sister is asleep in the guest room.

They're all finally resting.

Now I can maybe do the same.

My dad's going to be fine. The rest of my family is going to be fine. At least my immediate blood family. I need to get back to Chicago and make sure my family with Crew, Nathan, and Danielle is equally stable.

I have a niggling feeling things aren't completely fine there. I'm restless. I've been in Decatur for three days and have only been checking in with them sporadically. Nathan tells me that Crew is feeling a lot better, and that Dani has stopped Googling everything she can find about concussions and heart attacks. At least when she's around him. She probably does it at the bookstore.

Still, it feels strange to be apart from them.

"I told Danielle that you will be coming home soon."

I look over at my mother. "What?"

She's picking at her sandwich and watching me. "When she texted today, I told her that I thought you would be coming home soon. Maybe tomorrow."

"Danielle texted you today?"

"She's been texting me every day. And she sent me and your father those gorgeous flowers."

She points to the arrangement that's sitting in the middle of the dining room table. It's beautiful and sweet and colorful and instantly looks like something Dani would pick out.

"She also sent us some soup and dinner rolls and salad from our favorite place today. It will be perfect for dinner tomorrow after you go home."

I swallow. I haven't said anything about going home tomorrow, but a big part of me wants to. Now hearing that Dani's been communicating and checking in with my mom, I want to even more.

"She's been in touch every day." My mom pauses. "And she's been asking about you."

"She didn't need to do that. I've been texting updates."

"Don't act like she's bothering me, Michael Joseph," my mother scolds. "I'd want you to be with someone who would check in and I love hearing from her. She's also keeping me updated on Crew's recovery. And she sent me a couple of book recommendations when I asked. I was bored sitting in the waiting room."

I let that all sink in. Danielle and my mother have been in touch. That doesn't feel strange. I want my family to develop a connection to her. Of course, Dani checked in with her. My girl is sweet and loving. I feel my shoulders relax a little.

"But I *have* been keeping them updated," I say. I don't want my mom to think that I've been blowing my girlfriend and her boyfriends—my best friends—off.

"Yes. But what did you say in your texts?" My mother asks. Her tone indicates that she has her ideas already.

"That I'm fine. That dad's fine. That everything is fine."

"So you told the woman that you love, that you've chosen as a life partner, that you're "fine" after your father's heart attack."

I frown and look down at my own sandwich. "I am fine. And he's fine."

"And you have nothing more to share with her? No other feelings? No details?"

"I don't know how much I should be leaning on her. She's not just mine." I'm as surprised as anyone that I admitted that out loud to my mother.

"There it is," my mother says. She leans to set her plate on the side table. "Is that why she isn't here, Michael? Because she's not just yours?"

"Crew got hurt." I know she knows this.

"So, she thought he needed her more."

I nodded. "Yes. And he probably did. He always will," I say. I take a breath. This is my mother. She knows me very well. If I don't say the rest of what I'm thinking, she'll know I'm holding back. "If his dad had a heart attack, and I got injured, she'd go to him," I say. "Because Crew does need her more." I meet my mother's eyes. "So does Nathan."

My mother doesn't seem surprised by this. "Do you feel like you come in third place?"

I sigh and set my plate next to hers. I lean my forearms onto my knees and decide to be fully honest. "I think she loves us all equally. And she needs us equally for different things. But we all need her too. Nathan's never had love and acceptance the way Dani gives it to him. Crew's never had a woman who wants him for him. Not his money or fame or looks, but just truly him. He can really be himself with her. They both can. And this sweetheart of a woman loves them with all she's got." I'm quiet for a moment. "They need her because of that."

"And you don't need her as much?"

I look at her. "I've been surrounded by love and accepted for who I am all my life. I chose Dani because she's amazing, I love her for who she is, but…I don't need her like they do and…" I have to clear my throat to finish. "I want to marry her."

My mother nods, clearly not surprised by that. "I assumed you *would* marry her."

"But I don't get to do that on my own."

"Right. Do Nathan and Crew want to marry her?"

"Nathan does. Crew…will eventually."

"So, what's the problem?"

"That she'll never be just mine." I blow out a breath, having finally confessed the full truth to someone. "They need her and she needs them and I guess I'm trying to figure out if I can be okay with not ever being everything to her."

Again, my mother doesn't look surprised, but she looks a little sad. "Oh."

I nod. "I know. I want her to be happy and fulfilled. Nathan protects her and makes her life so easy. And she loves that. She deserves the pampering. I love that he does that for her, actually." I take a breath. "Crew wants to play and have fun and be spontaneous and over-the-top. She laughs and just blooms, like a little flower in the sun, with him." I swallow. "And I love that for her. I love watching them together."

"And you take care of her and love her," my mom points out.

"Yes. It's just a strange place to be. To love a woman the way I love her. To want Nathan and Crew for her on one hand and, on the other, wish I could give her *everything* she needs myself."

My mom reaches over and takes my hand, squeezing it. "Well, *I* want *you* happy and fulfilled," my mom finally says. "So you take care of you, okay?"

I nod. "Thanks mom. I love you."

"I know you do. And Dani knows you love her too."

Yeah, I know she does. I just hope it's enough.

CHAPTER 15
Nathan

"I SHOULD HAVE GONE TO DECATUR," I say to Crew, who is, frankly, driving me fucking insane.

He's holding court on the sofa like hockey royalty—which he is—surrounded by balloons and flowers and takeout boxes that have been sent to him by family and friends for the last three days. The damn doorbell is ringing every ten minutes and I have to keep answering it like some personal assistant to McNeill. Between that and the fact that Hughes is barely communicating with any of us, I'm a ball of tension.

More so than I usually am.

I'm worried about the playoffs without McNeill. Looking at him lying there reminds me of everything we have to lose these next few games without him. I don't want to lose the momentum that's been building all season.

I'm worried we let down Hughes, because we're all still figuring out how to do this thing, our complex relationship/family.

I'm worried about his father, even though Michael has told us several times there was no damage to his heart, because I know what it's like to lose a parent and it really sucks.

I'm annoyed that it reminds me that sooner than later I will lose my grandfather.

And I'm really annoyed that Crew is annoyed when he's the one sitting on his ass doing nothing.

Danielle has been waiting on Crew hand and foot, but she's at the bookstore working the afternoon shift and I'm stuck with this dickhead. He sucks at being out of commission. He is demanding and grouchy, watching endless videos on his phone with the volume turned all the way up. I'm one more falling-off-a-dock-into-a-lake-blooper video away from walking out the door and texting Lori McNeill to come and deal with her son.

I already tried texting his sister, and she just sent me ten laugh cry emojis back.

"I can't reach my chopsticks," Crew says, reaching out his arm a mere two inches.

He's like a Victorian heiress on a fainting couch with a bout of the fucking vapors. If the couch was the world's biggest one in existence. I'm also still annoyed by this oversized couch because Crew is usually the one sprawled on it, even before his injury.

I pick up the paper packet holding the disposable chopsticks and throw them at him. They bounce off his chest and land in his pampered lap. "Did you even hear what I said?"

"Yes. And for oh, about the tenth time, Doc didn't want you to go."

That's what's bothering me. "Yeah, and I didn't want any of you to go to the nursing home with me on Christmas Eve, and you did it anyway, and I was grateful. I was glad you were there. It made it easier. I feel like we fucked up here."

"I agree. But nothing we can do about it now." Crew pries open a box of lo mein noodles. "Can you hand me the soy sauce?"

"Get your own soy sauce!" I snap, annoyed by his nonchalance over Hughes.

"What are you so pissy about?" he demands, stabbing his noodles aggressively. "You're the one getting laid. I'm not. Listening to the two of you going at it four feet away from me in the same bed when I can't participate isn't helping my recovery."

Oh, so he heard Dani and I having sex. I should probably feel bad about that but…I only feel a *little* bad about that. "Payback's a bitch, McNeill."

"This is for fucking her in the bed first?" he asks, frowning.

"I'd be fucking her anyway. She's my girlfriend and I love to fuck her. But if you have to hear it, yeah, that's for fucking her in the bed first." I pause. "But I thought you were asleep."

"How am I supposed to sleep through that?" he asks, looking genuinely astonished and sounding very surly. "The bed is big, but it's not that big. I'd have to be in a coma not to hear the headboard hitting the wall and our girl moaning her way through an orgasm. 'Oh, Nathan, oh, God, yes, please.' You two are fucking killing me."

His imitation of Danielle is lousy, but on the money in terms of what she is usually saying to me while she's coming. His clear irritation makes me stop pacing long enough to stare at him. He sounds genuinely offended. Hurt. More than a little pissed. I'm surprised, I have to admit.

"Just because you can't have sex doesn't mean I can't," I point out. "Danielle starts it."

Sometimes. Once or twice. Okay, it's always me. But she doesn't stop me.

Crew snorts. "Look, I get it. She's curled up next to you and you're thinking, why not? I guess I just wish you would have asked me."

My eyebrows shoot up. "I don't need your permission to fuck my girlfriend."

"No, but we're all here, living together. It's like a common fucking courtesy to ask me how I would feel about it instead of waiting until you think I'm asleep. I knew you'd be a little annoyed that I took her to the bed first, but I also knew it'd give you a great excuse to spank her and dive right in. You weren't really that mad."

Now I feel like a prick and I don't like that. Because he's right. Having sex with him lying right there is a little rude and selfish.

But I still push back. "You would do the same thing if the roles were reversed."

"No, I wouldn't. Man, it's like…" He thinks for a second. "Okay, let's say you're getting bloodwork."

"Why am I getting bloodwork?" My tension eases. He sounds more like his normal self, and I'm kind of looking forward to hearing whatever brilliance he's about to spout.

"Because you're old, I don't know."

That's definitely more like him. He loves to grind on me about my age. "Fuck you."

"My point is, if they make you fast that morning before your bloodwork, do you think I would rub it in your face that I'm drinking coffee with cream and sugar and eating a giant danish?"

I look at him.

He looks at me.

"You absolutely would rub it in my face," I tell him.

He starts laughing. "Shit. You're right."

I laugh too. "Look, I'm sorry we've been disturbing your beauty rest. I didn't realize you could hear us. And you're right, it's not cool to be essentially sneaking around." I pause. "In my own bed. With my girlfriend."

He rolls his eyes, but still chuckles.

"Maybe we can work something out. You can watch, or we can involve you in a way that won't reinjure your groin."

"Thank you. I would love to watch. And thank you for being so concerned about my groin."

"You're welcome. And if something is bothering you, let's talk about it, okay? Even if it's awkward." Like the repeated use of the word 'groin.' "We can work this stuff out. Everyone needs to feel heard in this arrangement."

"Cool. I can do that."

"Wow," I hear from Hughes.

I turn around to see him stroll into the room, a carry-on bag over his shoulder. He dumps it on the living room floor.

"Listen to the two of you working out your feelings. I'm

impressed."

He doesn't sound impressed at all. He sounds annoyed.

"Hey," I said, relieved to see him for several reasons. If he's home, that means his father must be feeling better. I'm also not embarrassed to admit I want to be off Crew duty. I'm not wired for this nursemaid shit. "I'm glad you're back. How's Clayton?"

"He's good, actually. He's bounced back quickly and is resting mostly peacefully, aside from a constant parade of family who insist on seeing him."

"Not a bad problem to have people who love you," I say.

Michael kicks off his shoes and neatly slides them under the bench we have by the front door for shoe storage. "True."

"How's your mom doing?" Crew asks. "She must have been freaking out."

"My mom is one tough lady. She's holding it all together, as usual." Michael takes in the mess splayed out across the coffee table. "How's it going here? How are you doing, McNeill?"

"I'm bored, and Nate sucks at being entertaining."

That makes me roll my eyes. "Drama queen. Danielle has been indulging your every whim."

Crew grins. "Not my *every* whim. This no-sex rule is going to kill me."

His anger with me seems to have passed, and I smile back. "Then watch where you're going next time you're on the ice."

"What time does Dani get home from the bookstore?" Michael asks. "She texted me right before I left Decatur but I think I missed some of the details." He rubs his forehead with his thumb and forefinger, like he has a headache.

"She should be home any minute, actually. I wish you would have told me your plans," I tell him, guilt still sitting on my chest uncomfortably. "I could have flown you there and back in my jet, you know that."

"I didn't need a private jet. There's a million flights between Vegas and Chicago. And I wanted to escort Dani here. She was very worried about our star player here."

I hesitate, because I'm not sure if my opinion is wanted or needed. Michael's relationship with Danielle is his, even if we are all living together and sharing her.

I decide now isn't the time. Hughes looks like he's exhausted.

"Can you medically clear me for sex?" Crew asks.

"If you're not cleared to play, you shouldn't be having sex," I say, worried about the playoffs all over again. I don't trust this hotshot not to reinjure himself, because even though he prioritizes hockey, he also thinks he's invincible.

"We're not at work," Michael says. "Ask me tomorrow."

Crew's eyebrows shoot up. "Are you for real?"

"Yes. You wouldn't call or text another team physician at home to ask that. We should have boundaries. This is our personal space, not the office."

It's a fair point. But it seems damn near impossible to keep the two separate.

"We all are part of the Racketeers," Crew points out. "And we're all in love with Dani and living with her. There's going to be spill over."

Michael starts cleaning up the mess of takeout boxes on the coffee table, his lip curling in disgust. "Fine. Whatever. I'm too tired to have this conversation right now."

I'm stunned speechless. Hughes never 'whatever's' anyone.

Before I can respond, he heads up the stairs.

"I'm going to take a shower."

I look at Crew, who shrugs his shoulders. "Guess it's whatever."

I frown, debating if I should have forced a resolution or not. And if I do, am I doing it as a part of our family unit or as the boss mediating between my star player and team doctor? Damn, this is hard. Harder than dealing with eighty-seven steps in this house and Crew's poor housekeeping.

Before I can figure out what to do, Michael returns to the top of the stairs. "Who put all my stuff away?" he demands.

"I had people come in and do it. I didn't want you to come home to a mess."

The new house is four stories. The game room in the basement with the living, kitchen and dining on the first floor. There are private spaces for me, Michael and Crew on the second floor, and Dani's reading room and bathroom is on the third in addition to the main bedroom where we all sleep. Michael's office, closet, and bathroom had been full of floor-to-ceiling boxes, so I had an organizer come in and unpack it all.

"I would have preferred to unpack my own stuff." He rubs the back of his skull, his nostrils flaring. "Now I have to redo it all."

He's irritated, and that irritates *me*. "I was trying to help! That's what I do. I see a problem and I pay people to fix it. It's my fucking love language."

Michael just shakes his head and disappears again.

"What was that?" I ask Crew, gesturing to Michael.

He puts his noodles down and puts his fist to his chest. "I have no idea. Jesus, I have heartburn."

The front door opens and thank God, Danielle is home. I go to her and pull her into a big hug, squeezing her hard against my chest. I breathe in the scent of her shampoo and remind myself relationships take work but she, and those two guys I share her with, are all worth it. But it means all of us giving and taking.

"Hi," she says with a laugh, words muffled in my chest.

I kiss the side of her head and help her out of her denim jacket. "How was your day?"

"Great, actually."

"Are you hungry? Tired?"

She sets her purse down on the bench by the door and removes her shoes. "I'm good right now. Glad to be home. Is Michael home yet?"

"Just got here," I tell her.

Her smile is relieved but I can see tension around the edges. Things have been off for all of us. We need...each other. We need to all be here, *together*, all of us, to re-connect.

"I need you to do something for me," I tell her.

"Like what?"

I'm already tugging her forward by her hand. "Just tell me you'll do what I want, dirty girl."

The 'dirty girl' immediately clues her in. "Oh."

A glance back shows her cheeks are pink, her expression intrigued. She's caught on to what this is generally, if not specifically. When I look at Crew, he's eyeing me, a question clearly on his lips. I just give him my most reassuring smirk.

"Hi Crew," Danielle murmurs from behind me as I lead her to the couch. "How are you feeling?"

"Fucking great, now that you're home." He sits up straighter, shoving the fleece blanket that's been covering him off of his legs.

He's caught on that I'm offering him a *mea culpa*. I do owe him. Fucking Dani right next to him in bed was a dick move. I'm not *sorry* exactly, but I won't mind making it up to him.

She leans over and gives him a kiss. His hand goes to the back of her head as he holds her mouth to his a little longer and she has to brace her hands on his chest. She gives a little sigh and opens her mouth for him.

"Missed you," he tells her when he lets her go.

"Me too." She runs her hand over his chest. "I've missed you in a lot of ways."

"Tell me you'll do whatever I want you to," I order Danielle, moving in to hold her by the hips.

She looks back at me over her shoulder. "I'll do whatever you want me to."

I lift my hand, entwining my fingers in her thick curls, making her look at Crew. "I need you to get on your knees and suck McNeill until he comes in your mouth."

She tries to look back at me again, but I'm holding her too tightly.

"I don't want to hurt him," she says.

But I can hear the catch in her voice. She's missed being physical with Crew.

Danielle is a nearly insatiable lover. I would have happily died trying to keep up with her, but I've thought more than once how it's good she's got three of us to help with all of her needs.

She absolutely loves giving herself to us, over and over, in every way. She loves knowing she's the goddess who we can't live without, who can make her three men lose control and give up everything just for a taste of her.

I grip her hair a little tighter and squeeze her hip. "Crew promises to be very still. No grinding, no thrusting. He just misses you, sweetheart. Give him some love."

With that, I nudge her forward.

Danielle obediently descends to the rug, tentatively reaching out to stroke over the front of Crew's sweatpants.

He groans, letting his head fall back onto the couch cushion behind him. "Damn, I've missed your sweet touch. Take me out, baby. Show me you've missed me too."

When he shoves his gray sweatpants down, Danielle is there immediately, gripping the base of his shaft and stroking lightly up and down, like she's afraid to be too rough.

"Hughes," I call up the stairs. "Stop rearranging shit that's already been put away and come watch our girl get a mouthful of hard cock."

Crew is rock solid already. When I think about Danielle being out of town with Michael, then returning to Crew injured and unable to have sex, I feel for the guy. He must be damn near ready to explode, and here I was adding to the problem by going balls deep in Danielle the last three nights, a few feet away from him.

I put my own hand on the front of my jeans and readjust. I'm getting hard watching her delicate, tentative flicks of her pink tongue over Crew's head.

My fingers are still in her hair, and I push her. "Harder. Make it count."

Michael has come down the stairs and is peeling his sweater off over his head, leaving him in his T-shirt. Danielle glances over at him. "Is this okay?" she asks, lips hovering over Crew. "I'm not going to hurt him, am I?"

Crew makes a strangled sound. "You're hurting me by just breathing on me. Suck me, Dani, *please*."

It's the closest I've ever heard McNeill to begging.

"He's fine," Michael says. His voice is rough, eyes trained on Dani. "Show him how much you love him."

That hits me in the chest.

It is about love.

Yes, it's hot as fuck. Yes, McNeill needs this physical release. Yes, we're *all* going to get that, I have no doubt.

But this is about our connection. Something none of us has ever felt in this way ever before—this specific combination of four people found one another. Something I'm beginning to understand is we'll never feel this way again unless it's *us*.

As Michael joins us, with no question, no hesitation, things finally *feel* right again.

We're here, all together for the first time in almost two weeks. The house is new, Crew's injured, Michael's got a lot on his mind, Danielle's worried about all of us, I'm itchy with the need to fix everything, but *this* is good. Us, together. It's a connection that's only truly manifested fully when all four of us are here.

I should know. I've had Danielle to myself for the past few nights. And it's been awesome. I love her with my whole heart and I love having her full attention. But it's not *everything* it can be.

And if anyone would have told me I'd feel this way a year ago, I would have laughed in their face.

Michael's permission is all the encouragement she needs. Danielle slides her mouth down over Crew's swollen cock and his eyes drift shut on a low moan. The way she takes him fully, as deep as she can, with zero hesitation, is fucking beautiful. After several strokes, she pulls off to take a breath and I take the opportunity to quickly pull her colorful spring dress off over her head in one rapid motion.

It gives me a great view of her tight ass, panties driving up between her cheeks, her hair tumbling down over her pale back. We have a no panties rule when she's home, but in fairness, she did just get home from work.

I sink to my knees behind her and push her head down again. "Don't stop. Breathe through your nose, pretty girl, and give Crew what he needs."

She obediently opens her mouth wide and I push down and pull her back, over and over until Crew is swearing, I'm fucking turned on, and Danielle is making little sounds of pleasure. Goosebumps appear on her arms. Hughes sits down on the couch by Crew's feet, leaning back on his elbows so he can study the way our girl takes it hard and deep.

"That's it," he murmurs, reaching out with his finger to gently swipe under her eye.

I can't see her face, but I'm guessing her eyes are watering from taking Crew's dick so deep. Which is hot. "Our girl loves that," I say gruffly.

Danielle nods her head enthusiastically.

Crew is tense, jaw taut, gripping her shoulders as he holds on.

I know what he's feeling. When Danielle's slick warm mouth is gliding over your cock, it's hard to not just let go and fill that throat. Her left hand is squeezing Crew's balls, so I take her free hand and place it on Hughes. His palm immediately lands on her hand and starts stroking her up and down over his pants.

"Our little toy," I say. "What should we do with her, McNeill? Keep going?"

"I need to come," he spits out.

"No teasing?"

"It's been too fucking long. Open up, Dani girl." His whole body is tense from the strain of not thrusting up into her mouth.

Crew's willpower is admirable. Groin injury or not, I'm not sure I could resist pumping into her.

But then he's exploding into her and Danielle takes it all, swallowing like our good fucking girl. We've trained her well. Though she's been an eager student.

I release her hair so she can sink back against me, resting her shoulder and head on my chest, breathing hard. She wipes her bottom lip but doesn't pull her hand back from Michael, who is watching her with rapt attention.

"You really are a team player," I tell Crew. "I respect your dedication to the Racketeers season because I would have just fucked the shit out of her."

"You're welcome," he tells me, relaxing back against the cushions with a sigh. "Though Dani is the true team player."

She laughs. "Why thank you." Then she eyes Michael. "Your turn?"

My dick throbs. "Oh, is that what we're doing? Line us all up and suck?"

She nods, her cheeks pink. "That sounds fun."

"Then I should go next. Let Michael have your pussy, sweetheart. He's been gone three days."

"Do you want my pussy?" she asks Michael, with a sweet, fake-innocent tone that makes me moan low.

"Oh, yeah. I've been dreaming about you day and night."

"Same," she murmurs.

She leans in and Michael cups her face, bringing her lips to his. He kisses her hungrily, his fingers sliding deep into her hair as her hands cling to his shoulders.

Her words about Michael being on her mind every night, even though she's been with me, don't make me jealous. Again, I'm a little amazed by that. But he's a part of her. So is McNeill. I know when I'm making love to her she's with me, she's loving *me*, but I know they're always in her heart and mind. Just as I'm there when she's with one of them. It's so fucking hard to explain, even to myself, but my heart somehow understands it even when my brain can't put it into words. I love that they love her. I love the way they make her feel and the things they bring out of her.

The three of us together can love Danielle the way she needs to be loved, and I'm very good with that.

"Turn around and give Armstrong some attention," Michael tells her. "Then I'll make that ache go away."

I stretch to my feet as she obediently turns.

She's still on her knees and now looks up at me. "Is this how you want me?"

I tug my shirt over my head, needing to break eye contact. Sometimes I love her so fucking much it hurts. Especially when she's like this—submissive and eager to please.

I boss her because it's what she needs from me. It's so fucking hot for both of us. For all of us, actually. The way Crew teases her makes Michael and me hot. The way Michael romances her does the same for Crew and me.

"Undo my pants," I command gruffly.

She does, her lithe fingers quickly opening my belt buckle and unzipping my jeans. The warmth of her breath is a teasing little precursor to the tip of her tongue reaching out and flicking over my cock when I free it.

Michael shifts in behind her on one side, unhooking her bra so that he can tease at her nipples. Crew shifts as well, sweatpants pulled back up like he needs the barrier between him and her body. He pulls her hair back to the side, petting her and giving her praise. "Just like that, pretty girl. See how hard you can get Nate."

"I can get him so hard," she vows, then gives a little gasp when Michael pinches her nipple between two fingers. "Oh, God, Michael. That feels so good."

"*My* turn," I remind her, gripping her chin. "Open your mouth, Danielle."

She gives me a knowing smirk. She knows I'm not actually jealous but that I'm just being the boss. But she gives me a quiet, "Yes, sir," and opens.

I grasp my cock and slide it past her lips and into her hot, wet, perfect mouth. She closes around me and I suck in a breath. How can this feel this fucking good every damned time?

"Take him deep, Dani," Crew coaches, one big hand stroking down her back. "You look so damned beautiful with those pretty lips stretched around a cock."

She hums her pleasure at the praise and I groan, my hand going to her hair and sliding in deeper. Her eyes find mine and I can see the lust shining up at me.

Crew leans in, kissing her neck, running his lips up to her ear, then telling her hoarsely, "You're making me hard again. Even worse than those nights listening to Nate fuck you right next to me. What am I gonna do with you?"

She groans as he sucks on her neck and Michael plucks at her nipples.

"Nate fucked you right beside Crew?" Michael asks.

Danielle makes a noise, though it's impossible to know if it's a yes or no or some attempt at defending our actions.

I just grin down at her smugly, stroking her cheek. I didn't know that Crew could hear us, but the idea that he listened to her moaning my name and the sound of my cock thrusting into her sweet, soaked pussy definitely doesn't embarrass me. Part of me wants to crow, in fact.

"That's just cruel," Michael says. He squeezes one nipple a little harder, and she gives a little yelp. "I think when he's healed up, Crew gets to tie you to the bed and edge you for a few hours before fucking you, all by himself, while Nathan has to watch."

Danielle and I both groan at that promise.

Michael grins. He knows that would hardly be a true punishment. Sure, maybe at the moment, but we'd all enjoy it very fucking much.

"Jesus, Doc. You're killin' me here." Crew strokes a hand over his hard cock.

Michael looks at Crew. "She can ride you. You stay still and don't flex that hip. Don't let your head move around too much or get your blood pressure up too high." He puts his face against Danielle's neck on the other side. "She can sit on your face and you can suck on her sweet clit. You can make her come all over your face. Then she can turn around and straddle you. You can make our pretty little slut work for her pleasure. Considering we're constantly worshiping her, that only seems fair."

Danielle has to pull off my cock to gasp and moan at Michael's words.

But Crew gives her ass a little smack for that. "Keep your mouth full until you finish Boss off, Dani."

Every word Crew and Michael have spoken has resulted in her taking me deep and sucking hard. I'm in heaven.

"You're doing so fucking good," I tell her. "I'm so close, baby."

Danielle sucks more eagerly, Michael cupping both her breasts. Crew pulls her panties down and strokes over her ass, as if reminding her that he'll spank her if she doesn't obey.

"I'm going to come on your face," I warn her.

She nods rapidly.

When I pull back, I groan, giving my cock a final hard pump with my fist before a fast, pulsing release. Thick cum jolts out onto her cheek and her lips, her mouth still open. It coats her pink skin as her eyes widen in triumph and pleasure.

"Nathan," she breathes, sliding her finger over her bottom lip to catch the creamy fluid before it drips onto the couch. She puts it in her mouth and sucks.

"You are so fucking hot," I tell her, my thighs shaky as I let out an exhale and relax. I grab some of Crew's takeout napkins off the coffee table and clean her face before giving her a soft kiss. "You're perfect."

She smiles up at me.

"Come here." I help her to her feet, and take off her bra fully, which is dangling by the straps on her forearm, then hold her hand as she steps out of her panties. I give her another kiss before I pat her ass. "On the couch. Michael's turn. And you don't have to be quiet for this."

She gives me a wide smile. "Thank god."

When Danielle climbs up onto the couch on all fours to position herself on either side of Michael's legs, I ditch my pants and move in behind her. Skimming my hand down over the curve of her spine, I stroke between her ass cheeks. She's bent over Michael, pulling him out of his pants, but she pauses long enough to arch her ass to me in invitation.

"Shift around, Doc," Crew says, watching us with rapt attention from where he's sunk back onto the couch. "I can't see her pussy."

"Great fucking idea, McNeill." I grab her hips and pull her to the side and Michael scoots over, underneath her. "How's your angle? Can you see better now?" I ease her legs apart and lean back so he can get a good view of my finger stroking up and down, not entering her but teasing, light contact.

"That's perfect, Boss."

It's my turn to take a step back.

I've had Danielle to myself in bed the last three nights (even if Crew was technically in the bed) so this is my peace offering to McNeill. He has shifted back onto the couch, his legs stretched out. "Danielle, get between Crew's legs, facing him."

Hughes usually lets me and Crew dominate the choreography when we're in bed, but I'm hyper aware of this new dynamic now that we're living together, and that Danielle didn't go to Decatur with Michael. I almost want to compensate him for that fact, so I make eye contact with him. "If that's cool with you?"

He nods. "Cool with me as long as I can fuck our girl."

"That's the plan," I tell him. "Fuck her nice and good."

"Like this?" Danielle asks me, seeking approval.

Her knees are between Crew's thighs, and her arms are on either side of his waist.

"Perfect, baby. Give Crew a kiss and lift that ass for Michael."

The position allows Michael to move in behind her. He squeezes her ass cheeks hard, kneading them. Then he thrusts inside her. She's so wet that he slides in easily.

Danielle gives a low moan into Crew's mouth.

He has his fists in her hair, holding her tight against him so she can't move, allowing her the full feel of Michael's cock moving inside her.

I watch, my own cock throbbing, loving every second of her pleasure. Danielle comes alive with us, and I'll never get tired of seeing her lose herself in the moment. She breaks almost immediately, so turned on by blowing Crew and me both that she was already on edge. I know what Hughes is experiencing. Her pussy will be milking his cock right now, a tight wet fist.

The look on his face proves me right. He's swearing under his breath, gripping her ass so hard her skin has splotchy palm prints appearing.

Danielle has turned her head from Crew so she can cry out. "Fuck, yes, Michael, *yes.*"

Crew takes the opportunity to pull her nipple into his mouth, which makes her shudder in pleasure.

Michael looks like he's hanging on by a thread, his pounding hard and fast, pent-up frustration releasing. I'm guessing he's fucking away the tension and worry of the last few days.

His explosion is tight, controlled, quiet. His eyes are closed and when he pulls away, he opens them and drags in a deep breath. He shifts over and tells me, "Make her give us another."

That's the only invitation I need.

I'm behind her, and then I'm balls deep in Danielle.

Being on the back end of another guy coming in a woman was something I'd never experienced until Danielle, and when we first got together, I shoved it out of my head, not willing to think hard on the logistics of it. But now I've learned there's something hot as hell about knowing she needs all of us, that we all need to come inside her, giving her exactly what she wants.

She's trembling beneath me, her back covered in goosebumps and a flush of pink. Her moans have turned into one long exclamation of ecstasy, and her arms are shaking.

"That's it," Crew coaxes her, playing with her nipples. "You're almost there. We need another one, pretty girl. Come on Boss's cock, for us."

For us.

Her coming with me inside her is for all of us.

All my muscles are tense and I'm holding back, knowing I'm close, but needing her to shatter first. She's writhing now, bucking her hips, chasing the orgasm.

"Michael," I say through gritted teeth. "Get in there."

He knows what I mean, and without hesitation, slips a hand under her belly and clearly lands on her clit with the exact pressure she needs.

Danielle screams and shudders.

"That's it," Michael tells her. "Damn, baby, you're so fucking gorgeous right now."

"Oh, yeah," Crew says, voice low and gritty. "Soak that cock."

"I am," she wails. "Oh, God!"

I can't hold back another second and I explode with a shout of triumph, filling our girl up.

I stay buried inside her, taking in huge gulps of air. Then I squeeze her hips, leaning over to kiss her back. Crew is kissing her mouth deeply. Michael is slumped next to them, his hand lazily stroking up and down her back.

I let go of her hips, and she sinks onto Crew's chest. He tucks her head under his chin and closes his eyes.

I roll to the side opposite of Michael.

We all just lie there for several long, quiet minutes.

It's fucking bliss.

I study the high ceiling in our new house.

I still don't love the house, but I do love that I live here with these three.

"Yes, this couch is fucking amazing," Crew finally says. "And yes, I'll be happy to be in charge of all furniture purchases for us for the rest of our lives."

And I'm so happy about the idea of the rest of our lives together that, for the moment, I don't even immediately tell him that there's no fucking way I'm trusting him to buy so much as a kitchen stool. Even if this couch does have its definite advantages.

CHAPTER 16
Michael

"HE SHOOTS." Crew bends his knees and puts his hands up to throw a crumpled paper towel into the trash like it's a basketball. "He scores!"

"He gets the hell out of my kitchen," I say mildly, slicing olives for a salad. I have a lasagna in the oven already baking and the room is thick with the smell of my Bolognese and the béchamel. It's therapeutic to be cooking again.

"*Your* kitchen? Isn't that the point of buying this house? It's my kitchen too," Crew says, swiping an olive off of the cutting board and popping it into his mouth.

It really is a relief to be back in Chicago. Here, in *our* house. The last few days were stressful as hell, worrying about my father's health and my mother's reaction to my father's health. My siblings. The grandkids. What was going on back here with these three, in this new house.

"It's Michael's kitchen, honey," Dani tells Crew, patting him on the arm as she opens a deep drawer and lifts out four plates onto the island to set the table. "We just visit it when we're hungry."

Then she leans over and kisses me on the cheek with a smile. I set the knife down so I can cup her cheek and give her a proper kiss, grateful she's not at the bookstore tonight and we can have a family dinner. Her taste and touch ground me and I breathe deeply. "I love you."

"I love you too." She squeezes my hand before she picks up the plates again.

"Danielle is right, McNeill," Nathan says with his back to us as he makes himself an old-fashioned. "Stay in your lane."

Last night, the three of us guys had all needed to fuck Dani hard, to release our frustrations and fears and annoyances with life and each other, and she had needed to get fucked. To feel close to us and reassured that everything is fine in all of our various relationships, both with her and each other.

But tonight is about reconnecting as friends, as a family. This is our first dinner together in this home that we spent two months dreaming about and renovating. The whole time I was in Decatur, I was worried about what was happening here without me. If the woman I love was okay. If the two guys I have come to care about were getting along. If they needed me. If they were unpacking our new house and putting things where they don't belong.

They hadn't personally unpacked a damn thing, but the team Nathan had hired had botched my bookshelves big-time. I shelve by genre and theme, not alphabetically, otherwise you end up with a Neil Gaiman novel followed by a medical book by Dr. Graham, which is housed next to Lord of the Flies by William Golding. Which is a mess, in my opinion. It's just not the way I do it, and I admit, I'm a little set in my ways.

Today I had to remind myself Nathan had meant well. His love language is making our lives easier with his money. Mine is feeding and nurturing them.

"If you want me to cook dinner, it's my kitchen between the hours of five and seven every night," I tell Crew. I love cooking in general, but it's taking on a new meaning now. I love cooking for my family.

"Michael cooks, Nathan drinks, Dani sets the table. What the hell am I supposed to do then? I know, I'm the entertainment."

Crew picks up oranges from the bowl on the island and attempts to juggle.

I finish my salad dressing and dip a spoon in it to taste the flavor profile. "You are definitely entertaining."

Crew drops an orange, and it rolls across the island to rest against our ceramic salad bowl.

"Help me set the table before you break something," Dani says.

"I don't know how."

That makes me laugh. "That's code for "I'm lazy and I don't want to." I have younger siblings, remember?" I tell him.

"No, I'm serious. I don't know how. I mean, obviously, you slap a plate down, but the silverware and the glasses and all that, I have no clue. I spent most of my childhood at the ice rink or in a bus or car traveling somewhere. I'm super familiar with the continental breakfast at Hampton Inns all over the Midwest. Plus, my mother was amazing at packing lunches and snacks and full picnic dinner spreads that could be eaten in the bleachers during tournaments. But we didn't have family dinners at home all that often."

"I can't imagine what that was like," I say. I had played sports, but just for school. Never competitive or traveling teams. Crew had never gone to college either, going pro straight out of high school. I wonder how many miles of road he's covered in his life. A dizzying amount.

"Here, I'll show you," Dani says, taking an orange out of his hand and plopping it back into the bowl.

"You know how to set a table?" he asks her.

"Yes. My mother was strict about Sunday dinner being traditional."

Crew makes a face. "Your mother seems strict in general." But then, because he's Crew, and always optimistic, he nods confidently. "I think Mary is warming up to me, though. She texted me on my birthday." He takes the plates she hands him and follows her to the round table we have in the corner of the kitchen by the drinks station.

Dani had wanted a banquette but Nathan had told her he refused to sit on a bench to eat his meals because it would feel like a prison cafeteria. Crew *obviously* refused to sit on a bench. And even I had to admit, that sounded uncomfortable as hell. Besides, who would sit where? So we now have four very plush, easy on the ass, fabric chairs around a round table.

"Doc is really the only one who had a typical childhood," Crew announces.

I raise my eyebrows. "Well, I did have a typical childhood, that is true. For which I'm extremely grateful."

I refuse to let this conversation take me back to the fear of that first phone call from my sister, saying our father had a heart attack. That moment was honestly the first moment I had really addressed my father's mortality, and damn, it fucking sucked. The earth had shifted beneath my feet because my parents have been my rock since birth. But I don't want to ruin tonight by going there in my head again.

"I had a typical childhood!" Dani protests. She points to the table. "From out to in, Crew, that's what you have to remember. Salad fork on the outside of your dinner fork."

Nathan sips his drink, legs sprawled out as he lounges in his chair. He has an amazing ability to do nothing with such authority that you assume he is contributing when he's actually doing nothing.

"You're in the way," Crew tells him, kicking his foot as he tries to shift in closer to the table, holding floral napkins that Dani clearly picked out at some point.

"I'm inspecting your work. Switch the wine glass and the bread dish. If you can't remember, just do this." Nathan lifts up his hands to show Crew. He forms a circle with his thumb and index finger, other fingers straight up. "The left hand makes a 'b' for bread. The right makes a 'd' for drink."

"Look at that," Crew says. "Cool." He rearranges the dish and the glass and moves on to the next place setting. He puts his fingers up again. "I feel like a yogi. Oomm."

Nathan laughs and pulls Dani down onto his thigh. He brushes her hair back and kisses her neck. Dani squirms, trying to get back up to help Crew, but Nathan holds her firmly on his lap.

"How did you learn stuff like that anyway, Nate?" Crew asks. "Given the way you were raised."

"I'm not the fucking Jungle Boy," Nathan says. "I had parents until I was twelve."

That makes me laugh as I drop my tasting spoon in the sink. I carry the salad bowl to the table. "I'm picturing little Nathan wandering around the jungle in a cashmere sweater."

"I do look good in cashmere," Nathan says, his hand now under Dani's sweater so he can gently massage the small of her back. "My parents taught me a lot. My dad was into flying, and hockey, of course, and golf, which I didn't actually enjoy at all. My mother liked to take me shopping, to museums, to five-star restaurants. I had a nanny and a tutor, my grandparents. Then boarding school at eleven. I had a very normal childhood."

Dani snickers. "Oh, sweetie."

"What? That's normal," he insists.

"Well, so was mine, for living in small town Indiana."

"*I* never said you weren't normal, baby," Nathan tells her, removing his hand from under her sweater and smoothing it back into place. "Someone else said that."

"Why don't you think I had a normal childhood?" Dani asks Crew as he gives up on trying to fold a napkin and throws it down haphazardly by a plate.

"This ought to be good," I say, lifting the wine decanter from the drinks station. I pour the red into a glass for Dani and for myself. Crew doesn't like to drink alcohol with dinner. "From the Book of Crew there's no telling what his logic is going to be."

Crew puts a fork on the lumpy napkin and shrugs. "That's easy. You're an only child."

"So?"

"I think he's saying we're spoiled," Nathan tells Dani. "Which is ironic."

"Only children can't have normal childhoods. It's a rite of passage to trade secrets and insults with siblings, while both vying for your parents' attention and working together to get away with murder."

I go back to the kitchen and open the oven to pull out my lasagna.

Crew follows me, grabbing the platter with bruschetta on it. "Back me up on this, Doc."

"I enjoyed having siblings for all the reasons you mentioned." I put the pan on the stove and remove my oven mitts. "I think we're different because of our different backgrounds, and that's part of why this works. We all bring something to the table."

"Except Nate," Crew says with a grin. "He hasn't brought a damned thing to this table tonight except his drink."

Crew isn't wrong.

But I know my role here. The peacemaker. The calm one. This is what I bring to the table.

"Nathan's going to serve the lasagna."

Nathan gives a mighty sigh, but he sets Dani off of him and rises to his feet, drink still in his hand. The man was probably born with a bourbon in his hand.

"At your service, Hughes."

The kitchen is warm, and our vibe is relaxed as we sit down around the table.

"A toast," I say, lifting my wine glass. I wait for them all to raise their glasses. Dani is flushed and smiling, her eyes sparkling. "To Cookie & Co.'s first meal together in our new house. I'm happy to be here with all of you."

"To us, damn it," Crew says, lifting his water higher in the air. "Because we're awesome."

"To Cookie & Company," Nathan says. "And special thanks to Michael for cooking. It looks and smells amazing."

"To Michael for being the dad *and* the mom," Crew adds.

That makes me laugh.

Dani does too, but she looks around the table, making eye contact with each of us one at a time. "To my favorite guys. Thank you for being you."

"Cheers!" Crew says.

We all do the same and I sip my wine, both the rich red and my emotions warming my insides.

Our dinner is filled with good conversation and laughter.

I realize I'm fully relaxed for the first time in over a week.

Reaching under the table, I find Dani's hand with mine and lace our fingers together and squeeze.

I love you, I mouth to her as Crew gives us a play-by-play of his first junior hockey championship and Nathan pats his stomach even as he goes for another slice of lasagna.

I love you, too. She blows me a kiss.

This woman. Her green eyes shine with love for me, for Crew, for Nathan.

I wouldn't want to be anywhere else but right here.

No one has to leave and go home somewhere that means we aren't all together.

This is home.

This is us.

And it's pretty damn perfect.

CHAPTER 17
Nathan

"LASER TAG," Danielle announces as she reads the slip of paper she's pulled from a glass jar.

"No way," I say immediately. "Nope. Fuck that."

"Those are the rules," Crew says, lounging on the couch, feet propped up. "We all agreed we would respect what the jar delivers for date night."

Danielle gives me a sweet shrug and turns the paper around so I can read "laser tag" written in Crew's block handwriting. The only cursive Crew knows is his signature. Otherwise, he prints everything in capital letters. "You don't mind, do you, Nathan?"

As if I'd ever tell her no. I lean forward and haul her toward me with a hand on her neck. "Of course not, baby." I plant a hard kiss on her before releasing her. "But seriously, that's three times in a row Crew's idea has been pulled. Unbelievable."

"I'm just lucky that way," Crew says.

I groan and look at Michael. "Hughes, can you believe this? Is there a luckier guy on the entire fucking planet than Crew McNeill?"

Michael shakes his head. "He is pretty damn lucky." He laces Danielle's fingers through his. "But I'm game for laser tag. Dani in a dark room? Works for me."

She laughs, which never fails to get under my skin and soften me. But...laser tag? Fuck me. I'm forty-one, damn near forty-two actually since my birthday is in a couple of months, and I've never played laser tag in my entire life. Why would I start now?

But Crew is right. Rules are rules. We all put three date night ideas on slips of paper in a jar and twice a week Danielle pulls one so we can all have a shot at doing something we particularly enjoy. Which was great in theory. But now McNeill's on a hot streak. Last week we were forced to go ax throwing. Watching my girlfriend—who is a lot of things but *not* athletic—almost drop an ax on her foot just about gave me a fucking heart attack. And I'm not even going to talk about the karaoke night. Being forced to sing Meatloaf in harmony with Crew has given me permanent emotional scars.

"Yes, that's three in a row," Danielle says. "But that also means there aren't any more of Crew's ideas in the jar, so your odds are one in three for the next date."

I'm listening to her and also reading McNeill's expression. It subtly shifts when he processes what she's said.

Oh, that little *fucker*.

"You cheated, didn't you?" I demand.

"How could I cheat?" he asks, but his shoulders are tense.

"Give me that jar," I demand, reaching for it.

It's perched on the end table and Crew realizes my intention and launches himself toward it. But he's on that damn couch that acts like quicksand, so he gets sucked back into the cushion vortex, allowing me to yank the jar off the table and turn so my back is to McNeill.

"You're my witnesses," I tell Danielle and Hughes. I put the jar in Danielle's hands. "Please hold this, love."

Then I reach inside the jar and pull out a piece of paper.

"Wine and paint night." That's clearly Danielle's, given her handwriting and the suggestion.

Not as bad as Crew's suggestion but not my idea of a great night out either. If that's what our girl wants to do, though, I'll pick up a brush and make something happen. If I know Danielle, which I do, she was trying hard to come up with something that didn't fall in anyone's particular favor.

I fish around in the bowl and pull another suggestion out. "Take a cooking class." Michael's, obviously. I can definitely do that.

"This is proving nothing," Crew calls out. "Except ruining the fun. Now we know what they all say."

I ignore him and pull out another one. I know I'm right. He's rigged the bowl. "You already know what they all say, because most are yours."

"Pack a picnic and watch the sunset." I look over at Danielle, touched by how romantic she is, to the point that I momentarily forget about McNeill. "That's sweet, baby. I love this idea." God, she's so damn adorable.

She blushes. "Thank you. In a few weeks, the weather will be warmer too." She leans over and presses her mouth over mine.

It's tempting to be distracted right out of my irritation, but I am *not* playing laser tag.

I dig into the bowl again. "Mini-golf," I say grimly.

That's McNeill all fucking day long, which means he added extra slips of paper. I glare at him. "That's four suggestions for you when there were only supposed to be three."

"Guess I can't count."

Danielle's jaw drops. "Crew!" But she sounds more delighted than angry with him.

She's always delighted with Crew.

I grab another piece of paper. "Clubbing? You're an asshole, McNeill."

"How do you know that's mine?" he demands, sitting up. "That could be Doc's."

I raise my eyebrows.

Michael laughs. "That is not mine but I'm always up for a little dancing."

"That isn't helping," I tell him.

He shrugs.

"Where are mine?" I demand. "None of these are mine." I gesture to the pile of paper on the end table.

Crew groans and falls backward onto the couch. "Oh, come on, the opera? I just…traded that one out for something better."

"How is…bowling—I wave yet another slip of paper in the air—better than the opera?"

"That's not even a real question," he says. "You might as well have written "take a nap," on your paper."

"Crew," Danielle says. "That's really very naughty." She's trying to sound firm, but not succeeding at all. The corner of her mouth keeps lifting, and she is clearly trying not to laugh. "You shouldn't have done that."

"I'm sorry," he says, giving her puppy dog eyes as he holds his arms out for her. "Do you forgive me?"

"Of course," she says, immediately going to the couch and climbing on it to kiss him.

"Unbelievable." I shake my head. "You're going to the opera," I tell him, pointing my finger at him. "Tomorrow night. Pick out your favorite suit."

"Dani?" he asks, pleadingly. "Help?"

She takes a deep breath, like she's gathering herself. Then she pins him with a hard stare.

"It looks like we're going to the opera tomorrow night," she tells him. She disengages herself from Crew's hug and tries to extract herself from the couch. I hold a hand out to her, which she takes with a backward glance at him. "And you really should be apologizing to Nathan, Crew, not to me, since it's his ideas you traded out."

That makes me feel absurdly triumphant. "Baby, you sound so fucking hot when you're being forthright."

Her eyes are bright with amusement and arousal as I pull her up against my chest with a hard tug. "Really? Did I do good?"

"You did great," I tell her emphatically, cupping her breast tightly. "God, you're sexy. Isn't she hot, Hughes?"

"So fucking hot," Michael agrees, coming behind her and lifting the pile of her curls off her neck so he can kiss her.

She shivers beneath our touch.

"Okay, I'm sorry," Crew says immediately and with zero sincerity, peeling himself off of the couch so he can join the party. "Sorry, Nate."

But Danielle's hand comes out. "You can just wait there a minute, Crew. Until it's your turn."

"Yes, ma'am," Crew says, sounding shocked and totally turned on.

My feelings precisely.

"*Damn*," Michael breathes. "That's our girl. Learning to take charge."

"And you're about to get rewarded for it," I tell her, teasing her nipple between my thumb and forefinger. "Let's get this sweater off."

Hughes and I mutually worshiping her body is going to be a hell of a lot more fun than running around in vests total strangers have been in and out of all day.

Turns out it's my lucky day after all.

CHAPTER 18
Crew

THE ONLY THING worse than being hurt and not able to practice is being hurt and not being able to play. But I have to be a good teammate and sit my ass on the bench and cheer the rest of the team on as they face off with the Beavers.

Fuck. This.

The Beavers score again, and I run a hand through my hair in agitation. What the fuck are they doing?

Alexsei skates to the wall and vaults over, taking a break.

I stomp to his side. "You have to go after Simons," I tell him. "Take it right from him. He's not faster than you. What the fuck's going on?"

Alexsei glares at me. "Are you kidding me right now?"

"What?"

"Sit down, McNeill. I've got enough coaches."

"Clearly not. He's beat you three times."

Alexsei turns, facing me fully. The Ukrainian has only about an inch on me and maybe ten pounds. We're very evenly matched size wise. Demeanor wise too. Neither of us is really a brawler. But he looks ready to punch me.

What the hell is that? I'm just saying the truth. He knows it. What's his problem?

"Back off, McNeill," Alexsei says.

I straighten to my full height. Fucking bring it on. That would be a hell of a lot more exciting than sitting on my ass and watching my team lose to these dickheads from Minnesota.

"You want to go?" I ask, stepping a little closer.

"No, I don't fucking want to 'go'. Not with you," he says. He lowers his voice. "Jesus, I can't go after Simons like I want to. If I end up in the penalty box or hurt, what are we going to do? You're out. The rest of us need to be healthy and on the ice. So sit the fuck down and get better so we can do this the way we planned."

I stare at him.

"You want the Cup, right?" he asks.

I nod.

"Then get your ass back on the ice so we can really play hockey. We need you out there."

Fuck.

He's right.

It's not like we're the only guys on the team. The Racketeers are good. They were good before I got here. But now we're *great*. Because with me on the other side, my wingman can play hard. Because with him across from me, I can play with everything I've got. I'm not carrying this team alone. None of us are.

Unless I'm on the bench.

I take a deep breath. "Yeah. Got it."

"What are you two doing? Exchanging pedicure tips?" Coach Phillips asks. He scowls at Alexsei. "Is there a problem?"

Alexsei meets my eyes. I give him a slight nod that says we're okay.

"No way, Coach," Alexsei says. "No problem. I was just tellin' McNeill here how hot his sister is and how I think I should take her out after the game if we win."

Coach Phillips swings to look at me. I'm frowning at Alexsei. He's just fucking with me, but I know he knows I have a sister. He knows exactly who Luna is. They were flirting their asses off at my birthday party last month.

My eyes narrow. "And I was just telling him that there's no way in hell she'd go out with a hitless wonder like him."

Alexsei laughs. "You think your sister is keeping track of my stats?"

He says 'stats' as if it means something other than hockey.

I nod. "If she's paying attention to you at all," I say. "Fair warning, she's got high standards."

That's my not-so-polite way of saying my sister would never date a hockey player. My sister is a hockey fan. But she's been around hockey guys all her life thanks to my early interest in the sport and all my friends being around the house constantly growing up. And, of course, many of them hit on her over the years. She is not impressed by jocks. Never has been.

"Oh, fuck." Alexsei gives a little groan. "I do love a challenge."

Then with a grin, he flips his mask down and hoists himself back over the wall to rejoin the game as other players barrel into the box for their rest.

"Alexsei wants to date your sister?" Coach Phillips asks. "Oh, that will fucking end well for all of us."

I laugh. "Nah. Though that doesn't mean he won't ask."

"You going to sit over here and talk about women the entire game?" he asks, giving me a frown.

"I was just trying to loosen him up," I say, watching Alexsei go straight at Simons and bang him into the opposite wall. I grin. "And hey, if he actually does have the balls to ask my sister out, at least he'll finally get us some fucking points first."

As we watch, Alexsei picks up the puck mid-ice, passes it ahead to Lamont, who then passes it back and with a flash of his black stick, Alexsei sends it into the net.

I whoop and then grin at Coach. "See? I'm a fucking genius at the pep talk."

"I've noticed that you and 'fucking genius' are not put into sentences together very often," Coach points out.

"It's a travesty I'm not more appreciated around here," I say, nodding as if he was complimenting me.

Grinning, I return to the end of the bench where Michael is sitting.

"You're smiling," he says, surprise clear on his face.

I nod. "Yeah." I frown then. "Weird right? I'm still hurt, my team is losing, and I think one of my teammates might ask Luna out."

Michael lifts a brow. "That is weird."

We watch without saying anything for a few minutes. Then I finally ask what's been on the tip of my tongue all night. We'd agreed not to talk about it at home and I get it—we need to have some boundaries. God knows I don't want Nathan coming home as my pissed off owner-boss when I fuck up. And we all know I will.

Home needs to be home. Work needs to be work.

The fact that the three of us work together is how we ended up in our situation in the first place. If we weren't all a part of the Racketeers, we wouldn't have all been here the night Dani had come to the game with her horrible date and ended up on the Kiss Cam.

But the working together and living together could definitely, easily, turn into a lot of together.

"Hey, Doc?"

He looks over at me. "Yeah?"

"I'm asking this as number seventeen, not your…roommate, okay?"

We still haven't really settled on what we guys should call each other. We're not each other's boyfriends. We are friends. We are roommates. But we also feel like a hell of a lot more than that.

But Michael nods and I know he understands what I'm getting at. "What's up?"

"I'm ready to play."

He doesn't seem surprised by the topic. "Okay."

I lift a brow. "What?"

"I said, okay."

"That's it?"

"You can practice tomorrow, half-speed, and we'll see how it goes."

I turn on the bench to face him. "Seriously?"

He gives me a smile. "Yes. Seriously."

I search his face. He was definitely more conservative with me last fall when I sprained my thumb. Sure, a thumb and a groin are two different body parts, but when I previously injured my groin, the team doctor kept me out for almost a month.

But then I wonder…

"Is this because I didn't get to fuck Dani and you did and you feel bad?" I ask, my voice lower.

He actually chuckles. "That's not how this is going to work," he tells me. "You can't bribe me or guilt me…not even with Dani."

"Okay." Yeah, Doc definitely isn't the bribeable type. "So, what is this?"

"I trust you," he says simply. "If you think you're ready, I'm definitely willing to give you a chance. You know yourself well. You've been playing hockey for a long time. And I know your body, your game, this team, the playoffs all matter to you. I know you won't fuck around with any of it."

I watch the game for a little longer, thinking that over. I like that, of course, but…

"Is it about home?" I finally ask.

I look over to find him watching me. Then he nods. "Yeah, it probably is. For better or worse."

"It's not about Dani specifically," I say. "Or that you and I are friends, exactly. But you've gotten to know me better. Last fall, I don't think you would have let me make this call."

Now he's the one watching the game and obviously thinking things over. Eventually he nods. "You're right."

"Yeah?"

"Yeah. I know you and trust you because of our friendship. Because I've really gotten to know not just what your priorities are but how you take care of the things and people that matter to you." He looks at me. "This team matters to you. I respect that. I know you're not one hundred percent, but you need to be out there with them. For them. For you, too. At this point in the season, especially, they need you. If you're willing to play and risk a setback that will take more work in the off-season, I'm going to trust you." He pauses. "And I'm here for you to work through it all after the season's over. We'll get you back to one hundred percent eventually. But I won't keep you out of the playoffs."

I can't name the emotion I feel. Relief and gratitude, of course, because this means I get to play. But it's not just that.

Michael trusts me. Because he's gotten to know me. That makes me…proud, I guess. That makes me feel really stupidly good about myself. Like I earned something I didn't even know I was trying for. I respect Hughes a lot and I really like the idea that goes both ways. I like that he knows what's important to me and values my work ethic and knows that I'm willing to make some sacrifices for the greater good.

"Thanks, Doc," I finally say. "That means a lot."

He claps me on the shoulder. "I've got your back. I'll even run interference."

"You think Coach will be mad I'm rushing it?" Then I shake my head. "You think *Nathan* might be mad, right?"

He grins. "I'm more worried about your girlfriend thinking you're rushing it. And that I'm letting you."

I laugh. But he's right. "Good thing you know lots of ways to make her agreeable to your way of thinking."

He laughs out loud at that. "I'm willing to pull out all the stops. Just for you."

CHAPTER 19
Sammy the Malamute
(WADE)

THE RACKETEERS PULLED out the win!

Finally.

It went down to the last second and if Alexsei hadn't skated his ass off, they would have had another loss.

It's hard to be a team mascot when you really want to swear and yell stuff like "Pull your head out of your ass, Wilder! What kind of a block was that?"

But no. I have to be excited and happy about everything. All the fucking time.

I really need a new job.

Except, this one's pretty great for drama.

Like when Alexsei skated over to the wall just below where Crew McNeill's girlfriend and sister usually sit.

Only the girlfriend wasn't here tonight. It was just his gorgeous sister, Luna. Looking hot as fuck in her fitted Racketeers T-shirt and her jeans, her purple tipped hair pulled up on top of her head.

And he said, "Your brother said if I scored, I could ask you out."

And she said, "I don't need my brother's permission for anything. You need to ask *me* if you can ask me out."

And then Crew said, "What the hell are you doing here, anyway? I told you I wasn't playing tonight."

And she said, "You do realize you're not the only hockey player on the team right? You're not even my favorite hockey player on the team."

And the guy sitting behind her, who I think is Alexsei's roommate, said, "Damn."

He'd been watching her through the whole game.

He watches her through every game.

I only know this because I also watch her through every game.

Not in a creepy way.

I'm just a dude who thinks she's gorgeous and seems fun.

A dude dressed up in a big furry dog suit who always knows where she's at during the game, and that she has three Racketeers T-shirts that she rotates, and that she always gets popcorn with light butter and a diet soda and…

Okay, shit, maybe the roommate and I are both creepy.

CHAPTER 20
Dani

"THANK you for coming down here tonight. I love working here, but I've missed seeing you," I say, reaching out and covering Michael's hand with mine.

We're sitting at one of the tables in the bakery section of the shop. I wanted some quiet time to write tonight but wanted him to read through the pages that I've done since he's been gone.

I've had one-on-one time with both Nathan and Crew over the past few days, and I've missed having the same with Michael. I just wanted a chance to connect. We haven't had a chance to really sit and just talk and read. I thought it might be nice if we did it outside of the house, just us.

I'm also trying to make an effort tonight to show some interest in his life. It's a gesture that I want to be sure he sees and understands, and I thought it would be best if it was just the two of us, at least for a few hours.

He turns his hand up so we are palm to palm and laces his fingers with mine. "You know I always love coming down here and spending time with you." He gives me an affectionate smile. "Is business going well? How are things with the bookshop?"

I nod. "We're very busy. Things are going great. We started

another book club. We have two author signings next month. And our Blind Date With A Book book box project has been huge."

He squeezes my fingers. "That's amazing. I'm proud of you."

I preen under his praise. As always.

"I started a new story and I have four chapters for you to read. Is that too much for tonight?" I ask him.

"Of course not. You know I love helping with your work." He brings my hand up to his mouth and presses a sweet kiss across my knuckles.

I pass my laptop over to him. "Here you go."

"Are you going to keep working ahead?" he asks as I pull out some papers from a folder.

"Actually, I've got some things to read too."

He nods. "Okay. Sounds good."

He settles in to read over the chapters I've finished, and I start with the top page of the first article.

I was able to find the two articles that Michael helped author in his professional journal. It wasn't hard, and I'm excited to learn more about what he does.

But thirty minutes in, my eyes are glazing over and I'm feeling frustrated and bored.

I have no idea what most of this means. The first was an article about thumb sprains in hockey players. I didn't even know those were common. But apparently, Michael is an expert. I'd abandoned it on page three. The second is an article about groin strains in hockey players and I thought, with Crew's injury, at least it would hold my interest a little longer than something about thumbs. I was wrong.

I don't understand the anatomical references, so many of the terms are seemingly six syllables long, and I definitely don't understand the interventions or the medications that they're talking about.

I feel frustrated. I really want to be interested in his work, his life outside of the Racketeers and what we do at home, but what he does is very over my head.

Hell, I've just finished memorizing all the hockey terms I should know because of Crew's job.

Michael blows out a breath, and I look up.

He's frowning at my laptop screen.

"What's wrong?" I asked.

He glances up at me but hesitates. Then he shakes his head. "I'm not finished yet."

I lean in. "Tell me what you think so far."

Again, he seems to hesitate but then says, "Okay, I do already have some thoughts."

I push the papers I'm reading away, and lean in on my forearms. "Well, that's what this is for right? You always help make my writing better. Tell me what you're thinking."

He takes a breath, then says, "Honestly? I wish you weren't writing another mafia romance."

I frown. "That's what did so well for me before."

"So you're not writing it because you really love it or had a story that you were dying to tell. You're doing it because you think that's what you have to do to find success," he says.

"That makes sense, doesn't it?" I ask, rather than admitting that no, I'm not dying to tell dark stories about people in the mafia. I struggle with the violence.

"On one hand," he agrees. "But you've only written one story. You could have just as much success with something else."

"You don't like the story," I say. It's obvious, and I have to swallow down my disappointment.

"You're just not this person, Dani," he says, glancing at the screen. "You're not...dark and twisty. This feels very superficial. Like you're just writing what you think you're supposed to write. None of this feels natural or like your heart is in it."

I frown. "You think I don't like my own book?"

He meets my gaze. "I don't. I think this is something you feel obligated to do. It's not something you love doing. You should write something that excites you."

I force myself to really let his words in. Michael loves me. He's not trying to hurt my feelings. He is trying to help me. I know that.

Nathan and Crew would read it and tell me it was amazing and tell me they love it because I wrote it.

And they would mean it. Absolutely.

Or maybe they wouldn't actually love the writing itself, but they would never tell me.

Michael, on the other hand, can be proud of me for trying, for doing the writing, for starting a new project, and still think I can do better.

I take a deep breath. "So what about...a rom-com?" I ask, feeling a little panicked even saying it out loud. My readers, the only ones I have, know me as a dark mafia romance writer.

But I struggled to plot this book because I kept thinking of funny, light story ideas.

He lifts a brow. "I think that you could write a really sexy rom-com. Maybe with hockey. You're basically living a sexy hockey rom-com," he says with a small smile.

"Really?" I ask. But I know he would never tell me that if he didn't mean it.

"Of course. You're a light, happy, loving person. You're sexy, adventurous, and funny. You could definitely write something that's all of those things."

I feel a little flip in my belly. Michael truly cares. He wants my writing to be successful because he loves and respects me. He does believe that I can be the writer that I've always dreamed of being.

Nathan and Crew know about my writing. They've read my stories. They take me out to celebrate when the stories do well.

But my connection with Michael is different. He definitely understands what I'm trying to do. He helps me through plotting, and he helps me with the actual storylines and characterizations. He gets it all on a deeper level.

Part of that is why I feel like *I* have not taken as much interest in *him* as I should have.

So I let myself actually think about what he's saying and not just throw up defenses because he's critiquing what I've written.

I am writing very dirty but yes, definitely dark stories about mafia men who kidnap and force women into situations they don't want.

There's gun fighting, knives. There's definitely blood and sometimes people die.

I think about some of the other romances that I read. I love the light, funny ones. Some of the romantic comedies are extremely sexy, with multiple partners.

Finally, I nod. "Okay, but if I was going to write a romantic comedy that was super spicy, I don't think I would want to do it as hockey. I think that's maybe too close to home. What if I wrote about another sport?"

He nods. "Great. What other sports do you like or know a lot about?"

I shrug and laugh. "None."

He smiles. "Well, you can learn. Or doesn't have to be a sports romance. It could just be a romantic comedy. Friends to lovers. Enemies to lovers. How about best friend's brother?" he asks with a little smirk. "You know something about that."

I let that sink in and the flip in my stomach turns into a bigger swoop. "I could write a sexy billionaire romance too," I say. "Or a hot doctor."

He smiles. "Or all three."

I grin. "Okay. I will think about that. Maybe we can plot something together?"

"I'm happy to help. But I also know that you can do this. Just tell a sexy love story, Dani. You know all about that."

My heart softens a little as I look into his eyes. Yes, he's critiquing me. But he's not trying to tear me down. He's trying to make me better and not just tell me what I want to hear.

Yes, I definitely know all about falling in love.

My love story happens to be right in the middle, where the couple—or couples—are figuring out that things aren't always sunshiny. That there are real-life situations that we have to get through. But I'm still madly in love.

And it is very sexy.

"I need to ask you something," he says, his expression getting serious.

"Okay."

He reaches out and takes my hand. "What do you think about getting a critique partner or some online beta readers?"

I frown. "What do you mean? You don't want to do this anymore?"

"I don't know if it's good for us."

"Michael." I squeeze his hand until he meets my eyes. "Why?"

"Do you really want my critiques? I feel like it creates a tension for us. Nathan and Crew…they don't critique you. Ever. In anything. And…" He blows out a huff of air. "You like that. You like their adoration and…" He trails off again and then gives a little chuckle as he shakes his head. "Those guys think you fucking walk on water, Cookie."

I press my lips together and study him. I finally nod. "I know. You don't let me get away with what they do."

His frown is quick and deep.

I squeeze his hand. "But that's okay, Michael." I pause, then ask, "Can I say something without you thinking I'm happier with them? Because I'm not. You know that you're all three just different."

He thinks about it for a second and I appreciate that.

He finally nods. "Okay."

"Nathan has his life pretty well set up the way he wants it. He's old enough and rich enough to do that. The only thing that was missing was love. And he didn't even think he wanted that. Then he and I fell in love and it was the cherry on top. I know he's happy with me. Very happy. And I know I make his life better. I know he wants it, me, forever now. But in every other way, his life is set, and he's content. He doesn't like change at all and if nothing else ever changed for him again, he'd be happy."

I pause. Michael doesn't say anything. He's just watching me.

"Crew *doesn't* have his life set up yet, but that's okay. He's only twenty-three. He's right where he should be for his age and everything. He's very successful in his career. He knows what he wants from that. He knows what he wants from his life and as far as he's concerned, he's got time to make it all happen. He and I fell in love and it matches right up with his timeline and what he wants for his future."

I stop again. Michael is still just listening.

"And then there's you. You are at a place in your life where you're not quite set. You thought you'd have the life that your friends and colleagues have—kids, a house, a wife–by now. You have it figured out. You know *what* you want. You just don't have the person to move forward with."

"I have *you*," he says, his voice gruff.

I nod. "Then you and I fell in love. But I come with two other people. Two other *men*. I'm not just a partner for *you*. So I messed up some of your plans." I give him a wobbly smile and lift his hand to my lips for a kiss. "I know you love me, Michael. And I know I love you, so, so much. I'm just not who you were planning on. And so you're having to shift around some expectations."

He takes a breath and it sounds ragged. "You're…exactly right. I've been thinking about that a lot, actually."

"Are you thinking good things about it?" I ask.

"Just how it will all work. How Nathan and Crew fit into the picture I've always had of my future."

So he didn't say it was *good*. But he didn't say it was bad. I chew on my bottom lip for a moment.

"Are you okay with the three of us being different in *these* ways?" he asks. "I know in other ways–the way we romance you, our interests, even the way we make love to you–we're different and that's a good thing, but is it okay with you that we're all in different places in our lives? And that our one-on-one relationships with you are a little different?"

I think about it for a moment, but that's easy to answer. "Of course. I need all three of you. I *want* all three of you. And it's *because* you're all different. I don't expect any of you to have exactly the same outlook on life."

He studies my face as I speak. He nods, seeming pleased by my answer. "I agree. Even though we're all in this relationship together, it's important we all continue to respect that we're each individuals. And that we each have a relationship *with you* that's different from what you have with the other two."

I nod. "I agree."

He smiles. "Great." He leans in and kisses me. "I love you."

"I love you too."

He sits back in his chair. He seems mostly mollified by our conversation. His gaze lands on the papers on the table. "What were you reading about?"

I quickly move to cover the papers with my hand. I'm not sure I want him to know that I have absolutely no clue what any of this means.

But the title of the first article peeks out from underneath my hand. He frowns, then looks up at me. "You're reading one of my papers?"

I sigh and lean back, pushing all of the papers toward him. "Both of them. Or maybe you have even more? These are the ones that you were talking about in Vegas."

I can't read the expression on his face.

"Why?" he asks.

"Because I want to know more about what you do. Because I realize that I know a lot about what Nathan and Crew do, but I don't really know many specifics about your job. And I don't want you to think that I don't care. I want to be more involved in your life. I want the next medical conference to go better."

"Danielle," he says firmly. His full use of my name always makes me pause. "You didn't do anything wrong. We're okay."

I nod. "I know. But I want to show you that I care."

"I know you care."

"What you do is just so far beyond what I understand. I don't mean that hockey isn't impressive. It totally is. It's just a little easier to understand. And Nathan is just…rich."

Michael chuckles at that, and I smile. "I'm sure there's more to it than that, but he sits in meetings and tells people what to do. It's basically exactly how he is at home."

Michael's grin grows.

"I just know that you have a bigger life. And you had a lot of life before I came along."

He puts a hand over his chest. "Ouch. A dig at my age?"

I grin and lean in, grabbing his hand. "No. Except, kind of. I'm just saying that you've done a lot that I haven't. And I don't want you to think that you can't include me. That I can't keep up."

He studies me for a moment. Then he says, "Dani, you don't have to read my papers. Or listen to my lectures. Or understand everything I do at work. That's not the important part."

"But being a part of your life outside of watching you on the bench during hockey games and at home when we're all together is important."

He nods. "I understand what you're saying. It's like me being involved in your writing."

I nod. "Exactly. I want to show you that I want to know more about you."

"Okay. I have an idea. You don't have to know the ins and outs of orthopedic rehabilitation. Or the research I do. But what would you say to another dinner with my friends? We can go out with one of the couples that we met in Vegas. They're going to be in Chicago this weekend. They asked if we wanted to get together and I've put them off."

I grimace. "You've put them off because you aren't sure I can handle it?"

He shakes his head. "I put them off because I wasn't sure what we were all doing. There are four of us and I don't know what our family plans are."

I feel a little warmth in my stomach. *Our family plans.* I love that.

"I assume you don't mean to invite Nathan and Crew to dinner?"

"How about just you and me this time? We go to dinner with Garrett and Deb like we did in Vegas but it's kind of a do over. They know about our bigger situation, but I would love for you to get to know them better. It will just be casual. It won't be a professional setting. Just friends going out for dinner."

I nod. "I'd really like that. They can tell me stories about you from before we met, right?"

He smiles. "Definitely."

I suddenly feel excited. I would love to hear people tell me more about Michael. I love the stories his family tells, but I'm guessing that friends will tell different kinds of stories.

"I'd love to go."

"I'll text him back right now."

He starts to withdraw his hand so that he can grab his phone. But I tighten my fingers on his for a moment and then say when he meets my eyes, "I love you. So much."

He leans over and gives me a soft, sweet kiss. "I love you too, Dani. So much."

CHAPTER 21
Crew

"OH, my God, Crew. Oh my *God*," Dani moans.

Unfortunately, she is not in the throes of an orgasm brought about by my tongue, or fingers, or cock—I clear my throat and adjust myself at the thought of that—but bouncing up and down on the balls of her feet as she nervously watches the delivery of our four-person hot tub.

Technically, it's *my* hot tub, since I'm the one who wanted it and I paid for it, but in spite of the general grumbling from Cookie & Co. about this purchase, I know we'll all be enjoying it.

"Are you sure this is *safe*?" Dani asks.

"Of course," I say with total confidence as the hot tub dangles high up in the air, hoisted by a crane above our just-renovated pricey piece of real estate. "These guys are professionals, sweetheart."

But I take her hand and tug her back toward the street because, to be honest, it looks like the claw game at the arcade where you try to delicately grab and hold an object like a stuffed animal or a pair of fuzzy dice. Only this is life-sized and capable of killing us.

"It's insane, that's what it is," Nathan says. "As is putting a hot tub on a rooftop deck."

Nathan has had lots of grumblings about the expense—which makes me laugh because he has more money than Oprah, as he pointed out himself once—and the lack of privacy on the rooftop. Which is Nathan code for he thinks it's ugly or tacky or something. But I don't give a shit. A deal's a deal and I asked for a hot tub so I'm getting one.

Even if my asshole is clenching a little right now watching this delivery. Damn. It's spring in Chicago so you guessed it, it's windy. Like, really fucking windy. The hot tub is swaying a little too much, even for my own personal comfort, but I am not about to admit that.

We're on the front sidewalk, necks straining as we watch a guy who looks like he's been operating that crane since the beginning of time, a cigarette dangling from his lips. The truck is blocking a portion of the street and we have safety cones preventing anyone else from entering the zone of death. Which probably means we shouldn't be standing directly behind it, but someone has to supervise this shit, and it's obviously going to be Nathan.

"The neighbor's four doors down have one too," I point out. "And it's for my health. It helps with inflammation." Mostly I'm envisioning making out with Dani in it while she's in a bikini, but no one can argue with the health benefits. "Ask Doc."

Nathan's not even listening. He's on the verge of having a heart attack as the hot tub again sways dramatically. "Watch the fucking house!" he yells, charging toward the edge with his hands waving. "Watch the neighbor's house, for fuck's sake!"

The edge of the hot tub grazes the copper gutter on the second floor as it makes its ascent up and over the roof. It does appear to be defying gravity right now.

Michael's head pops out of our front door. "Dani, come inside. This is making me nervous." He gives me a look, like I should have known not to have Dani on the sidewalk.

Which irritates me a little. I don't need to be told to take care of our girl. I was already concluding on my own we should go back into the house. But that's the downside to being the youngest in our foursome. I'm not always taken seriously. Just because I like to play strip video games doesn't mean I'm an idiot. The fact that they *don't* makes them idiots.

Dani waves Hughes off, though, before I can tell him to kiss my ass. "Inside or outside, I don't think it matters, Michael. If they drop that, we're all in serious trouble."

"Good point," I tell her, squeezing her hand. "Let's walk down the street a little bit."

Our neighbors, Mark and Marissa, are watching wide-eyed from their front steps, mugs of coffee in their hands, their pug and their young daughter running around the little patch of grass between the house and the sidewalk.

"If that falls on my house, you owe me Racketeers season tickets for the rest of my life," Mark says, eyeing the hot tub. His tone is casual though, like he assumes this will all be fine.

Mark and I have hung out a few times already with Michael. Mark's around Nathan's age, but he's chill. He likes to brew his own beer and talk hockey with us. He's the kind of guy who assumes things will work out for him because they usually do, and he parents from a chair, letting his kids have more independence than Marissa does. She's the anxious parent, hovering, and she's doing that now, eyeing our delivery with genuine fear, which is fair.

"Mark!" Marissa jumps and grabs his arm, spilling his coffee down the front of his T-shirt. "Jesus, do something!"

Mark shakes coffee off of his hand. "I am doing something. I'm getting us hockey tickets."

Marissa makes a sound of disgust. I don't think we're her favorite neighbors. I've gotten the impression she doesn't approve of our relationship. Either that, or she's just anxious in general and it's nothing personal. At any rate, she and Dani haven't really connected. Dani squeezes my hand now.

"Sorry," she says. "The crane operator assured us they do this all the time."

"I doubt that," Marissa mutters.

Mark sighs. "McNeill, how about legacy hockey tickets that can be passed down to our kids? Season tickets in perpetuity."

"We'll get you box seats for the playoffs," I tell him. "It's the least we can do." They've already tolerated our remodeling and they're about to endure many nights of me making out with Dani in the hot tub.

Nathan is probably right. There isn't enough privacy, but hell, we live in the city. Privacy is at a premium. We all agreed for various reasons this house is the best option for this phase of our lives and relationship, so even though Nathan hates having to interact with the neighbors, he's going to have to play nice.

"This is the last of the home improvement projects," I tell Mark. "Aside from Michael's plans for a garden. I heard talk of a living greenery wall and a fountain. I'm trying to talk him into letting me add a rock-climbing wall and a trampoline."

Marissa just grabs her daughter by the arm, turns, and goes back into the house without a word. I watch her retreating back with chagrin. "I was kidding about the trampoline."

Mark scoffs. "Don't worry about it. It's your yard, do what you want."

"Michael wants to do a salsa garden," Dani tells him.

"What the hell is a salsa garden?" Mark asks. "It sounds amazing."

"We're going to have tomatoes, onions, and peppers we don't know what to do with, so we'll be dropping off produce for you."

"Excellent, I'm looking forward to that. And cilantro, right?" Mark asks. "I love cilantro so much I've contemplated rolling it up and smoking it."

That makes me laugh. There doesn't seem to be much Mark isn't willing to smoke.

Several other neighbors have wandered out of their houses to watch Operation Hot Tub.

"Hi," Dani says, turning to greet a couple I don't recognize from a few doors down. "Sorry for the noise."

The crane is loud. As is Nathan, who is now stalking over toward us, swearing repeatedly.

"No worries," a woman who looks around my mother's age says. "I would love a hot tub myself. Aching joints."

"Same," I tell her. "Occupational hazard."

"What do you do?" she asks, her smile friendly but blank. "You're so young, you can't possibly have bad knees yet."

"Trust me, they've gotten pretty banged up over the years." I realize she has no idea who I am. I also realize I've gotten used to fans recognizing me and this is a little… *humbling*. I fucking hate it. "I play hockey."

"In university?"

Dani smiles broadly. "For the Racketeers," she says. "Crew is the top scorer."

I appreciate that she's proud of my achievements, but now I feel a little sheepish. Like I need my girlfriend to point out that I'm legit.

"Oh, is that the local team? And you play for them?"

This is from a man who is obviously her husband. He's come up next to her and put his hand on the small of her back. He has a British accent, which makes me feel better that he's not a hockey fan.

I nod. "Yep. Play for them, get paid by them, turned their whole franchise around, gonna win a championship for them."

Nathan has also reached us in time to hear that and he clears his throat. "Turned the franchise around is a strong statement. We weren't losing without you." Nathan puts his hand out and introduces himself. "I'm Nathan Armstrong, the owner of the Racketeers. I'm really sorry about all the noise on a Saturday morning. It's nice to meet you both. Which house is yours?"

I realize I should have introduced myself and Dani.

"We're Peter and Bev," Peter says. "We live in the brick house right there." He points. "Horrible monstrosity. Who builds a salmon-colored brick house with sandstone accents? We're having it painted in a few weeks, so I'll see your crane and raise you four-story scaffolding, Armstrong."

Nathan laughs. "This is Crew, and this is Danielle," he says, pointing to us. "It's a pleasure to meet you Peter and Bev. We'll have to have you over to commiserate over construction headaches. Mark, you and Marissa need to join us too. I told Crew this hot tub was ridiculous but he had to have it."

For a guy who didn't want to meet the neighbors, he's all on board now. I feel that twist of competitiveness that is part of the dynamic between me and Nathan. The neighbors can't like him more than me.

"This is my first house. What's the point of a whole house if I can't have a hot tub?" I protest.

"So you bought the house for your son and his wife?" Bev asks Nathan.

I almost laugh out loud. Nathan's face goes as red as the tomatoes Michael is going to plant in his salsa garden.

Mark coughs.

Dani turns pink.

I grin.

"He's not my son," Nathan says. "Danielle is *our* girlfriend. Both of ours."

Bev looks confused. Peter looks stunned. Mark looks highly entertained.

"So you both…with her. And she…" Peter trails off.

I nod. "We do."

"I see," Bev says politely, when it's clear she doesn't get a damn thing about it. "How lovely."

That's one way to put it. My grin spreads.

"You like the young ones, huh?" Peter says, clapping Nathan on the shoulder. "Can't say I blame you. Men our age can't be afraid to lean on our pocketbooks, am I right?"

Nathan looks like he's going to have a stroke. I love Peter with my whole fucking heart right now.

Michael comes out the front door. "The eagle has landed," he said. "The hot tub is in place."

"Who is that?" Bev asks, her jaw dropping. Her hand raises to her chest as she ogles Michael. "Now that's a handsome gentleman," she murmurs, as if she's forgotten her pot-bellied husband is standing next to her.

"That's my other boyfriend," Dani says. "Dr. Michael Hughes."

"A doctor?" Bev murmurs, still staring.

Peter shakes his head. "Your other boyfriend? What the devil is going on in your house?"

Mark actually laughs out loud now. "More than in my house. My wife makes me sleep in the guest room because I snore."

"Peter snores too," Bev confides. "Too much meat and cheese. You should try one of those sleep apnea machines. I tell Peter all the time he needs one."

"And look like bloody Darth Vader?" Peter demands. "Then you'll never shag me."

"I'm with Peter on this one," Mark says.

I glance at Dani. She gives me a bewildered look, but she's smiling. I lean down and whisper in her ear. "Let's go test out our hot tub. They'll never even notice if we leave."

She bites her lip in amusement but shakes her head. "Be nice."

"I'm always nice. Except when I tie you up and tease you."

Her eyes widen, and she sucks in her breath. "Is that what you're planning to do?" she whispers.

"Come inside and find out." I wave to everyone. "Great chatting, Dani and I have an appointment we need to run to."

"Don't you even—" Nathan starts to protest but Michael gives him a small head shake.

I'm counting on the two of them to be too polite to scrap with me in front of the neighbors or to blow them off, and I'm right. They continue to chat and I make my escape, hauling a giggling Dani behind me.

CHAPTER 22
Michael

"SO MICHAEL HID the beer in the washing machine of the dorm laundry room and then sat on it when the dorm supervisor came into the room," Garrett Baker, my oldest friend from undergrad, says. "Like sitting on the lid would make it seem super casual, that we weren't breaking dorm rules by drinking."

I shake my head in amusement at the story. "Really? You have to tell my girlfriend about my college antics?" I ask him. Poor Deb, his wife, has already heard this story but she's smiling too as we sit at a table with Dani, drinks and appetizers laid out in front of us.

"This is my favorite Michael story," Deb says. "Hands down."

I groan and lift my wine glass. "This is embarrassing. Seriously. Keep in mind I was eighteen, please, and panicking because I was on a full scholarship and didn't want to get busted."

"What happened?" Dani asks. "Did you get in trouble?"

"This genius," Garrett says, finger pointing at me, grin on his face, "is sitting on the machine, assuring the dorm supervisor up, down, and sideways that we are in fact, just doing our laundry and studying in the laundry room on a *Friday night,* until the guy, who was like forty years old and no idiot, asks why the washer isn't actually turned on. It's not running. Dead giveaway."

"Here's the part where I panicked entirely," I tell Dani. "I was scared witless he would make me lift the lid."

"Oh, no, what did you do?" she asks sympathetically, a smile playing about her lips. "Did you do what I think you did?"

"Oh, yeah. One hundred percent. Without even thinking, I just turned it on so he wouldn't look inside. At first it was fine, just water filling the tub with two twelve packs. I was actually relieved, feeling like we got away with it. Then the agitator started to oscillate. Things went downhill from there." I wince even now at the memory.

Garrett grins. "The second the dorm supervisor was out of there, we tried to recover the beer but the machine was locked from the starting cycle. We could hear the beer cans clanking around in there. So Michael unplugged the machine."

"Why?" Dani asks me, looking bemused.

"To stop the beer from being shaken up. Plus, what do they always tell you with electronics? Turn it off, then turn it on again."

Deb is shaking her head and gives Dani a smile. "My God, I'm so glad I was never an eighteen-year-old boy. It's a wonder any of them survive."

Dani laughs. "To be fair, I would have probably just blurted out everything to the dorm supervisor in my panic. Confess and cry, that's more me. I've never been the naughty girl."

"Want to fucking bet?" I ask Dani with a grin, unable to resist. I reach down and squeeze her thigh.

"Michael!" she says, her cheeks turning a fiery red instantly. "Oh, my God, I can't believe you said that."

She looks genuinely shocked, but not upset. Just startled.

With Nathan and Crew around, there isn't much opportunity for me to shock her with innuendos, but here, at a casual dinner with my oldest pre-med buddy, I can. It feels good to be here, with her.

Dani looks beautiful, wearing a teal dress that complements her eyes, an ivory sweater draped over her shoulders. She's drinking sparkling water instead of wine and I know it's because she still feels bad about the work dinner in Vegas. I appreciate so much her willingness to be present with me, trying to get to know my friend and his wife, who also went to college with us.

Deb laughs. Garrett says, "Hey now, we're in public." But he's grinning too.

I know my friends are happy for me that I've found my person. Deb spent half of our twenties attempting to set me up on blind dates with her single friends.

"I'm just saying you're not as innocent as you pretend to be," I murmur and lean over to kiss the side of Dani's head. "I like that about you."

"Anyway," Dani says, shooting me a look that tells me I'm going to pay for my comment later, in the most delicious way possible. "What happened when you plugged the washer back in? Was the beer saved?"

"It wouldn't open. It was still locked, though to this day I wonder if that's true or not or if we were just panicking so hard we couldn't get it open. And this was right before you could use a debit card or your student ID to pay for your laundry. It took quarters and it wouldn't start without more quarters, so Garrett had to go scrounge up some change from the guys on the floor. Then we had to wait out the whole wash cycle."

Garrett shakes his head. "By then, the cardboard had gotten soaked and torn. The cans got all shaken up and several exploded. The washer was full of sudsy, cheap light beer. The cans that were still intact blew up in our faces when we tried to open them in Michael's room. Beer everywhere."

"The little that was left was flat. A complete waste of money and a Friday night."

"We ended up playing video games." Garrett laughs. "Dreams of being cool completely shattered."

"But we didn't get caught. There's that."

"You still owe me ten bucks for that beer."

This has been a long-standing joke. "It was as much your fault as mine. I don't owe you shit."

But I like that Dani is hearing about my youthful stupidity. I think sometimes she thinks I've never misstepped, and that isn't true. I've had an evolution into adulthood just like anyone else. There is a little bit of spilled beer in everyone's past.

"To think they both became brilliant doctors," Deb says ruefully.

"Terrifying," Dani agrees, shaking her head with a smile. "So what do you do, Deb? Michael told me your degree is in history."

"I was a high school history teacher until we had our third child, then I stepped down. With Garrett's schedule, it was too hard to juggle work and the kids. I'm a domestic goddess, as I prefer to call it."

"And she's amazing at it," Garrett says with clear pride. "I couldn't do what I do without her holding down the fort at home. Kids are a lot of work."

"You think?" Deb says with an eye roll. "But honestly, raising three under six years old is easier than teaching history to teenagers who think the Boston Tea Party is an indie band."

Dani asks to see pictures of their brood and I eat some of the calamari that's in the center of the table for us to share. Dani isn't the type to ask out of pure politeness. She loves kids, and it warms my heart to see her genuinely oohing and aahing over the photos on Deb's phone.

"That one is the holy terror," Garrett says, glancing over at Deb's phone. "Our youngest, June. She's the reason we're stopping at three kids. She's broken us."

"Stubborn doesn't even cover it," Deb agrees.

"She looks so sweet."

"Don't let the blonde curls and big eyes fool you. Behind the adorable exterior hides the soul of a warrior. She'll let blood be drawn before she gives in."

"If you ever need a sitter, Michael and I would be happy to take your kids for a night so you can get a break."

"You have no idea what you're offering, but thank you."

Garrett shakes his head. "I love her, but I'm genuinely scared of that kid."

I laugh.

Deb smacks his arm. "Stop, Garrett. She's *two*. Dani, do you want kids someday?"

"Deb, that's a little personal," Garrett says, reaching for his martini. "Don't put Dani on the spot."

We've talked only briefly about kids and so I'm curious to hear what Dani's response will be. She doesn't hesitate. "No, no, it's totally fine. Yes, absolutely I want kids."

That warms my heart. "And she'll make an excellent mother. She's very caring and generous."

Dani glances over at me and gives me a smile that makes my heart swell. "Thank you," she says softly. "You're going to be a great father too."

I reach over and take her hand, lacing her fingers with mine. I lift her hand to my mouth and give her a light kiss.

It's been two weeks since I got back from Decatur. Things have been good between all of us in the new house. We've settled into a pleasant routine with the four of us. But also, since our date night at the bookstore, Dani and I have been communicating well, and it feels like we're rock solid. I can't imagine that life could be any better.

Unless Dani was my wife and we were expecting a baby together.

That would be everything I've ever wanted.

"I see," Deb says, and her voice is gleeful.

"You've stepped in it, Hughes," Garrett says dryly.

"I haven't stepped in anything," I tell him. "I'm happier than I've ever been."

I am. This is my idea of a perfect night out. We're in a small, intimate restaurant with ambient lighting, excellent tapas, with old friends and my favorite girl. The conversation flows for the next two hours with lots of laughter until finally Deb calls it.

"I'm getting drunk," she declares. "And tomorrow I'm going to regret it if we don't head out now."

Garrett sighs, but he nods. "Baby Satan, I mean June, gets up at five a.m. most mornings. Deb is right."

"Do not call our daughter Baby Satan," Deb says, though her eyes are sparkling with humor and love for her husband.

"I call 'em like I see 'em." Garrett raises his hand for the check. "You two can stay if you'd like but I'm ready for bed."

"We might stay out for a bit," I say, when I look over at Dani. She nods in agreement. "It's only ten."

"Oh, my God, this is the latest I've been out in three years," Deb says. "When did I get old?"

Garrett must be a little drunk too, because he says to me, "You have the right idea dating a younger woman." Then he realizes instantly that was the wrong thing to say. "Fuck, that didn't sound right. Deb, baby, you know I think you're young and hot and… and…everything." He gives her a sloppy kiss on her cheek.

"Just shut up, please, you're making it worse." Deb rolls her eyes but she doesn't look offended.

I know she feels secure in their relationship and Garrett thinks she hung the moon. He knows he couldn't survive without her.

"I mean it, you're my life."

"Just take me home and put your tongue to better use."

I almost choke on my wine.

Garrett falls back in his chair. "Damn. Okay. Done and done." He starts to pull his wallet out.

I wave him off. "Don't worry about it. This one's on me. For the spilled beer. Take your wife home."

"If we get pregnant tonight, I'm blaming you," he says as he pushes his chair back.

"If *we* get pregnant tonight, likewise." I gesture between me and Dani. I mean it as a joke, but Dani's eyes widen a little.

"Oh, Jesus," Deb says. "On that note, I'm taking my drunk and sweaty husband home. Garrett, order an Uber."

We all stand up and Deb hugs Dani. "It was delightful to meet you. Michael is a great guy, though I'm sure you already know that."

"He is," Dani agrees, hugging Deb back.

"And it's obvious to me why he's fallen in love with you." Deb pulls back and smiles at her. "Let's go to lunch some time."

Dani looks pleased and agrees. I'm happy as well. Deb wouldn't extend the invitation if she didn't genuinely like Dani. She would be polite when needed but nothing more.

I shake Garrett's hand and give Deb a hug.

"I'm glad you finally stopped dating those type A women," Deb says. "Dani is so much a better fit for you."

"I totally agree."

Then it's just me and my girl.

"That was fun," she says, and she looks like she means it. "They're very nice."

"It was fun. Thanks for doing this, Cookie. It means the world to me."

"Of course. I was nervous." She shakes her head a little. "I've never done this. Been part of a couple having dinner with another couple. My last serious relationship was in college, you know that. We weren't socializing at nice restaurants with other couples."

Technically, we're not just a couple either. We're a couple within a larger poly dynamic. But right now, I'm enjoying having Dani all to myself.

"But you genuinely had fun?" I ask her.

She nods with a smile. "Not one medical term was used, *and* I got to hear about your college years."

I finish my glass of wine. "All the conversation about kids doesn't bother you? I admit, sometimes I get tired of that myself because it reminds me of what I don't have. It seems like everyone my age has already started a family."

She shakes her head. "I don't mind. While I can't relate to the struggles of parenthood, I find conversation about kids entertaining. And I guess I'm not old enough yet to yearn so deeply for a child that talking about them is painful."

I absently reach out and take her hand. I want to feel her skin, her warmth. "That makes sense. I wouldn't say I've reached that point either. It's not exactly painful for me." I shrug. My father's heart attack reminded me that nothing in this life is guaranteed. He and my mom already had three kids by my age. "I just want children. That's all."

"I want to be the woman that you want the future with," Dani whispers. "The kids, the house, the vacations, the experiences, the memories."

Her words and the emotion behind them makes me sit up straighter in my chair, casual contentment turning into something deeper, something powerful. This woman next to me is one hundred percent who I picture as the mother of my children. Who I picture as my *wife*.

I don't ever want her to doubt that.

My voice is thick when I say, "You *are* that woman, Dani. You are."

She smiles at me, love in her eyes. "I believe you want me to be."

I wait for her to elaborate on that but she doesn't. She doesn't sound upset. If anything, she sounds more sure of herself in our relationship than she has in a while.

Stroking her palm, I'm overcome by the need to touch her. I can't resist the urge to lean over and brush my lips across hers. "Do you want a drink now that we're alone, or would you like to take a walk by the lake?" I ask, cupping her smooth cheek, studying her serene expression.

"A walk would be perfect."

"You're perfect." I kiss her again, briefly leaning my forehead against hers, before bowing to convention and pulling back. I don't want to wind up making out at a dinner table and I just might with the way I'm feeling. "I love you."

Everything inside of me is screaming that it's time to lock this in. That I need my girl to know that I am in this for her, with her. That we're a team and that in ten years we'll be trading war stories about our devilish toddlers with Deb and Garrett while they warn us about the teen years.

That thought hits me so hard I suck in a breath.

"I love you too."

I stand up and pull her chair out for her. After taking care of the bill, I take Dani by the hand and in a few minutes, we're strolling slowly alongside the river.

"I can't believe how warm it is for this time of year," she says, tipping her head back to inhale deeply the crisp spring air.

"What's your favorite season?" I want to know everything there is to know about her down to the smallest detail.

"I do love spring. It's the season of new beginnings and blooming bulbs and grass turning green. But I also love summer. Swimming, fireworks, barbeques. Oh, and fall. I'm a pumpkin spice girl all the way. But then there's winter and the holidays and snowflakes and honestly, I can't choose."

I had planned to find the perfect spot but hearing her and all her joy in living life has me deciding now is the time. Here and now is perfect. "Of course you can't choose," I tease her, squeezing her hand.

Dani laughs lightly. "I guess I can never live in San Diego. I need all four seasons. What's your favorite, Michael?"

We're walking on a bridge that goes over the river. A boat is lazily floating past, and the city is lit up in a colorful backdrop.

"I love all the seasons, too, for different reasons. But spring is going to be my favorite after tonight."

"Why is that?"

I pause and turn to her, love and admiration for this woman swelling up inside of me. "Because I'm hoping it's the night you agree to be my wife."

Dani gasps. "What?"

I go down on one knee. "Danielle. Cookie. I've been waiting a long time for the woman who is just right for me and then there you were, on the KissCam, as big as can be."

Her fingers are trembling now in mine, her eyes wide, free hand pressed against her chest.

I continue, because I don't want to rush. I need her to hear what she's brought to my life. "You were adorable, of course, but then I got to know you and see what a generous, loving, intelligent, and compassionate woman you are. You have a heart so wide you can love three men and I know that, I respect that, but aside from Crew and Nathan, there is you and me and I love you with all of what's inside of me." I put a fist on my heart. Tears are in her eyes now and she's already nodding in agreement, which emboldens me to finish. "You own my heart, Cookie, and I want to have that future with you that we talked about. Lake houses and babies and rocking chairs on the porch when I'm retired. *You* are my soulmate. Will you do me the absolute honor of becoming my wife?"

"Yes! Oh my God, Michael, yes! Of course!" She lets out a sob, tears of joy streaming down her face.

Euphoria fills me, lifts me off the ground, and I grab her, swinging her into my arms.

I suddenly realize there is clapping. Several people had been observing us from a distance and now they're beaming. I give them a victory wave, grinning, before returning my full attention to the woman I love.

"Danielle," I murmur, kissing her hard before pulling back to study her, to memorize this moment. "You make me so damn happy."

"You make me happy too. I can't wait to be your wife."

"Whatever souls are made of, yours and mine are the same."

"That's Brontë," she whispers.

I knew she would get the reference. Because we're made for each other.

Her eyes are shining with love, her cheeks flushed. She's glowing and she's never looked more beautiful. She has her arms wrapped around my neck and she's standing on her tiptoes so our lips can touch.

"I want to put a baby in you," I say against her mouth.

Dani nods with a smile, but says, "Maybe not *tonight*. Let's talk in a year or two."

"Deal. As long as you're mine, forever."

"I'm yours," she whispers.

CHAPTER 23
Nathan

I HEAR the door open and my heart rate picks up.

Every time. My heart does this every time I know Danielle has just walked into a space where I am. It never gets old.

I shift on the couch that I will never admit to Crew is actually very comfortable. It's too big. It doesn't fit the aesthetic of the house. But it's comfortable.

I've been reading while Crew has been watching television propped right in the center of the monstrosity so he can see the screen.

The television that is also a monstrosity and hung over the fireplace. He couldn't miss seeing it. But Michael had sided with Crew on the purchase, saying that movie nights with us all on the couch together would be great with a television that size.

I don't really care. I'm not a TV guy but I can let them have whatever screen size they want. I just can't not express an opinion.

"Hi!" Danielle greets us as she steps through the door with Michael right behind her.

Crew mutes the television and gives her a big grin. "Hey, pretty girl. Did you have fun?"

I lay my book down and take my reading glasses off, studying her across the room. She looks absolutely gorgeous in a teal dress that's tighter than what she normally wears. But it's her smile that really catches my attention. She's glowing.

Wow, that must have been some dinner.

"It was such an amazing night," Danielle answers Crew as Michael takes her purse and sets it on the table just inside the door. He also offers her a hand while she balances first on one foot, then the other as she takes her shoes off.

She sighs happily and then comes into the living room with that radiant smile still in place.

Crew notices it as well and gives a low chuckle. "I guess so. Did you get frisky in the car on the way home? Or…" He looks up at Michael. "Did you sneak into the ladies' room at the restaurant?"

Danielle laughs. "Not that."

I try to catch Hughes' eye to try to gauge what's going on but he's watching Danielle with his own serene smile. He's got his hands tucked in his pants pockets. He's still in his jacket but his tie is loose and the top button is undone. He looks…maybe happier than I've ever seen him. What the hell is going on?

Not that I don't want him to be happy. But it was just dinner with old friends.

Wasn't it?

"We have something we need to talk to you both about," Danielle says, smiling at Crew. She's standing near where his feet are resting. Then she turns her smile on me.

I lift a brow. For some reason, I feel anticipation knot my stomach. And it doesn't feel like good anticipation.

Crew shifts to sit up straighter. I glance at him and see that he's not grinning the grin he usually wears when our girl is around. It's as if he senses something is up that he's not sure he's going to like either.

"Did something happen tonight?" Crew asks.

Danielle nods, then glances at Michael, her smile still bright.

Michael gives her a look full of love and tenderness.

My chest tightens.

That's never how I feel when these two men look at this woman. At least not since the very beginning when I believed there could only be one of us in Danielle's life. Since we all realized we could be with her together, make her happy together, I haven't resented a single loving look or a private conversation or memory between Danielle and Michael or Danielle and Crew.

Until now.

And I don't even know what's going on.

"What happened?" I ask, the first words I've said.

Danielle looks at me, biting her bottom lip. Usually, that makes me want to kiss her. And bite that lip too. And bite other things.

But this isn't a coy look. Now she looks nervous.

Crew glances between her and me, a slight frown pulling his brows down. "Yeah, what's going on?"

Hughes steps forward, putting his hand on Danielle's lower back. I notice how she leans back into his touch.

"I proposed tonight," Hughes says simply.

His words hit me as if he just punched me.

There is dead silence in the room for several ticks.

I watch Danielle the entire time.

Her cheeks are flushed. She's breathing faster now. Her lips are pressed together.

And she's not looking at me.

She's watching Crew. As if she doesn't want to see my expression. Does she know that I'm not going to like this?

She should.

I finally pull my gaze to Crew. He's staring at her as if he's confused.

I, however, am not confused in the slightest.

I push myself up from the cushion—and get pissed all over again about how huge and soft the fucking thing is because pushing up is a lot less assertive than I'd like it to be—and face them.

"You did what?" I ask Michael.

Not because I didn't hear him. Not because I didn't understand exactly what he meant. But because I'm accusing him of a crime. A serious one. And I want to hear his confession again. And I want to give him this one chance to add on some kind of caveat or explanation if there is one.

He faces me, his hand still on Danielle. My girlfriend.

"I proposed to Danielle tonight." He pauses, meeting my gaze directly. "I asked her to be my wife."

I hold his gaze steadily, waiting for something more. There has to be more to it than him just jumping the fuck ahead like this and doing this on his own.

I feel a very strange sense of loss. And fear. And rage.

Michael just came in and pulled the damned rug out from underneath everything I thought we were doing.

Crew scrambles up from the couch now. "You fucking proposed? What the hell, Doc?"

"I did," Michael says.

"And what did you say?" Crew asks Dani.

Her cheeks are pink now. "I said yes," she replies. It's clear. She doesn't stutter or even hesitate, but she does say it quietly. "But we, obviously, need to talk to you both about it."

I see Michael's jaw tense and I watch Crew try to wrap his head around this. He looks from Michael to Danielle, then back.

"But...why?" Crew finally asks. He directs it at Michael. "We fucking talked about this."

I see Danielle's shoulders straighten and Michael sighs.

"You...what?" she asks.

But Michael answers Crew first. "Because I love her, Crew. Because I want to spend the rest of my life with her. Because I want the world to know that I'm fully committed to her, and vice versa. Because I want to have a family with her. And tonight, I wanted her to know that. The timing was right."

"The timing was right? How's that work when the two of us were sitting here at home thinking we were all going to fucking wait?" Crew asks, waving a thumb between him and me. "You know how we both feel and you just went ahead without us?"

"Tonight was a moment between Dani and me," Michael says, a stubborn set to his jaw. "I'm not leaving you two out, but I wanted to tell Dani how I feel and let her know what I want. I want everyone to know what she means to me, who she is to me. I want a family. I want a future."

I'm watching Danielle. She's looking back and forth between Crew and Michael, worry and confusion in her eyes. "I want those things too," she says. "But…you've talked about this?" Her eyes land on me. "The three of you?"

"We have," Crew says, barreling ahead. "We talked about proposing and we tabled this whole thing because we're not ready."

Danielle actually pulls back slightly at that.

"That is not true," Michael says, angrily. "Some of us are very ready."

Crew shoves a hand through his hair. "We're not ready as a group. We couldn't figure out how it would work," he says. "It all seemed too complicated, so we decided to wait." He scowls at Michael. "Or so I thought."

"It is a little complicated," Danielle agrees. "But that's what we need to talk about." She steps toward Crew. "Just because it will take some talking and compromise and unconventional thinking doesn't make it impossible, though." She hesitates. "Does it?"

My chest is tight and I'm definitely feeling an unreasonable but unmistakable instinct that someone is trying to take something that is mine away from me.

"We can't all marry you," I say. Since I've been mostly silent until now, they all turn to look at me. "That's impossible. No matter how much talking we do."

Hughes shakes his head. "We can make it work."

"No, we can't." I nearly bark the three words, my frustration spilling over.

"Nathan—" Danielle starts.

I hold up a hand. "No," I say. "Legally we can't all marry you, Danielle."

"He's right," Michael concedes. He takes her hand. "But we can have a commitment ceremony. We can do everything but the legal paperwork. We can do the part that really matters—stand up in front of family and friends, exchange vows, declare ourselves."

I'm trying to choose my words carefully. "Which will still mean that you don't have a legal husband. In the eyes of the law, you are still single."

"Which won't matter," Michael insists. "You'll have our full financial support. We'll live together. The kids can take your last name, but Crew and I can be listed on the birth certificates."

"For fuck's sake!" Crew exclaims. "We just moved in together!"

Danielle looks at Crew, then back to me. Her smile is definitely gone now.

But fuck...I can't believe Hughes did this without us.

"You don't want to get married?" Danielle asks Crew.

Well...shit.

That's the question. Just laid out there between us all.

And Crew is very likely going to fuck this part up.

He swallows hard. "Sure I do, baby. Eventually. But this whole damned thing has already moved so fast. I did not think we'd be talking about all of this so soon."

She nods. "I understand." Then she looks at me. "What about you, Nathan? Do you want to get married?"

I don't have to even think about it. "I do."

"To me?" she presses.

"Only to you." There's not one single question about that in my mind. Or heart.

"So, why are you so mad?" she asks.

"Because Hughes fucking proposed to my girlfriend after we specifically agreed to do that together."

"Actually, I proposed to my girlfriend," Michael says. His

voice is low and tight. "Which I have every right to do. Without anyone's permission."

I meet his eyes.

He goes on. "I decided to tell my girlfriend that I am so in love with her that I want to spend the rest of my life with her. It wasn't about you, Nathan."

"And that's the entire problem," I snap. "We are a *we*. We all decided to be a we. There's not a you and Danielle, and a me and Danielle, and a Crew and Danielle, and you fucking know it!"

My cool is officially used up now.

He said he would know what to do if they were a couple and didn't have two other people to consider. Yeah, so would I. So would Crew.

But that's not our reality.

"Crew's right. We did talk about this," I say. "We all have our own relationships with her but when it comes to the big picture, like where we all live, how we all fit into her life, and what fucking forever looks like, it's a we. And it's because of you and Danielle!" I wouldn't call this shouting, exactly, but from the way Danielle pulls back and presses closer to Michael, she might define it differently. "You and Danielle were the ones who first suggested this whole fucking sharing thing. You're the ones who assured us this could work. And you–" I point at Michael, "are the one that keeps things from unraveling!"

He blows out a frustrated breath. "The dad. I know that's my place in the relationship but fuck, you guys, I don't want to always be the glue. Not when I know what I want and Dani wants the same thing and you are two grown-assed men who say you're committed to this thing. Why can't I be the one with big emotions and you and Crew be the ones to figure things out this time?"

"You want me to be the glue?" I ask, taking a step forward. "You want me to give a solution? Fine. Danielle and I get married. We go on our honeymoon. We get back. You and Danielle have your commitment ceremony, go on your honeymoon—"

"We did not decide who would be her legal husband!" Hughes roars.

"Exactly! Because we didn't talk about it again!" I shout back.

"Holy shit!" Crew exclaims. "Can everyone just slow the fuck down?"

"*Hey*!"

We all stop and look at Danielle.

She's stepped away from Michael and is standing in the middle of us.

She looks pissed. She's breathing hard as she looks from Michael to me to Crew. She looks at Michael when she asks, "You all talked about this?" she asks again.

He nods.

"You told them you wanted to propose?"

"Yes. I've been thinking about it for a long time."

"But you all discussed a bunch of different possibilities, about how this would all work, who I would be married to, who I'd have kids with, all of that…without me."

He sighs, but admits it. "Yes."

Now she looks at me. "And you didn't come up with a situation where you were all happy?"

"No. We all had different ideas about how it would work."

She looks at Crew. "And you're freaking out."

He shoves a hand through his hair. "Not freaking out. Just feeling a little…steamrolled."

Her eyebrows rise. "Because you don't want to do any of that. The marriage or commitment ceremony or anything."

"We just moved in together," he repeats, but he sounds less frustrated and more apologetic now.

Danielle swallows hard. She looks from him to me, then up at Michael. Then she takes a deep breath. "I need some…space. Right now."

She steps away from Michael and starts toward the stairs.

"Dani," Michael says softly. "This doesn't change things between us."

"The fuck it doesn't," I say, angrily. "You're not going to be The Husband with Crew and I as the extra boyfriends or sidekicks or whatever."

"That's not what I meant," Michael says, clearly frustrated.

"So I'm the asshole, right?" Crew asks. "The three of you want something I don't. Are we going to vote or something and then I'll lose and just have to go along with it?" He looks angry.

I glance at Danielle. She's on the verge of tears. My heart squeezes, but I know she will not welcome my reaching for her.

"Of course not," Michael says, falling into his role of trying to work things out despite what he just said a minute ago. "No one loses here, Crew. But no one gets forced into something they don't want either."

Danielle takes a deep, shaky breath, and heads toward the stairs.

"Dani–" Crew starts.

"No," she says, starting up the stairs and not looking back at us. "I'm going to go before you keep talking. I'm really glad I wasn't included in the first conversation either." She stops midway up the staircase, though, and turns to look down at us. "I'm sorry. I know none of you expected this…thing we're doing…to turn out to be such a problem."

Her words hit me in the chest. I've hurt her. I've ruined this happy night for her.

Actually, *we've* hurt her and ruined her happy night.

See? The three of us can function as a unit.

A mix of emotions are still roiling through me. Ironically, this feels like something I'd typically talk to Michael about.

We all stand in tense silence, looking at one another. We know that Danielle doesn't want any of us to follow her upstairs. But it feels fucking wrong to let her stay up there alone and angry and hurt.

"Fuck," I finally say.

"That went really badly," Hughes agrees.

I look at him with brows lifted. "You couldn't have truly

thought that was going to go well, did you? That Crew and I would be happy, or even fine, with you proposing tonight?"

"I wasn't thinking about Crew or you at all," Michael says with a frown. "I was thinking about Dani. And me. And I was happy and in the moment and it was right to tell her this was what I want."

"Jesus Christ," Crew mutters, thrusting his hand through his hair. "Married? We just had our first dinner in this house together." He glares at Michael. "Why does everything have to be on the fast track with you? You were the one that suggested we all date Dani. You made that seem like the perfect solution. You said it would be great. Then you were the one that suggested getting a house and moving in together. You made that seem like the most logical fucking thing. You said it would be great. And now you fucking proposed. What the hell is your deal?"

Michael's jaw definitely tenses now. He takes a deep breath. He rolls his neck. He clearly tries to calm down.

And I just stand back.

Because I know for a fact, that Crew McNeill absolutely can and will, eventually, push every single person he spends a great deal of time with to the lose-their-shit-point.

And Michael Hughes is about to prove that fact to me.

"All of us dating that amazing, sweet, loving, beautiful woman upstairs was the best solution," Michael says. "And fuck you if you're going to stand there now and try to tell me that it wasn't. That you're not a thousand times happier now than you were before she, and yes, Nathan and I, came into your life. And moving in together was the right answer for us. For all of us. There is no reason for the four of us to live apart. This is where we all want to be. Where we all need to be. And fuck you again if you try to tell me that being here in this house with us isn't your safe place. Isn't the place where you feel the most loved and supported and accepted that you've ever felt." He takes a menacing step toward Crew.

Crew, for his part, just stands straighter, meeting Michael's gaze directly. He's still scowling, but he doesn't argue any of that.

"And yes, I think having a commitment ceremony, publicly declaring our feelings and essentially becoming her husbands is a great idea. I am ready for that. I acknowledge that I'm older than you, further along in my life. But I want a wife. I want *Dani* to be my wife. I want to start a family with Dani. I want to stand up in front of everyone who is important to my life and declare to them that she is my wife in every way possible." He turns to include me in his next statement. "I didn't intend to leave you out. Tonight wasn't about me being first or the only one. It was about declaring my feelings to Danielle. And her declaring those feelings back. What you guys do is up to you."

"So, you might have a commitment ceremony with her now, and then Nathan and I wait?" Crew asks.

I hate that idea. But I want to see what Michael says first.

Michael shrugs. "I don't think that's ideal. I think that leaves all of us in kind of a shaky situation. But that's up to you. We can't force you to do this just because we're ready and you're not."

"I'm ready." They look at me again. "I am ready now," I repeat. I look at Michael. "I'm pissed you did this after we talked, without coming back to us. But Danielle knows how I feel. And I'm more than happy to stand up in public and say so. I want her to be my wife as well."

Michael opens his mouth to respond but our attention is drawn to the staircase where Danielle is descending again.

Carrying a suitcase.

"No," I say firmly.

She looks over at me. She looks tired. She also looks angry.

"I'm going back to the apartment with Luna. I'm spending the night there. At least tonight. I need time to think."

"Danielle—" I take a step toward her.

"Dani—" Michael says on top of me.

"Fucking hell," Crew mutters.

But she just holds up a hand, stopping all of us. "What you just said is very true, Nathan," she says, looking at me. "No matter where I'm at in my life, we have to be honest about the fact that you are all at different places. I don't want to be with just one of you. Just because Michael and I happen to match up where we are right now and what we want, does not mean that I don't love you and Crew just as much. I want to make this work, but I think we all need some space and time to figure out what that looks like. And, frankly, I don't think I can be here with you right now to do that."

"You can't just walk out, Cookie," Michael says, his voice quiet and calm. "We can talk this through."

"I just need some time," she says to him. There's a honk at the curb outside. "Andrew came to get me," she says by way of explanation. "And I think the three of you need time."

At least she called my driver and not a random taxi or Uber.

"One night," I tell her.

She shakes her head. "I'm not promising anything. We need time to work this out." She looks at Crew. "And I'm not testing you. I'm not saying that you have to agree with me on everything for us to be together or anything like that. But I really feel like we all need time to think about what happened tonight. This is real life. This is how a relationship progresses and gets more serious. We obviously need to think about how we all feel about the situations ahead of us, what we want the future to look like before we really talk about it together. Because obviously when we try to talk about it before we have really considered all the possibilities, we end up hurting each other."

And then she's gone. Out the door, down the steps, and into our waiting town car.

Crew gets up from the couch, shaking his head. "An hour ago, I was sitting here watching television, hoping you guys are having a good time at dinner and looking forward to seeing my girlfriend when she got home. Now my girlfriend is engaged to another guy, and she's moved out."

Michael scowls at him. "You mean the girlfriend that you have because of me?"

"Fuck off, Hughes. You think that Dani is with me just because you had the idea that we should share her? What's to say that she wouldn't have picked me if she had to choose between us?"

"Obviously, I'm the one who's best suited to give Dani what she needs," Michael says.

That is probably the most combative Michael has ever been with us.

"Enough of this," I say firmly. "This doesn't do any of us any good. We are all with Danielle. She is all of ours. So we need to figure out what we all want going forward."

"I'm going downstairs," Crew says, stomping out of the room and toward the door to the basement where his game room is.

So I guess we're not going to talk about it tonight.

"I'm heading upstairs to bed," Michael says. "In my room."

Yeah, there's no fucking way we're all going to be sleeping in the family bed together tonight.

But I stop him when he gets to the bottom of the stairs. "Do you think she's okay?"

He blows out a breath and shakes his head. "No Nathan, I don't think she's okay."

"Should one of us go after her?"

He shakes his head again. "I don't think she wants any of us right now. At least she's going back to the apartment. Luna will take care of her."

I sigh. "Luna is going to be so pissed at us."

Michael meets my gaze. "Maybe rightfully so."

Then he turns and heads upstairs without another word.

I sink back onto the couch that I hate in the living room of the house that I thought I hated.

Yeah, maybe, rightfully so.

CHAPTER 24
Dani

I USE my key and let myself in through the bookstore. It's dark and quiet and peaceful. The smell of the books mingling with the scent of vanilla and cinnamon that drifts in from the bakery is comforting and I take a big, deep breath.

Part of me wants to sink into the huge, soft armchair in the corner and just be alone. But the chair is in the romance section and that makes me want to cry.

My heart feels bruised but I managed not to cry in the car on the way over.

I don't think that's going to last, though.

Obviously, Andrew knew something was wrong, but he didn't ask. Even when he loaded my suitcase in the back. I simply told him, "Take me to my apartment, please." He's made the trip to my apartment several times over the months I've been with the guys, so he didn't need anything more than that. He just let me sit in the back and quietly nurse my emotional wounds.

I can't believe what just happened. I went from the highest high, from Michael proposing to me to the lowest low, realizing that Nathan was turning this into a contest and that Crew didn't want any of this to happen at all.

Crew didn't want any of this to happen.

That shocked me.

Sure, it was all a bit of a shock. And I should've thought more about that. I guess, as is typical, when Michael has an idea and is in charge of something, I just assume it's all going to be okay.

The proposal was obviously very spontaneous, which was what made it so romantic and amazing. I love that the careful, rational, always-in-control one of our foursome had been so wrapped up in his feelings for me that he'd just dropped to one knee. Even now, the butterflies in my stomach love that.

But I'd assumed we'd include Nathan and Crew.

And I guess I figured we were all on the same page when it came to our future.

We're in love. We've moved in together. Isn't forever a given?

I climb the stairs up to the apartment and let myself in.

I don't even know if Luna is home tonight. All I know is that I have to sleep here. This place is familiar. This is comfortable and cozy and while I don't consider it home anymore, it is a place where I feel safe.

And it's away from the guys.

I hate that I want to be away from the guys right now, but I do. I couldn't imagine spending the night in our house together and continuing to talk about this, or, maybe worse, avoiding talking about the subject of our future.

I did know that I could not sleep in that bed with any of them, not to mention all three of them. I'm not sure they would've all slept there together. There was so much tension and anger in the room that I just needed to get away.

The door swings in and I roll my suitcase across the threshold.

Luna is sitting up from where she had been obviously lying on the couch. "Oh my God, Dani!" She leans to put her plate of cookies on the coffee table. "You scared the absolute shit out of me! What are you doing here?"

"Sorry, I probably should've called or texted. Are you alone?"

She gets up from the couch and crosses the room. "I am. But it doesn't matter. You're always welcome here. Even if someone else is here. What's going on?" She's looking at me with sincere concern. Her eyes drop to my suitcase. "Oh, no. What did they do?"

That's what makes the tears start. Not just that my friend is welcoming me and obviously concerned for me, but that she immediately assumed the guys had done something. And that she's blaming all three of them.

"Michael proposed."

She frowns. *"What?"*

I nod. "Michael proposed. It was really romantic. And I said yes."

"Did he do it in front of the other guys?"

I shake my head. "We were alone."

She whistles low. "And Nathan lost his shit, right?"

I nod, the tears streaming.

"Come on. I have more cookies. Tell me everything."

She grabs my suitcase, shoves the door shut, then rolls my bag to the doorway of my old bedroom. I toe off my shoes, then take a seat on the couch.

She comes back over and tosses me one of our fuzzy, soft throws. She's in loose pajama pants and a tank top. Her hair is up and she's without makeup. I look around. The coffee table has cookies and a mug of tea. Two used tea bags lie on a plate. An old rom-com, *French Kiss* with Meg Ryan, is paused on the television.

"Why aren't you out?" I ask.

"Didn't feel up to it," she says.

"You've been flirting with Alexsei," I tell her. As if I didn't notice. As if I haven't told her repeatedly, I need to know more about that whole situation. As if she hasn't been avoiding that subject and further conversation every day in the shop.

"So?" She climbs under her own throw blanket and reaches for her mug of tea.

"So, what's going on there?"

"Oh, no." She turns to face me, leaning against the arm of the couch. "You show up on my doorstep with a *suitcase*, crying? *You* have some talking to do."

I blow out a breath. She's right.

It only takes me a few minutes to tell her the whole story. Which is surprising. The biggest heartbreak of my life seems like it should take longer to recount.

Her eyes are wide when I'm done. "Those fuckers."

I shake my head. "They're not."

"Oh, but they kind of are," she insists. "Every single one of them messed up tonight."

"Michael *proposed*," I say.

"Yes. Knowing the other guys would be pissed."

"He shouldn't have to ask permission to have his feelings and to move our relationship forward," I argue. But the words feel weird even as I say them.

Luna pulls her knees up, wrapping her arms around her legs, and leans in. "But he does, Dani. You are *all* in a relationship. It's not just you and Michael."

I feel tears threatening again. "I know. But Michael had a point. Why does he always have to be the reasonable, rational one that considers everyone else's feelings first?"

Luna laughs softly. "Because that's who he is. That's what he does. I mean, he could still want to express every desire he has for you, ask you to be his wife, make a big declaration, and lock you down. But he has to respect the other guys and their feelings about it. And Michael knows that as well as anyone."

I think about that. It's true. And I don't know what exactly got into Michael tonight. I like to think he was just overcome with love and passion.

"I want that," I finally say softly. "I want the proposal. The engagement. The wedding. The husband. Kids. The house." I sigh. "Our new house is a dream. It's more Michael and me than it is Nathan and Crew, but I thought them going along with it meant they were on board. I guess I just thought we were all moving in this direction. And..." I take a deep breath. "Maybe I thought

Michael's proposal would push the other two in that direction. Instead, I think it pushed them away."

"You know they love you, right?" Luna leans over and takes my hand. "I have no idea how or why you want to live with three men. But if you're going to, you have three really great ones. They, appropriately, think you walk on water. They adore you. They take really good care of you. Every one of them fills a place in your life that has made you into an even warmer, more open, more confident, happier person."

My tears start again, but I nod.

"You're good for them too, Dani. They are all better with you than they were before you. You all can figure this out."

"I hope so."

"Well, they will. Or you will. But maybe some time away is good. They'll figure out what they really want. So will you. But yeah, Nathan and Crew need to come around. Michael needs to figure out that he can't just go off half-cocked like this. That's not him. That throws everyone off. And that's okay. Everybody has a part to play in this. There are four of you. You're not just trying to figure out how to deal with and respect one other person's feelings, you all have three other people to consider."

I nod. Then I ask the question that I've most been dreading the answer to. "What will I do if Nathan and Crew don't come around?"

"I thought you said Nathan already said he wants to get married."

"But does he?" I ask. "Or is he just competing with Michael? Did he say it because he can't imagine letting Michael have me to himself?"

Luna shakes her head. "If that's it, he's an idiot."

I give her a sad smile.

She laughs softly. "Yeah, it is possible that Nathan is an idiot."

I swallow. It's difficult with how tight my throat feels. "And Crew doesn't want this."

She squeezes my hand. "I never thought I would see my

brother actually consider anyone else's feelings but his own. His default is to think about how everything affects him first. But he loves you. And he knows that Michael and Nathan are good for him too. He'd much rather be with you than without."

"But do I want him that way?" I ask. "I thought maybe this would push them to want the same things but now I realize that I don't want to push them. They need to want it. Not because Michael does. Because *they* do."

"You all have some stuff to figure out," she agrees, almost apologetically. "Relationships are hard. And you've got three. Four really. It's you and each guy, and then all of you together."

Yeah. What the hell am I doing?

"Do you think Crew wants to get married? Someday? Maybe?" My voice breaks slightly. "To me?"

She squeezes my hand. "I mean, are you sure *you* want to marry *him*?"

I know she's trying to lighten the mood, but I give her a little smile. "I love your brother with everything I have."

That sobers her quickly. "I know you do. He's fucking lucky as hell that that's true. And, fortunately, he knows that."

Yeah, I hope he feels that way after being pushed into this corner.

"I'm just going to hang out here tonight. Maybe tomorrow. I don't know. I think we all just need to think things over."

Luna slumps back against the arm of the couch. "Man, you make me glad I stayed in with cookies tonight. Men are a lot of work."

She's not kidding. But I don't want my situation to turn her off of trying to find love.

"Luna—"

She holds up a hand. "Nope. We're not talking about my love life, my lack of, how I can't believe there's actually a hockey player that I like talking to and not just ogling from the stands, none of that."

I lift my brows, but I can tell she means that she does not want to talk about Alexsei tonight.

"You know you're welcome here as long as you want to stay," she adds. "Hell, this is perfect. We can share our period snacks and hot pad like we used to do."

I frown at her. "What?"

She reaches down between our throw blankets and pulls out the heating pad she has plugged in. She lays it over her tummy. "I started yesterday, so my cramps are especially bad today. Are you not cramping yet? We were always so synced up. You haven't lived apart from me long enough to be off, are you?"

I think about that. We always were within a day of each other. It actually was kind of freaky. But now that I think about it...

My heart starts pounding as I start counting from the last time I had my period. Nathan went to the store for me for tampons. I would have given a thousand dollars to actually witness that. He'd also come home with twenty boxes of every type and size of tampon known to man.

Finally, I look at my best friend. "Luna?"

"Yeah?" She hands the plate of cookies toward me.

"I...haven't started."

Her eyes widen. "You're late?"

I nod. "Yes. But just a few days."

"But you could be–"

I shake my head. "I've just been under a lot of stress."

I'm on birth control. There's been *a lot* going on. The move, Vegas, Clayton, Crew's injury, the tension, not to mention tonight.

She watches me carefully for a long moment. Finally she just says, "You know I'm here for you always. For anything."

"I know." I force a smile. I need a distraction. "So, tell me all about Alexsei."

Luna groans. "He is a man, he plays for the Racketeers, the end."

"He's *really* cute."

"You want another boyfriend? Go for it."

"No!" I laugh. "God, that's the last thing I need."

Luna laughs too. "Drop it, Dani, or I'm putting on a slasher movie."

She knows I hate those. I sigh. Fine. I won't be distracted by my best friend's love life tonight. But I don't want to think about mine anymore right now. I pull the blanket closer to my chest. "Anything but a romance."

CHAPTER 25
Crew

WHAT THE ACTUAL *fuck was that?*

I came downstairs to try to distract myself with video games but instead, I'm pacing back and forth in our game room. The game room I love. That I've coaxed Dani down into on more than one occasion to play silly games and laugh and kiss on each other.

That's what we're doing.

We're laughing. We're having fun. We're *living together.*

Why the hell isn't that enough?

It's not like I *never* want to marry Dani. If I'm going to marry anyone, it will be that girl. I don't want to be with anyone else, that's for sure. I don't want to let her go, either.

But *fuck,* it seems to me like we've gone from zero to ninety as it is, and I'm good, I'm happy. I want to be with Dani. We're living in the moment.

Then Hughes had to go and fuck it all up by making it as serious as it can possibly get. And shine the spotlight on me and Nathan and what *we* want right this very minute. Or what we *don't* want right this very minute. Jesus.

It's not like I don't think about how Michael is more stable, and more romantic, and more mature than I am almost every damned day as it is.

I can hear his fucking footsteps upstairs in his fucking kitchen right now, as a matter of fact. Because the kitchen is his. And now, apparently Dani is his because I wasn't thinking we were renting tuxes and sweating at the altar, watching Dani walk down an aisle in a white dress any time soon.

I've been focused on adjusting to the fact that there are no paper plates allowed in this house, so I have to actually load the dishwasher, and my recent medically dictated bench time to give any sort of thought to something like *marriage*.

I mean, we kind of feel married in a lot of ways already, in my opinion.

And a poly marriage sounds like a lot of work and I don't know if I have this in me. Not right now, anyway. I need to save my best efforts for the ice.

I can hear Nathan's footsteps up there too. If I know him, he's headed straight for his bourbon. Staying here, listening to them, is giving me anxiety I don't need right now.

Pulling my phone out of my pocket, I text Alexsei. He's single and goes out all the time and is the perfect guy to hit up at the last minute.

> Hey, what's up?

To my relief, he answers right away.

> Hey. Nothing. Hanging out at McGintys. Come up if you're not busy. And if your girlfriend will let you.

Except my girlfriend has gone to my sister's house and I'm stuck here with two guys who want to marry my girlfriend. The walls are closing in on me.

> Be there in twenty.

My plan is to leave without saying anything to Nathan and

Michael but Hughes sees me grab my keys and head for the front door.

"You're not going to Dani, are you?" he asks. "We should wait for her to tell us when she's ready."

"Oh, like you waited to ask her to marry you?" I ask in disbelief. The fucking nerve of this guy. "I'm going to the bar, Dad. Don't wait up."

It feels satisfying to slam the front door behind me. I'm not usually a guy who gets pissed off the ice. But I'm angry that I got sucker punched by Dani and Michael and I'm also scared. Will I lose Danielle if I'm not ready to put a ring on it?

McGinty's is a pub near the arena where players like to hang out because it's quiet and chill. Fans do hang around trying to grab a selfie or an autograph but they're usually respectful. There's a decent number of people here tonight but it's not a mob scene. I instantly spot Alexsei at the bar with his roommate, Cameron.

He sees me and waves.

"Hey, what's up?" he says as I approach. "They let you out tonight, huh?"

I almost groan but instead I steel my shoulders and grab the placard with the QR code to scan the drinks menu. I put my phone to it and pull up the menu. "I do what I want," I tell Alexsei.

He lets out a snort of laughter. "Damn. Sure you do, man."

I do. But honestly, what I want to do is almost always on the ice or at home with the three people I live with.

And I'm pissed that *all* of that is currently fucked up and feeling out of my control.

Alexsei claps me on the shoulder. "Grab a stool. You remember Cameron?"

I nod and turn to his friend, who is the total opposite of Alexsei, who is loud and a goofball. Like me. Cameron is an intellectual, not an athlete. Slim build, rarely smiles, he puts the "tense" in intense.

"Hey man, what's up?" I say.

Cameron just nods in return. No smile. I've never been able to figure out if this guy hates my guts or if he just doesn't give a shit. Or hell, maybe he likes me. I have no clue. Right now, I don't really care.

Dani was so upset.

It shreds me inside to think that I've hurt her.

"You getting a drink?" Alexsei asks when I raise my hand for the bartender.

I'm scrolling the menu on the phone. He sounds surprised, which he should. I don't usually drink. "Me and Dani had a disagreement at home tonight. It was kind of my fault." I don't want to go into specifics because that's our personal business, but I do need to talk about it with someone.

"Yeah, well, it's hard to keep three people happy. Hell, it's hard to keep one person happy." Alexsei points to his beer. "You like oranges and pine notes? Try this beer. It's like a fucking walk through the Illinois woods."

"That sounds like shit," I tell him, honestly. "I want a Coors Light. I want to pretend to drink, not actually drink."

Cameron startles me by giving a sharp laugh. "I can appreciate a man who knows himself."

"I thought I knew myself." I take the stool on the opposite side of Alexsei and drop my phone on the bartop with a sigh.

"Want to talk about it?" Alexsei asks sympathetically.

I shrug. "Dani wants to get married. I'm not sure I'm ready for all that."

Alexsei whistles. "Marriage, huh?"

"Damn," Cameron says. "That's a big step."

"Exactly. Armstrong and Hughes are all on board." Even though they both had fucked up tonight too, Dani will forgive them. Because they are committed to her and she knows that. It's what she wants. It's what she deserves. "But my life is crazy and I just want to enjoy *now*. What's wrong with that?"

"Nothing," Alexsei says. He finally flags the bartender down.

"You've earned the right to just ride the wave, especially after the season we've had. Dave, my man, a Coors Light for the Racketeers MVP, please. Put it on my tab."

That perks me up a little. "I can't wait for the playoffs. We're going to destroy those pussies. Top scoring team in the league right here." I point between me and him.

"You are the hat trick whore."

I grin. "Jealous?"

"Always."

But he doesn't sound jealous. He sips his woodsy beer and glances around the room, scanning.

I know what he's doing. Looking for a hot chick to potentially hook up with. Which makes me happy because he's been sniffing around my sister recently and I'm not sure how I feel about that.

I also notice something that makes me double-take. Cameron has his hand on Alexsei's thigh. Like, *on* it, on it.

What the hell? Fuck it. I just don't have time to finesse the question. "Are you two here *together*?" I ask.

They exchange an amused look.

"We did arrive together and we are going back to the same apartment together," Cameron says. "Take that how you want."

"But..." I knit my brow together. I look pointedly at Cameron's hand.

"But what?" Alexsei asks, meeting my eyes directly.

And I just know. They are *together*.

Okay, then.

"I've seen you with women. Both of you," I say.

"Says the dude in a poly relationship. Yes, I date women. And Cam and I have shared women."

"That's actually the way I prefer women," Cameron says, letting his hand fall away before pushing his glasses up on the bridge of his nose. "Together."

Alexsei nods. "Nothing hotter than that, seriously."

"But the two of you are also into each other?"

They exchange a look, then Alexsei looks at me. "Yes."

"Why don't I know that about you?" It feels like I should have noticed that before."

They exchange another look that leads me to believe there's something simmering beneath the surface that they're not intending to share with me. Then Alexsei cracks a grin toward me.

"Maybe because you mostly pay attention to yourself," he says. "It's McNeill's world and we're all just living in it."

He's ripping on me and it's a joke. But he's also serious.

It hits me hard.

Maybe he's right. Maybe I've just been living in my own fucking world and not seeing what the three people I'm in a relationship with want or need.

I grab Alexsei's beer and take a huge swallow. I grimace. "That's horrible."

"Then don't let other people tell you what you might like," Alexsei says, retrieving his beer. "Decide for yourself what's right for you."

I sigh and accept my Coors Light from the bartender with a thanks. "You may be a mediocre defenseman but you're a wise man, Ryan. You make a lot of fucking sense."

I have a lot of thinking to do. About Dani, about Nathan and Michael.

About me.

And what I want.

CHAPTER 26
Michael

I PICK up yet another pair of Crew's dirty socks off the kitchen island with salad tongs and carry them to the laundry closet next to the powder room. Opening the door, I flip the lid of the stackable washer and dryer up and fling the socks into it. Back in the kitchen, I toss the salad tongs in the trash.

Ever since Dani left for Luna's twenty hours and some odd minutes ago, Crew is behaving like a frat boy, even more so than usual. He's nesting in the basement and emerging only to crap up the kitchen with his takeout boxes and dirty clothes that he seems to peel on and off and then forget about.

I'm frustrated and I'm fucking over it.

Between Crew's slobbish pouting and Nathan's belligerent cold-shoulder, I've had enough of these two assholes.

I know they're still mad about being caught off-guard by my marriage proposal to Dani. I get it. But I maintain that I'm allowed to be impulsive too. They do it all the time. It's not fair that I don't get to just go with my gut and let Dani know I want forever with her.

Pulling out the disinfecting spray, I make liberal use on the island, wiping it down three times before I finally feel like it's free of Crew skin cells and sweat and I can start cooking.

I get onions and peppers on the stove and then I text Dani.

> I respect your space but I just want you to know I love you.

> I love you too. I'm staying at Luna's again tonight but I'll talk to you tomorrow.

She has ended it with a kiss emoji, so I'm not concerned she's planning anything drastic, but I'm not sure what I can do to ease her mind right now. I'm also frustrated that she chose to run off to Luna's instead of staying and talking.

Crew emerges from the basement like a teenager who has smelled food. He sniffs the air, hands stuffed into the pouch of his hoodie. He's wearing basketball shorts and yet another pair of socks that I'm sure I'm going to find on the furniture later. "What's for dinner?"

I grab my pan by the handle and shake it to stir the vegetables. I eye him. "I'm having fajitas. You're having whatever the hell you can cook or buy for yourself."

His jaw drops. "Are you for real?"

"Yes, I'm for real. Why the hell would I cook for you right now?"

"This is just great," Crew snaps. "I'm not the one who decided to rush things and get *engaged* and I'm being punished?"

"You're being punished because you've left clothes and dirty dishes all over the house and because I don't feel like sitting across the table from you right now." I don't care if it's not rational. I'm tired of being taken for granted as the fixer. Right now, I don't want to fix this. I want someone else to do the heavy lifting.

Nathan is coming down the stairs. "What's for dinner?"

"He's not feeding us," Crew tells him. "He's only cooking for himself. We're having meals withheld for not jumping up and down in excitement when he went and proposed to our girlfriend behind our backs."

Nathan is scowling. "Hughes, what the hell?"

He can scowl all he wants. These are fucking fajitas for one.

"You locked the bedroom door," I tell Nathan. "That wasn't cool."

"It's *my* bedroom."

"No, it's not. It's *our* bedroom. You don't get to lay claim to it solo just because Dani isn't here."

"The fuck I don't. Crew has the basement. You have a pull-out sofa in your office. Where am I supposed to sleep if not in the bedroom?"

He did it to stake a claim. That the bed that Dani sleeps in belongs to him, because he designed it and paid for it, and because Dani is his, not mine. It was a dick move solely based on my asking Dani to marry me without his permission.

"I don't see what that has to do with starving Nathan and me," Crew says.

Because again, everyone gets to be an asshole but me. "Maybe I'm just in my asshole era. I don't know what to tell you."

"Wow," Crew says.

"I've seen you order a single pack of M&Ms for home delivery," I tell him. "You're not going to starve."

"That is not the point."

"What is the point, McNeill? What did you think we were doing here if we weren't aiming toward marriage and kids?" I demand. "Playing house?"

"That's not fair," Crew says. "We are in a relationship. That's what we're doing."

Nathan, who is dressed casually in joggers and a sweatshirt, runs his fingers through his hair, mussing it up. "Danielle said she's staying at Luna's again tonight. Can we just agree to stay out of each other's way until she gets home?"

I turn off the stove and take a deep breath. I'm frustrated with the whole situation. Last night by the river with Dani was one of the best moments of my life, and I feel like these guys stole it from me.

Yes, I should have talked to them first.

But in that moment, it would have been nice to just have their support.

"Yes, I'm more than happy to stay out of your way. I think I'm going to stay at my apartment tonight," I announce. "I agree that we all need space."

"Your apartment?" Nathan frowns. "What apartment?" Then it seems to sink in and he stares at me. "You still have your apartment?"

I nod. "Yes, I haven't gotten a decent offer on it, so I told the agent to just take it off the market."

Crew actually puts his phone into his pocket and eyes me. "Why?"

"I figured I would just keep it as an investment until interest rates go down again." I don't like the way they're looking at me. "What? It was a business decision."

"Are you sure that's all it was?" Nathan asks.

"What do you mean?"

"Maybe you thought you needed a place to go if this all went south?" he asks.

Crew swears under his breath.

"Maybe." I shrug. That very well could have been subconscious on my part. I can admit that. "This is all a huge commitment for four people to make together. To all be in agreement and on the same page. And clearly we're not. Last night proved that."

"But you didn't tell us," Crew points out.

"Because the dad can't share everything," Nathan says. "The dad has to hold it all together." He gives a sigh. "Listen, Michael, we joke about that being your role, but it doesn't have to be. We're all adults."

"None of us are acting like adults today." Even me. Anger deflating, I point to the pan. "The chicken is cooked and it's in the fridge, already cut into strips. Just warm it up with the vegetables. The tortillas are in the oven."

I don't know what I'm feeling.

But I understand Dani's decision to take some time away a

little better. It's hard to think with so many voices in your ear. I suddenly don't know what my role is in this relationship. Or maybe even what I want it to be.

I do know I don't want to feel frustrated with these guys I've come to care about as true friends.

Crew goes to the fridge and pulls the door open. "Let's just eat dinner."

Something has been nagging at me. I turn to Nathan. "Why didn't you tell us that you couldn't have kids?"

"It never came up."

"Because you thought it was something between you and Dani. Not the four of us."

He frowns but he nods.

"Something that affects all of us." I turn to Crew, who has the plastic container with the chicken I cooked yesterday in it. "And you didn't tell us you're not ready to get married."

"I didn't know I had to."

"Exactly." I sigh. "I get where you're coming from. I understand where Nathan was coming from by not confiding in us. But we're either all in this—all of this—or we're not."

But it's clear we're not. At least, not yet.

If we were, my proposal wouldn't have gotten the reception it did.

"This is a mess," Nathan says after a moment.

"Look, this is a lot. It's all a lot." I need to get my head on straight. "I'm still going to head out."

Crew shakes his head but he says, "Do whatever you need to do, Doc."

The use of the nickname indicates he may still be mad at me but he cares about me and I appreciate that. "I'll be back tomorrow."

Nathan watches me but he doesn't say anything, so I head for the stairs to pack an overnight bag. I miss my girlfriend. We didn't even get to celebrate our engagement properly.

And now I'm not even sure if we *are* engaged.

CHAPTER 27
Sammy the Malamute
(WADE)

THINGS ARE good again in the Racketeer-verse.

There's an amazing energy in the arena tonight.

McNeill is not only back on the ice, but he's playing like he hasn't missed a beat. We are absolutely going to the playoffs and you can feel the electricity in the air.

His girl is back too. Danielle has missed a couple of games and no one has really said anything about it but everyone has noticed. There's been some social media speculation, though people have mostly just assumed she's been absent because Crew hasn't been playing. But fans have been a little pissed about that, feeling she should have been here supporting the team anyway, which I agree with.

But it's all been forgiven as of tonight. Crew's back. The Racketeers are going into the third period up by two. And Danielle's here, wearing Crew's number, cheering them on like always and sitting with the radiant, beautiful, *amazing* Luna.

I don't know if it's just because we're on the verge of the playoffs, or if it's the edibles I had just before I pulled on the fuzzy Sammy head, or if it's because I just can't hold it in any longer, but tonight is the night. I am shooting my shot.

It's good to know all the people who work for the arena.

Especially the KissCam guys.

I make my way down to the seats where Luna and Dani are sitting.

The guys in the booth know that when I get to the end of the row, they're supposed to put Luna and Dani up on the screen. They're here together, so obviously they don't have anyone to kiss and they won't kiss each other.

Not that I'd mind *that*. Pretty sure a lot of people in the arena would also enjoy that…

I shake my head, forcing my focus back to my plan.

Tonight, Sammy the Malamute is making a move on Luna McNeill.

And then Wade is getting her number.

As soon as I arrive at the end of the row, the kiss cam flashes her gorgeous face on the jumbotron. Okay, Dani's too. Which causes the arena to go crazy. Everyone loves Dani because she's a member of the most popular and famous hockey family in Chicago. Maybe in all of pro hockey. Also because everyone knows how her romance with Crew, Doc, and Bossman started on the KissCam.

They also love Luna because they know she's Crew's sister and Dani's bestie.

Both girls grin and wave to the camera and blow kisses.

But that's not enough. And the guys upstairs know to keep the camera on them.

The girls are only two seats in from the aisle, so I step past the two guys on the edge and hold my hand out to Luna.

She looks at me with an arched brow.

I motioned for her to give me her hand.

The crowd is cheering. And then they start chanting, "Sammy! Sammy! Sammy!"

She rolls her eyes and shakes her head.

I put my hands on my hips and nod my head. Then I point to my mouth and beckon with my hand again.

Dani is laughing, and she finally elbows Luna, as if she's trying to get Luna up out of her seat.

Luna sighs. She's definitely not the sweetest of the two ladies, but she's a good sport and she's been around hockey and hockey fans for years.

Finally, she stands and the crowd cheers.

She faces me, smiling in spite of herself.

And in that moment, I'm Wade, not Sammy, looking at the gorgeous woman I've been pining over for months now.

But…I'm still dressed as Sammy.

I reach for her as I take a step forward, but Sammy's feet, belly, and huge hand all get there way ahead of my own and I somehow step on her foot while bumping into her while smacking her all at the same time.

She starts to fall backward, but with my foot on hers, she can't step back to catch herself, so her arms flail and she punches Sammy in the face, which knocks my mascot head askew, so now I can't see through the eye holes.

I don't know what happens next, but I'm imagining her falling backward into Dani's lap, whacking her head on the seats the way Dani did the time I tried to kiss her, Crew and Doc Hughes storming up here the way they did that time, and Bossman yelling in my ear.

But…I don't hear anything except sudden loud cheering.

I reach up and yank my Sammy head back into place so I can see what's going on and…

See the guy who has been sitting behind the girls—and low-key stalking Luna—all season holding her.

He's leaning over the seats, with an arm behind her, his other arm grasping her forearm, and somehow, he doesn't look clumsy or stupid or even uncomfortable.

The arena loves it.

There are dozens of phones out, recording the whole thing. Dani has her hands over her mouth, watching with clear delight even though they're practically hanging over her.

And Luna is gazing up at him as if he's her hero.

Which I suppose he kind of is.

This is Cameron. I don't know anything about him except that he sits here in the family and friend section because he's Alexsei Ryan's best friend.

Now the crowd has switched from my name to "Kiss! Kiss! Kiss!"

And Cameron, being such a great guy, does just that.

He lays one on Luna.

Who does not seem to mind at all.

Well, that's just fucking great.

I finally tap him on the shoulder. Which everyone thinks is hilarious and which I play along with as Sammy the mascot, when Wade the person, really wants to punch the guy in the face.

When he lifts his head after what feels like an hour, I hear him say, "I've missed this."

Whatever the fuck that means. Wait. He's kissed her before?

I reach out and grasp Luna's hand, finally helping her upright.

Not that she even spares me a glance. She's still staring at Cameron like they're in a romantic movie. Cue the swelling music.

Damn. My shot is too late. That's pretty fucking obvious.

I risk a glance at the bench.

Crew is still sitting, but he's frowning up at us. Okay, at Cameron and Luna.

Looks like I'm not the only one who doesn't like the two of them making out on the KissCam.

I don't see Doc Hughes anywhere though.

Luna didn't actually fall or hit her head, thanks to Cameron, I guess, so she probably doesn't need medical attention. That will spare me getting yelled at by Hughes.

But there's no way in hell I'm looking up at the owner's box.

I shudder to think what the Bossman might have to say to me right now.

Not that it was really my fault. I didn't mean to knock her

over. And I could make a case for how *glad* he should be that I knocked Dani over that first time…

Just to be safe, I take my earpiece out.

CHAPTER 28
Dani

GOD, I miss my guys so much.

I have tears in my eyes as I'm reading back over my story for Habanero.

It's about them.

Sure, I've changed all the names and details about them and none of the things I wrote actually happened, but I was able to write this fun, sexy, romantic love story from my heart because of them.

And it makes me ache, feeling every minute of the forty-eight hours we've been apart.

I came straight home after the hockey game. I definitely wanted to show up for Crew. It was his first game back and the one they needed to win to clinch the playoffs. He did an amazing job, played so damned hard, even though I could tell he did have a little pain. But he stayed out there, fought hard, and they pulled out the win. I'm so proud of him.

But I wasn't quite ready to go back to waiting in the back hallway.

Luna was headed back there, and she was very coy about whether she was going back to congratulate her brother, Alexsei, or because Cameron was going to be back there.

That kiss Cameron laid on her was something. As someone who is somewhat of an expert in how KissCam kisses can turn into so much more, I cannot wait to talk to my bestie.

But I needed to get out of there.

If I'd gone to the hallway to wait with the other WAGS, I know I would've run into Michael. Nathan probably would've come down too.

I'm just not quite ready to see them all. I don't know if we've figured anything out. I don't know if anything's changed.

I was really clear about what I want.

I guess I feel like the ball is in Nathan and Crew's courts.

They need to figure out what they want and then let Michael and me know.

They know what we want.

Nathan and Crew need to come to me when they're ready to discuss the future. Not necessarily together. But when they each *really* know what they want and when it's not a competition or contest for Nathan and when Crew is sure what he wants our future to look like.

My stomach cramps as I think about how there's a possibility that I might be facing a future with two of my three guys instead of all three. It's not the first time that's occurred to me, but I've tamped it down each time it crosses my mind.

It's just not right. I don't want just two of them. I don't want just one of them. I want all three. It's the four of us. It's Cookie and Company. The Company is all three of those guys. It would never feel right without them all.

But I also don't want to give up my dreams of marriage and children and a future that is lake houses and family vacations and holidays with *all* of us in a crazy RV going to all the family get-togethers.

The dinner with Garrett and Deb the other night really showed me what I want. They made it real to me. I want to have stories to share at dinner with friends. Memories, past experiences we laugh about for years, trips, adventures, a home, private jokes, intimate moments, and eye rolls, sighs, and laughter about our kids.

But while I can *clearly* see having those things with Michael, I can't imagine having those things with *only* Michael. I can also clearly see both Nathan and Crew as fathers, as much as that might shock them. They'll all three be amazing. I want my children to have all three of those men in their lives.

I feel that so strongly in my heart, so deeply in my soul, I can't give it up.

I already love my future children so much that giving them anything less than the presence and love of Michael Hughes, Nathan Armstrong, *and* Crew McNeill is not even a possibility.

Finally, my story is done uploading and I click the *finish* button.

I'm eager to see what my readers think of this.

A little nervous, but mostly excited.

Michael was right. Not that I'm surprised. But over the last few days without the guys, I've had plenty of writing time and I have poured myself into a new story.

I've changed direction, away from the dark twisty stuff, and it's just poured out of me because it's felt so good and so natural.

I've just closed my computer when the bell over the front door jingles. I frown. I was pretty sure I locked the door. Maybe it's Luna. But it's early. I assumed she'd go get a drink with Alexsei and Cameron. Or something.

I click off the lamp on my desk and round the corner.

I come up short.

My heart immediately starts hammering in my chest and my eyes fill with tears.

It's Nathan and Crew.

They came to me.

They've figured out what they want.

Thank God.

They're both dressed as if they came straight from the arena.

Crew is in his game day suit and Nathan's in jeans and a button-down, looking nothing like a regular guy despite the denim.

"Oh my God," I say, my voice shaky. "Hi."

Nathan's the first one to speak. "Clayton had another heart attack. It's more serious this time."

My heart turns over in my chest. But not in a good way.

My hand flies up to cover my mouth. "Oh no."

They both take a step forward, their eyes on my face. They look concerned. But I know it's not for me. It's for Michael.

"He's okay," Nathan says. "For right now, anyway. He's at the hospital, stable. Michael got the call during the game. He's on my jet, and he's already on his way to Decatur."

"Oh, good." My throat is tight.

I just stare at my guys. They both look so worried.

And in that moment, I realize that nothing else matters. Everything from the last few days just disappears.

Nathan doesn't care about competing with Michael for anything.

Crew isn't worried about his own personal feelings about the future.

Right now we are all aware that the man we want to make a life with, the fourth part of our foursome, the guy we all depend on and love, needs us.

I nod. "I'll go get my stuff."

"Our bags are already in the car. I've chartered another jet."

Of course he did. That's what Nathan does. He pays to fix things. And this time it's absolutely perfect.

"I'll help you pack," Crew says, his voice rough.

I take a moment to do the one thing that we need most. I cross the floor and pull them both into a hug.

The three of us embrace for the first time in days.

But it's not about making up or saying we're sorry.

We don't need to do those things. We're okay. We're all here because our family needs to be together right now.

No matter what we argued about, no matter whose feelings

got hurt the other night, no matter what confusing thoughts we're dealing with, we're family.

We were all there for Crew tonight for his first game back, and we'll be there for Michael. He doesn't need us any more than Crew did, really. We couldn't play hockey for Crew tonight, but we were in the stands supporting him. We can't make Clayton be okay, and we can't do anything for Michael that he can't do for himself. But we can be there.

"Should I pack for a few days?" I ask, letting them go.

"Just something quick. We can buy whatever else we need."

I smile at that. My billionaire would very much love to buy us all things. That would make him feel useful.

I nod. "Okay."

I head up to the apartment. They're both right behind me and I pack quickly. Crew grabs my suitcase and then links his fingers with mine. As we go back downstairs, Nathan's right behind us, and then strides past us to open the door of the SUV.

"Evening Ms. Larkin," Andrew greets me.

"Hi, Andrew."

Nathan takes the passenger seat and Crew and I sit in the back, holding hands the whole time.

But none of us speak.

Even when we get on the jet and take off on our way to Decatur, we don't say much.

But we really don't need to. We all know where we're going and why.

Finally, as we're making our approach to the Decatur airport, Crew asks, "What are we going to do?"

I know the answer to this and I feel a strange sense of calm fill me as I say, "We don't need to *do* anything. We just need to be there."

Crew nods and Nathan reaches over to squeeze my hand. My heart swells. These two men are so good. All three of my men are so good.

I won't let them go.

. . .

Forty-five minutes later, we step into the waiting room.

Michael's sitting with his mother, his forearms on his thighs, his head hanging.

Lorraine gives us a soft, loving smile.

"Michael." She nudges him.

He looks up at her. Then she nods towards us.

He looks over to us. His eyes widen for just a moment. Then he's up off his seat, coming for us.

He wraps his arms around me, but quickly pulls the other two into his embrace.

"I love you guys," is all he says.

That's all he needs to say.

CHAPTER 29
Michael

I DON'T KNOW if it's wrong, but I'm sitting in the waiting room waiting for news about my father, knowing it could be bad, and still feeling like my heart is full and I'm happier than I've been in days.

And it's all because of three people.

My people.

Across from me, Dani is lying across the padded waiting room bench, her bare feet in Nathan's lap, his hand cupped around one of her feet. His eyes are shut and his head is propped against the wall beside him as he dozes lightly.

Her head is in Crew's lap, and he's absently playing with her hair. His eyes are not closed, but he seems lost in thought.

They're here.

All they've done is hug me and say, "We love you too," but they're here and that means the world.

I don't need anything else. At least nothing they can give me.

I need to have a cardiologist tell me that my father's going to be okay.

I need to see my father sitting up in bed, grinning at me.

I need to see a heart monitor hooked to my father's chest, recording a steady, strong rhythm.

But Dani, Crew, and Nathan can't give me any of those things.

Still, just looking at them across from me, having them here, seeing them together, makes everything feel better.

Sitting here in this waiting room feels like déjà vu. The last time I was here, the circumstances were similar. My father was back with a medical team working on him and we knew nothing.

All I had was my mother's reports about how he had been standing at the kitchen sink, helping with dishes, and suddenly he gasped, clutched his chest, and slumped forward.

She helped him into a chair, looked at his ashen face, heard him say that his left arm hurt, and then she immediately called 911.

This time, he lost consciousness. He did not wake up before the paramedics got there. My mom rode in the ambulance with him and he was out the entire way to the hospital.

Last time I was here, I was worried and felt at a loss, with nothing to do. I didn't know what to say to my mother, I couldn't do anything medically, and I really couldn't give my sisters or Nathan any answers when they asked.

This time feels different.

Yes, my father's condition seems worse. The team has been back with him longer, with no news. His symptoms sound worse.

But I called Nathan and said, "My dad had another heart attack. I need to go to Decatur."

All he said was, "Go to the airport. My jet will be ready."

That was it. But this time I, for once, just said, "Okay."

I let him take care of that part.

And I'll be honest, showing up at the airport, being escorted out to a private jet with no standing in a long security line, no waiting to board the plane, no sitting amongst a bunch of strangers as I'm worrying and praying was such a huge fucking relief.

I had texted him.

> I'm on the plane. Thank you.

And his answer had been simple.

> Of course.

Those two words had meant the world to me.

Even after everything that had happened over the last few days, all the tension, the blame we've all tossed back and forth, the actual anger between us, and the fact that things within our little family are not necessarily okay, he still gave me exactly what I needed and made it seem as if I hadn't even needed to ask.

And truthfully, I know I didn't.

Not only would Nathan do that for me, but he was glad to do it.

I also knew that he would tell Dani and Crew, and I knew that they would worry. Not that I want them to worry, but it felt good knowing that regardless of what happened over the last few days, they would be concerned about me. I would probably get texts, maybe phone calls. I can call Dani at any time, and she will pick up, and I can hear her sweet voice.

But when I looked up and saw the three of them standing in this waiting room, I'm not sure I've ever felt more loved and supported.

I grew up knowing that I was loved unconditionally, and that there was nothing I could do to make my parents not be proud of me or not want me.

But I guess I also grew up believing that parents had to love their kids.

Of course, as an adult, I've learned that's not always the case, unfortunately. But I'm very grateful that my childhood made me believe that parents always love their kids.

Having a family like the one I have with Crew, Nathan, and Dani is different. We're choosing this. And more, we're choosing this in spite of the fact that it is not the norm, it is not traditional, and we will get pushback. Hell, we're giving each other pushback.

But we're still here. We're still us.

Seeing them in this waiting room felt right.

Me, the guy who never really needs anyone, the guy who fixes things for our family, the one they lean on for everything from fajitas to groin strains to emotional healing and working through healthy, productive communication, needed them.

And they showed up.

Without me asking, without any questions.

No one is insisting on doing things for me, no one is forcing sandwiches on me, no one is asking over and over how I am.

And yet, I know the second that I need a sandwich or a hug or an ibuprofen, I have three people who will give me whatever I need.

And they'll take care of each other, so I don't have to worry about *them* needing sandwiches or hugs or ibuprofen.

Fuck, this is amazing.

And yes, I absolutely want to marry Danielle Larkin.

But I don't want to do it without Nathan and Crew.

Ten minutes later, my mom stands up and stretches. "I'm going to get some juice."

I nod. "Sounds good."

She gives my shoulder a squeeze before making her way across the waiting room. Like Dani, Nathan, and Crew, she doesn't ask if I need anything, knowing that I'll tell her if I do.

After she leaves, I lean forward, resting my elbows on my thighs and study my three…roommates. Best friends. Life partners.

That's what they are. My best friends and my life partners.

I take a deep breath. "Hey," I say softly.

Crew looks up. He reaches over and pokes Nathan, who opens his eyes and then rolls his neck and straightens.

"What's up?" he asks, his voice a little gruff.

"I want to talk," I say.

"She need to hear this?" Crew asks, looking down at Dani.

I nod.

He runs a finger down her cheek. "Hey sweet girl, wake up," he murmurs to her softly.

Dani stirs, rubbing her cheek against his thigh. Then her eyes flutter open.

Her gaze finds me immediately. She gives me a soft smile. "Hi."

I smile back, feeling so damned content, in spite of the reason we're all here. "Hi,"

"Michael wants to talk," Crew says.

"Okay." She pushes herself up to sit and runs a hand through her hair to straighten it.

Nathan's arm immediately goes to the back of the bench, behind her, and Crew's hand rests on her thigh.

I know that they don't consciously think about touching her. They do it instinctually. They just all want to be connected.

I completely get that.

We all need to be connected.

"I'm really fucking glad you're all here," I start.

Dani leans forward and reaches for me. "Come closer."

I scoot my chair close so my knees nearly touch hers and we can link our fingers.

"What do you want to talk about?" Dani asks, reaching up with the hand I'm not holding to stroke her fingers over my cheek.

"I love you. And I definitely want to marry you."

She smiles and nods. "Me too."

I look at Nathan, then Crew. "But we can't be without these guys. The four of us work best together. We're all in this together."

Her eyes fill with tears, and she swallows, then nods. "Yes. I know. I want you all."

I see Nathan's arm move from the back of the bench to Dani's shoulders. Crew's hand tightens on her leg.

I take a breath, and then again look from Nathan's eyes to Crew's.

"We're all in this together, right? It's all four of us. For good."

"Yes," Nathan says. His voice is firm, and he answers without hesitation. "But we don't have to talk about this right now."

I shake my head. "This is the best time. We're never going to know what tomorrow holds. I'm learning that with my father. We are never guaranteed tomorrow. Or the day after. We have to celebrate what we've got right now. Love and family are the most important things. And I'm not saying we're never going to have disagreements again. I'm not saying we're never going to wish we could spend the night apart. And I'm not saying there won't be times when one of us wants some time alone. But I want to know that no matter what amazing things happen in Crew's career, like the playoffs, or awesome things Dani has ahead with her writing, or Nathan has with the Racketeers, or what scary things might happen, like with my dad, I want us all to know, without a question that we're going to be there for each other."

Nathan takes a deep breath and leans in. "Absolutely. There is nowhere I'd rather be, no matter the circumstances, than with you three. Whether I'm the supporter or…" He clears his throat. "I'm the one needing support."

I know he's thinking of his grandfather. I nod.

Nathan looks at Dani. "This isn't exactly how I planned this, but hell, baby, we don't really do anything the way most people do, right? The four of us have upended pretty much every plan any of us has ever made."

She sniffs and laughs softly.

"So, Danielle," Nathan says. "Will you marry me? I would love nothing more than to make you my wife."

She gives him a dazzling smile and leans over to kiss him. "Yes, Nathan. I would love to marry you."

He cups the back of her head and deepens the kiss. Crew and I just look on, grinning happily.

When they finally pull apart, we all take a deep breath, almost as one.

Then we all look at Crew.

He has a contemplative look on his face.

And even though I've recently felt like I haven't been as tuned in to these men as I'm used to, I know what he's thinking and feeling right now.

I hope he knows he can be honest with us.

I let go of Dani's hand as Crew reaches for it.

He links his fingers with hers and lifts it to his lips, pressing a kiss to the back. Then he looked her directly in the eyes. "Dani, I love you. I love you more than I ever imagined I could love someone else. And you're it for me. You are the woman I want to spend my life with. I don't want anyone else. And I don't want you with anyone but us."

She presses her lips together and nods, watching him closely.

I watch Nathan's fingers curl into her shoulder slightly.

I wonder if he's suspecting what's coming next the way I am.

I reach out and settle my hand on Dani's knee.

"But I'm not ready to get married," Crew says.

Dani doesn't look surprised. She puffs out a little breath of air. Then she smiles at him like she absolutely adores him. "I know."

He doesn't seem surprised by her reaction, either. "It doesn't mean I don't love you. It doesn't mean that I'm going anywhere. But...can I have a little time?"

She nods. "Yes. Of course. I mean, it doesn't really change anything. Does it?"

He shakes his head. "I don't think so."

Then they all three look at me.

And I step firmly, and without pause, back into my role in our family. I'm the calm one, the rock, the one with the right words in these emotional moments.

"Crew, even though we are a foursome, we are still four distinct people. We all have our own hopes and dreams, personalities, and ways of looking at the world. That doesn't have to change. Just because Nathan and I are in a different place in our lives and are ready for this, doesn't mean that you have to be. And just because the three of us are ready to take this next step right now and you're not, doesn't mean that you can't still be a part of us."

Crew takes a deep breath and nods. "I would actually love nothing more than to watch the three of you have a commitment ceremony. That would be amazing. You are three of my very favorite people. Probably my three favorite people, if I'm honest, but if you tell my mom that, I'm denying it." He gives us a lopsided grin. Then sobers slightly and says, "Knowing the two of you are committed for life to my girl…" He trails off and chuckles. "It's fucking crazy but I love that. I know I'll never have to worry about Dani with you two loving her."

He looks at her. "It's not like *any* of this has been traditional or typical, so I guess I'm just going to say it out loud. I don't mind if you marry Michael and Nathan right now and you and I just wait." He winces. "Damn, that still sounds so fucking weird." He shakes his head. "My mother is going to kick my ass." He groans. "My *sister* is going to kick my ass."

Dani laughs lightly and puts her hand to his face. "It might sound weird, but it doesn't *feel* weird. Other people don't have to understand, as long as *we* all do. I love you, Crew, and I know you love me. And you and I are going to take *our* relationship at *our* pace."

"I am not walking you down the aisle, though, so don't ask," he says, leaning in to rest his forehead against hers. "Because I'm not giving you away."

Her smile grows even as a tear slips down her cheek. "You're damn right you're not." She presses her lips to his.

I exchange a look with Nathan.

Crew's right, that all sounds bonkers. Who would do this? What guy would let his girlfriend marry two other guys but plan to stay in the picture?

But Dani is also right…this feels right.

We can't bully or pressure Crew into doing something he doesn't want to do. That wouldn't be right. He has to make this commitment when he's ready. He's a twenty-three-year-old kid.

Okay, *kid* isn't fair. He's an adult. He's already achieved great things at his age. But he has his whole life in front of him. He and Dani need to take their relationship on the path that it needs to take, even if there are two other guys involved.

But Nathan and I shouldn't have to wait. Not if Dani is ready for the next step too.

As always, we all fill in different parts of her life. Nathan and I can give her the wedding-husband-kid part, but Crew will still be there for the fun, the romance, the dating and growing and learning about themselves that they both need.

As I watch Dani smiling and wiping her happy tears away, Nathan hugging her, Crew holding her hand, and then her eyes meeting mine, my heart feels like it's going to burst out of my chest.

This woman is going to be my wife. We're going to start a family. I'm getting everything I've ever dreamed of.

Then I look at Nathan and Crew.

Everything I ever dreamed of and then some.

CHAPTER 30
Crew

"YEAH!" I yell as I run up the stairs to the Racketeers jet after we sweep the first playoff series against Houston, right fist up in the air.

That game was fucking fire. Bursting with adrenalin, I grab our goalie, Blake Wilder, who is waiting on the platform at the top of the stairs to enter the plane. I fling my arms out and yell, "We're kings of the fucking world!"

"Get the hell off of me," Blake says, but he's laughing and grinning as he glances back at me. "You're such an idiot."

"But I'm also awesome." I shake his shoulders and turn to look at the other guys climbing the steps behind me. *"We're* awesome! We killed it tonight, Racketeers! Fuck yeah!" I bounce on my heels, too pumped up to stand still. I don't know how I'm going to sit for the two-and-a-half-hour flight home.

A cheer goes up from my teammates.

Nathan is inside the plane by the cockpit, shaking each guy's hand and clapping them on the shoulder as they enter and head for a seat. I stick my hand out to him when it's my turn and say, "You're welcome," with a grin.

There is no standard Nate scowl. Instead, he just shakes his head and my hand with a strong grip. "Good game, McNeill."

"Thank you, Mr. Armstrong." In public, on a night like tonight, I owe him the respect he deserves as team owner. But I add a wink, just for his benefit.

The mood is jubilant, rowdy. We're going into the next series confident given our sweep and how much we outscored our opponent. I flop into a seat next to Alexsei and drop my gym bag on the floor. I loosen my tie a little and give Alexsei a fist bump.

"Good game, man," I tell him.

"You too. Let's do it again."

I nod. "It's not going to be as easy." We don't know who we're playing yet, but the other two teams currently battling it out have better defense than Houston. "That ice was wide open tonight."

We go over the game in detail, before Alexsei invites me to hang out with some of the other guys when we arrive back in Chicago.

"We're not getting home until like two in the morning," I say, shaking my head.

"So? What are you, forty?"

"I need to get home. Get some victory love from my girlfriend." I grin.

It's been a couple of weeks since we got back from Decatur. Clayton is out of the hospital and recovering at home under Lorraine's watchful eye, with help from Michael's sisters. Michael is going back down there again this weekend to check in. That night in the hospital, I was really worried about Michael. It also made me think about my own father, and how much he means to me. Then I'd thought about Nathan, being so damn young when he lost both of his parents. Made me more determined than ever to win over Dani's parents.

It had definitely brought all of us closer, and things have been great at home.

"I never thought you'd be the settling down type," Alexsei says.

I shrug. "I don't know. I love being in a relationship."

"How is that going? With all of you? I know you hit a rough patch there for a minute."

"Really well now. I feel like we've all figured out our place with each other a little better. Dani is engaged to Michael and Nathan and I'm the boyfriend." I know the reaction I'm going to get to that and I don't care. We're doing what works for all of us.

As predicted, Alexsei's eyes bug out. "No shit? Damn. And everyone is cool with that? Are *you* cool with that?"

Jack Hayes claps me on the shoulder as he makes his way down the aisle past us. "Good game, McNeill."

I scored two goals and assisted in a third. Not a high-scoring game for me, but solid. It was a team effort tonight.

"Thanks, you too, man."

Returning to the conversation with Alexsei, I nod. "I'm very cool with it. Dani wants a commitment from me, which she has. But marriage feels like a big step and I want to feel a hundred percent ready for it. I want to have that moment, you know, where you *have* to propose. When you can't imagine *not* proposing. It just doesn't feel right yet. But I'm all in and she's all in and I feel good knowing I don't have to worry about her being lonely or that she's not having all of her physical and emotional needs met at any given moment."

"When you put it like that, it sounds like less work." He shoots me a grin. "God knows you probably have some shortcomings."

"Kiss my ass." I say it lightly. I'm not offended. Because hell, it's true. We all have shortcomings.

That's why Cookie & Company works so damn well. Nathan brings the intensity, the dom vibe, the quick decision making. Michael is the rock, the mediator, the one who keeps us fed and on schedule. I bring the fun and keep things from getting boring.

"I'm the hot sauce," I tell Alexsei. "I bring a little kick."

He groans. "That's so bad. But if you're happy, I'm happy for you."

"I am." I've never been happier. "Just one more thing needed to make this year the best one of my life. Time to win a championship."

With my girl, and Nathan and Michael cheering me on, it's pretty much a fucking guarantee.

CHAPTER 31
Nathan

IT'S a good day to be me. Some would argue every day is a good day to be a billionaire hockey team owner, but I've had my fair share of heartbreak. Losing my parents, my grandmother, watching my grandfather's slow slide into dementia. Missing out on the ultimate sports goal—winning a championship—the last three years in a row.

But with McNeill acquired for the Racketeers this season we've just swept the first series of the playoffs and the guys have four days to rest before they have to take on their next opponent. I feel it in the air. This is the year.

For the Racketeers. For me.

Because this is also the year that I'm getting married.

It took me forty-one years to find love, to meet a woman who softens all my hard edges, while still allowing me to be myself. I'm bossy, quick to get irritated, and I lean on money to fix anything that it can fix. But Danielle understands me, appreciates me, and loves me in a way that feels better than any championship ever could.

The unexpected bonus to my relationship with Danielle is I now have a found family that includes not just the girl, but two best friends in Michael and Crew. We've had a learning curve as to how to do this as a foursome, but we've gotten to a really amazing place together.

But I still want the Cup, and we're going to get it.

McNeill is high from the wins and he bounds up the steps to our brownstone with an energy that makes me envious. "There better be a naked Dani waiting for me on the other side of this door!" he says with a grin as he punches in the code to automatically open the heavy front door.

I'm going on adrenaline, too, given how late it is, so normally I'd be eyeing these fucking steps like they're Mt. Everest but tonight feels different. Since we've moved in, I've found it ironic that I can do the elliptical at the gym for forty minutes but a dozen steps make me hesitate.

I know now it's because this house wasn't my first choice and I was compromising. It was Danielle and Michael's dream and I struggled with that, just like I struggled with Michael popping the question without talking to me first. It's different now though.

Danielle has agreed to be my wife and I'm in this relationship for the long haul, compromises and all. They have made sacrifices and compromises as well. Danielle has to juggle our three very different personalities, which I think all of us would admit is not easy. Michael has had to take on the role of family mediator. And Crew has had to watch the two of us move ahead in our relationship with Danielle because we're at a different place in our lives. But with honest communication, respect, and love, we're making this work.

We're a team. And there's no fucking "I" in team. I'm taking that seriously.

Except when it comes to my shower. And my body wash. I draw the line there. No one is allowed in my shower except Danielle and even she can't use my body wash unless she's massaging it all over me. Or herself. When she's naked. And wet. Hell, I guess she can use it.

Hughes is right behind me, pressing the button to lock the car. I've started letting him drive when Andrew isn't available because no matter what time of day it is, Hughes always manages to find a premier parking spot. He has a gift for street parking.

I jog up the steps after McNeill, Hughes on my heels, already anticipating the reception we're going to receive.

Danielle does not disappoint.

I hear the timbre of Crew's voice change. "Now that's what I'm talking about, baby. *Damn.*"

Shifting to his right so I can block the view from our front door in case any of our neighbors are out walking their many, many dogs, my mouth goes dry. Danielle is wearing the Racketeers T-shirt I gave her the night we met—the one that is way too tight and has a plunging V neck—and nothing else. No panties. Just smooth pale legs and a bare pussy.

She's holding a bottle of champagne. Her hair is down, her red curls tumbling around her shoulders, and her smile is as bright as any Racketeers fan. She looks ecstatic.

"That was such a great game, congratulations!" she says, as if she isn't mostly naked. She throws her arms around Crew's neck. "I'm so proud of you. You were *so* good."

His hand goes to her ass, squeezing a cheek in a way that makes my dick hard. "I definitely deserve *a lot* of accolades."

She laughs lightly and extracts herself from his hold so she can turn to me.

Hughes enters the house and shuts the door behind him. "Holy shit, Cookie," he says when his eyes land on Dani.

"Right?" Crew says, sounding amused. "And here I was worried Dani would be asleep already."

"How can I sleep when I'm so excited for you guys?" She wraps her arms around my neck. "Your team did you proud, Mr. Armstrong."

It's my turn to slide my palms down over the curve of her ass and haul her tight up against me. "You're doing me proud too. My very good girl is following the no panties at home rule."

"Of course." Her eyes are sparkling. "I follow *all* of your rules."

That's debatable. But in the bedroom, she definitely does. "Then you should be rewarded." I kiss the delicate skin behind her ear. "What do you have planned for our star player and the happiest team owner in the league?"

Her breath hitches. "Anything you want. I've been *so* lonely without you."

Her bottom lip pouts and I catch it between my thumb and finger.

Danielle traveled to the playoff games with Crew's mom and stayed with her in a hotel suite, so she wasn't a distraction to our star player. Or me. Or Michael. Which she definitely would have been. We saw her for breakfast each morning and briefly after the first three games, but otherwise, we had all agreed to stay focused and save the celebrations for when we got home.

"Say hello to Michael first and then we'll give you all the attention you deserve, you poor little hockey widow."

She gives me a saucy smile. "It's been *four days*." Then she reaches out for Michael. "I missed you."

One of his big hands grasps her upper arm while the other cups her ass as he hauls her against his body, covering her mouth with his and kissing her deeply.

She's still gripping the neck of the champagne bottle.

And I've got ideas.

But when she pulls back, laughing breathlessly, she says, "You all deserve champagne." She gives us a sexy smile. "Served ala Dani."

"Fuck yes," Crew mutters, his hot gaze sweeping over her. "Just tell me where you need me, pretty girl."

"All over. Everywhere," she tells him but she simply trails her fingers over his chest as she sashays past him on her way to the steps.

His breath hisses out between his teeth, and he starts to follow her.

"We're not getting champagne on the bed," I say. Weakly. That will make such a mess but I suppose we can just wash the sheets…

"Shut the hell up, Boss," Crew tosses over his shoulder. "I'll buy a new mattress or whatever. I'm getting my celebration."

He's following Danielle up the steps and the sway of her bare ass and the little smile she gives me makes my cock impossibly hard. Fuck the mattress. I start after them.

But then she says words that make me fall in love with her all over again.

"Don't worry, Nathan. I got us special sheets just for *really* messy nights." She gives me a wink.

"What kind of special sheets?" Crew asks.

"Waterproof," she confirms. "And they're not plastic or anything weird. They're kind of soft even."

"You're the perfect woman," I tell her, pulling my tie loose and only three steps behind Crew now.

She laughs as she leads us to our bedroom like the damned pied piper.

At the foot of the bed, she turns and gives us all a dazzling smile as we all start shedding clothes.

The bed is covered in a large black top sheet. She giggles, watching me take it in.

I grin and shake my head. "When did you get this?"

"I ordered it a couple of weeks ago."

"What were you planning a couple of weeks ago?" Crew asks, stalking toward her in only his boxers now. He cups her face, then runs his hands through her hair, tipping her head back and kissing her throat.

"This. A big celebration after you won tonight."

He lifts his head, his expression soft. "You were that sure we'd win?"

She nods. "Of course."

"I love you," he says gruffly. "So damned much."

"I love you too."

"Good. Because I think I'm going to fuck you like I hate you a little."

A smile plays at her lips, but she nods, almost solemnly. "*Please.*"

He chuckles, low and rough. "Don't say that. I'm on edge as it is."

It occurs to me that even though they've had sex, Danielle has been careful with him. She's been on top, controlling the movements. Crew hasn't really *done* much. He certainly hasn't thrust and pounded into her like he loves to do. It's all been very careful, protecting his hip before the game tonight.

Now, the game's over, it went well, and he can let loose.

I hope Danielle's ready.

"I need you, Crew," she tells him, gripping his wrist where his hand is against her face. "It's been *four days* with *nothing*. And I haven't had you be *you* in even longer."

I grin. Our girl is always ready.

"*Fuck*," Crew breathes out. He runs his hand through her hair again. "You feeling needy, pretty girl?"

"So needy."

God, the way she's so insatiable makes me crazy. I love the way we all three have to work to keep her satisfied. It's such a turn-on and almost impossible to believe. This woman could have never been content with just one man.

"Get on the bed and spread those pretty legs for me," Crew says. "I need this pussy like I need my next breath."

She does as she's told, as always, and Hughes and I strip down to our underwear and step to the bed.

Michael immediately stretches out next to her. He works her shirt up over her breasts. He doesn't take it off, just bunches it up, then leans in to take a nipple in his mouth.

Crew strokes his hand up her inner thigh, making her spread her thighs wide. He groans. "Fuck, yes. I haven't really fucked you well in too long, Dani girl."

She's arching and moaning, her hand at the back of Michael's head. "I know," she manages for Crew. "I need you so much."

I lean over and take the bottle from her hand. I think our girl's already forgotten about it and her plan. "Well, Crew definitely deserves some champagne for his efforts tonight." I hold the bottle over Danielle's stomach as I pop the cork from the bottle.

The cork goes flying and the bubbly liquid foams out of the top, landing on Danielle's smooth, pale skin and she sucks in a breath. Crew moves to take a sip from her belly button but I pour some of the champagne over her mound so it runs over her clit and down between her legs and he instantly shifts direction, lowering his head and catching the liquid with his tongue. He licks over her clit and she lifts her hips, trying to get closer.

I pour more champagne for Crew. "Good game, McNeill."

"Thanks, Boss," he says, giving me a grin before he goes back to "drinking" his champagne mixed with the taste of our girl.

As he laps at her pussy, I move the bottle up to Danielle's breasts, tipping champagne out over her nipples for Hughes. He licks, then sucks the sticky, sweet liquid from her skin. Some dribbles to the sheet underneath her but he gathers a lot of it with his tongue and lips.

"So fucking good, Cookie," he murmurs, dragging a finger through the champagne and then around her nipple, plucking and squeezing.

"It's even better mixed with Dani." Crew holds his hand out toward me and I pass him the bottle. He pours more over her pussy, then rubs the mouth of the bottle through her folds.

Danielle gives a little gasp.

"That feel good, greedy girl?" he asks, pressing the tip of the bottle into her slightly.

Her eyes go wild and she squirms. "*Crew.*"

He chuckles, wiggling the bottle, then rotating it against her sweet, pink opening. "*Dani.*"

I watch as he pushes the bottle in just half an inch or so, teasing her.

"Crew, oh my God, you're not going to…"

"Fuck you with this bottle of champagne?" he asks. He presses it another half inch in. "I don't know. That's new. Sounds fun."

"But…" she gasps as he rubs his thumb over her clit. "I want…"

He wiggles the bottle again while circling her clit. "What do you want, sweet girl?"

"You. Michael. Nathan," she says, panting our names.

"We're right here," he teases.

"Your *cocks*," she says, her voice full of pleading. "No toys or… other things. Just you."

Crew chuckles low. "You're getting a little demanding, Cookie."

She gives him a lusty look. "I just want to be fucked hard and deep by my guys."

He blows out a breath and I feel the same stab of heat that I know just jabbed both him and Michael. When Danielle talks dirty to us, we all have no hope of resisting.

He pulls the bottle from between her legs and hands it to me.

"Have a taste, Boss."

My eyes lock on Danielle's as I put the bottle to my lips. I lick the glass edge, tasting her, then take a long pull of the sweet drink.

She's breathing hard, her breasts rising and falling, her lips parted as she watches me.

"Delicious," I tell her, dragging my thumb over my lower lip.

"I would let you taste it right from the source," Crew says, scooping his hands under her ass and lifting her hips. "But I am the fucking MVP and I'm not sharing." Then he lowers his mouth and starts licking, sucking, and tongue fucking her with enthusiasm.

"Yes! Crew!" She cries out, her hand gripping his hair as her head presses into the bed, her neck arching.

Michael's mouth goes to her neck, kissing and talking to her.

"Let it go, Dani. Give it all up to him. Let our big star have all your sweetness. At least this first time."

She's panting and her eyes squeeze shut. "Oh my God!" She's pulling Crew's hair and gripping the duvet with her other hand.

"That's right," Michael says. "This is just the first of many, so let go, let that pussy get nice and hot and wet for us because we are going to treat it *so, so* good," he promises against the front of her throat.

She moans loudly, and I move to join the fun. I often hold back because once I touch her, I can't stop. And I want to dominate everything. So when I'm giving the other guys the first touches and kisses and orgasms, I'm better with standing back and watching.

Sometimes.

But, as Danielle has pointed out, it's been *four days.*

I lean over and grip her chin, bringing her mouth to mine. I kiss her deeply, stroking her tongue with mine, swallowing her cries as her other men take her up to the peak and then over it.

Her body ripples with her orgasm and Crew relentlessly sucks on her clit even as the shudders keep rolling over her.

She pulls her mouth from mine, begging, "I can't. It's too much, Crew."

He finally lifts his head. "My mouth or my cock, Dani. Your call. But some part of me is staying right here."

"Cock. Please fuck me. Please."

"You better be sure you're ready," he says, running his hands up and down the backs of her thighs. "I'm not taking it easy on you."

Michael's hand strokes over her stomach. "You're ready for him, aren't you, sweet girl? You're ready to take him deep. I'll hang onto you while he pounds your pretty pussy."

She takes a deep breath. "Yes. God yes." She looks at me. "Come closer. I want you too."

"You touch me and I'll go off," I tell her as I set the champagne bottle on the floor next to the bed and stretch out on her other side. "So keep your hands to yourself. For now."

She grins. "But I love when you go off."

I growl and lean in to say against her lips, "I want to be buried deep when I do. Be good."

She bites her lower lip as if considering what will happen if she's *not* good.

"Be. Good," I repeat.

"Yes, Sir."

Fuck, even that makes my cock ache as if she's touching me. I wrap my hands around her wrists and tug them over her head, locking them together in my grip.

She takes a ragged breath. She loves to be restrained like this and it will save me from coming with one even accidental stroke of her hand against my cock.

She's now trapped between me and Hughes, her hands are confined, and she's not going anywhere until we say so.

"Take your victory spoils, McNeill," I order. "Fuck her."

Crew gets to his feet and strips off his boxers, then he grips her hips and sinks deep.

He groans as she gasps. "Oh God, Crew. Yes. You feel so good."

"Hang on," he says through gritted teeth.

Michael presses the heel of his hand against her belly, his thick middle finger against her clit. "We've got her," he says, watching her face with clear lust and love.

I cup a breast and put my face against her neck as I tease her nipple. "We've definitely got her."

Crew pulls back and thrusts again, deep and hard. He sets up a punishing rhythm that has Danielle crying out and babbling a litany of *yes, oh God, more, Crew,* and *fuck.*

Michael and I hold her tightly between us, feeling every thrust, worshiping her from head to toe with our hands and mouths and dirty praise.

"You're such a good fucking girl, taking that cock," I tell her.

"Your pussy was made for three cocks wasn't it, dirty girl? One would never be enough. Your gorgeous, greedy cunt needs filled up over and over again."

She whimpers and turns her head to kiss me.

"You were made for us," Michael tells her, circling her clit as Crew fucks her. "We'll never get enough. We're so fucking addicted. You might be the one spread out and held down but you've got all the power here. We're so fucking weak for you."

A shiver goes through her body, and she turns to kiss him.

I suck on her nipples.

Hughes fingers her clit.

Crew picks up the pace, swearing.

"Fuck, Dani. Goddamn, how is this so good every fucking time? Yes, squeeze me like that pretty girl." He's watching her with an expression full of lust and awe at the same time. Like he can't believe she's here like this with us.

I know how he feels. Sometimes this all feels surreal. How was it that the four of us found each other? Especially when none of us knew we were even looking for *this*?

"I'm coming, Dani. I can't hold on," Crew tells her, fucking her even faster.

"Yes, Crew. Yes," she urges.

Not even a second later, he's squeezing her hips, and groaning out his release.

Hughes and I barely give him a chance to pull out before we're dragging Danielle up the bed and into position.

Michael rolls to his back, pulling her on top of him, kissing her deeply.

I move in behind them, running my hand up and down her back.

She seems boneless and sated as she lies draped over Michael, but we are definitely not done with her yet.

I lean over and kiss her shoulder. "Oh, no, dirty girl. You've got two more men who need to fill you up."

She moans. "Oh, *yes*."

"Spread your legs and take Michael into that sweet, hot pussy, Danielle," I tell her, still stroking her back. "While I take your perfect ass."

I feel the shiver of desire that goes through her and she immediately shifts so she's straddling Michael.

I was the last one to be introduced to fucking her ass while another man was buried in her pussy but…fuck. It's so good. I don't mind if I'm the pussy or the ass guy, but double-penetrating Danielle is a favorite of all of ours.

Without needing to be asked, Crew tosses the lube from the bedside table onto the bed beside my knee.

I look over. He's stretched out on the bed, positioned just where he wants to be for the best view of his girl getting double-teamed by two other men.

It should be weird.

It's most definitely not. We all love it and I can't imagine having a relationship any other way.

With any other people. Ever.

I can't wait to go engagement ring shopping for Danielle with Michael.

"Oh God, Michael," Danielle moans as she sinks down onto his cock.

"I love it when you've already been worked over and are all soft and hot and sensitive," he tells her, moving her up and down his shaft.

"Me too," she says, her voice breathy.

I coat my fingers with lube and slide them between her cheeks. "Lean forward, baby," I tell her.

She immediately assumes the perfect position. She loves this as much as we all do. Hell, maybe more. It doesn't matter how many times she's come before we take her like this, she will always come again.

I work one finger, then a second into her as she slowly moves up and down on Michael. He's gripping her hips and gritting his teeth. I know he wants to go fast and hard, but we have to get her ready.

"We need to get that pretty plug into this pretty ass again," I say, stretching her.

"The plug makes me *so* horny," Danielle says, moving against my fingers. "I wear it all day and think of you all and I can't concentrate on work."

I withdraw my fingers and press the head of my cock against her tight hole. "Good."

"I'm serious," she said, pressing back against me. "That day was torture."

"That night was worth it though," Crew reminds her. "You jumped us the second we walked through the door and were *begging* for it. That was almost as good as the night with the vibrating panties."

"We are *not* doing that again," Danielle protests. "I was so stupid for thinking that wearing those to a hockey game would be fine. You were so me–"

She breaks off as I press into her.

Her head falls forward. "Oh, God, Nathan."

I reach around, resting my hand at the base of her throat. "You'll wear the plug, or the panties, or nipple clamps, or whatever else we tell you to, won't you, Danielle?" I pull back and then thrust forward, sinking in a few more inches.

"Fuck," Michael swears from under her. He's stopped moving for the moment.

I put my mouth to her ear. "You are such a gorgeous, dirty slut for us. You'll do whatever we want you to just to have our cocks filling you up." I slide all the way in on my next thrust.

She gasps, and Michael swears again.

Yeah, it's fucking *good*.

I squeeze her throat slightly. "You're a slut for our cocks, aren't you, Danielle?"

She nods as much as she can with my hand there. "Yes," she gasps. "I'll do anything."

"Good." I pull out and thrust in. "Girl."

Michael does the same and soon we've got our rhythm perfected. Danielle takes everything we give her. Crew brushes her hair back from her face and leans in, giving her dirty words and praise and love while Michael and I fuck her.

It's the perfect combination of everything she needs and soon she's climbing again.

"I'm going to come," she cries.

"Yes, you are," Michael tells her. He thrusts up into her as he takes a nipple between his finger and thumb, squeezing. "Give us everything you've got, Dani."

I feel the tightening around my cock and I can't hold on.

"Danielle, come for us," I growl against her ear. "Come apart, baby."

She does with a beautiful cry, her back arching, her body gripping Hughes and me. I roar my orgasm and Hughes is right behind me, shouting her name.

I wrap my arms around her, holding her to my chest as we all come down from the high.

Eventually, I let go, and she seems to melt into Michael. His hands stroke up and down her body as I step back, breathing deep.

We all clean up, Crew carrying Danielle into the bathroom first. We all need to shower because of the champagne, but Crew makes their shower quick, much to my surprise.

We remove the amazing waterproof sheet, and all slip into bed in our usual order: me, Danielle, Michael, then Crew. Sometimes Crew cuddles up next to Danielle, but he's the one who is most often up in the night, usually to eat at some point, so his typical spot is the outside.

We all wrap around each other and Michael turns off the lamp.

It's not even five minutes before I hear all of them breathing deep, and I fall asleep with a smile and a single, happy thought: This is all so good. It's the four of us against the world.

There's nothing that can shake us up now.

CHAPTER 32
Crew

I'M up only two hours later. I often get up in the night. My stomach seems to think it needs to be fed every three to four hours and going even six to eight without when I'm sleeping is too much.

Tonight, though, I'm not sure it's just my stomach that got me up. My head's been spinning a lot the past few days, and it's not because of my concussion.

I'm not surprised that by the time I finish spreading the peanut butter on the bread, I hear soft footsteps behind me.

Dani seems to have a radar for when I need her. And even though I'm not sure exactly what to say, I do need to talk to her tonight. Just the two of us.

Yes, I wanted to celebrate when we got home. That wasn't the time for deep emotion and soft words.

But now is.

Her arms steal around my waist and I cover her hands with mine, giving her a little squeeze. "Hey pretty girl," I say.

"Hey. Is there a sandwich in here for me?"

I look at her over my shoulder. She's in her silky short little robe, her hair tousled, and her eyes sleepy. She's so fucking soft and beautiful like this. "You hungry?"

"Well, I burned a lot of calories a couple hours ago."

I chuckle. Yes, she sure did. "Want strawberry or grape?" She's an equal opportunity jelly user.

"Whatever you're having."

I'm only wearing athletic shorts and her hands stroke over my bare stomach as I make a second peanut butter and strawberry jelly sandwich.

I put them both on plates— real ones, Nathan would be so proud. I turn and lift one triangle of sandwich to her mouth and one to mine. Our eyes lock as we both take our first bite.

She takes the tiny portion of sandwich from my fingers, and with my hand freed, I run my fingers through her hair, brushing the deep red tresses back from her sweet face.

I swallow, then say, "I love you so fucking much."

I've never felt anything so deeply in my life. I've been lucky enough to be part of teams where I felt a connection with other people on a level that's very difficult to explain. I was raised in a family where I was loved unconditionally, and I knew that every single day.

But I have never felt the way I do about Danielle. Just her being around—whether she's in my arms or across the room—makes something inside me settle into place. She makes everything right.

She swallows, and then her tongue licks over her bottom lip. "I love you too," she finally answers.

"I want this forever, Dani. I want to fuck you forever. I want to wake up in the middle of the night with you forever. I want to make you sandwiches forever. I want you there when I'm hurt or sick, and I want to be there when you're hurt or sick. I want to come home to you every day forever. I truly do want to be with you. Forever."

She puts her sandwich down and cups my face between her hands. "I know that."

"Then why doesn't it sound fucking stupid for me to not marry you? Why does it feel all right for me to let Nathan and Michael marry you but for me to not be ready yet?"

Whenever I say it out loud, it sounds ridiculous. If someone else said it to me—that they were dating someone who was going to marry someone else and they were totally fine with it and, by the way, they were going to keep dating that soon-to-be-married person, I'd think they were insane.

But this really does feel okay between us.

"I don't know," she says honestly. "Because we trust each other? Because we really are in love and that doesn't have to mean anything specific other than what we want it to mean? I know it's in part because we both understand who and what Michael and Nathan are to me. To us."

I take a deep breath and blow it out. Then I drop my hand from her face and turn and pick up both of our plates. I carry them to the breakfast bar and then tilt my head towards the stool next to me. "Let's talk."

She slides up onto the stool. I turn and position my knees on the outsides of hers, caging her in. I rest one hand on her thigh and the other on the counter next to her. "At first, I thought I was able to be content with all of this because I knew that Nathan and Michael were giving you what you wanted right now so you could be happy while you and I took our time and figured things out slowly."

She nods. "That makes sense."

"It does. And maybe that's part of it. I want you to have everything you possibly want or need. And right now, I think that Michael and Nathan are better at giving you those things. But I want to be a part of that. I want to be a part of your life. I want to be your husband someday. So none of this changes how I feel about you. None of this changes my plans. And I realized tonight, coming off the ice after the game, what maybe some of this is."

She leans over and rests both of her hands on my thighs. "Okay. Tell me."

"We're on the way to the championship. It is the thing that I have been striving for my whole career. Probably, honestly, since I started playing seriously. It's certainly a big part of why I came to the Racketeers."

She nods.

"But, as I skated off the ice with that win behind me, it hit me that it's not the most important thing anymore. I skated off that ice realizing that I was deliriously happy, but hockey and those wins were not the highlight of my life anymore. You are."

Her brows lift and she smiles softly. "Wow."

I grin and lift my hand to her face, stroking my thumb over her cheek. "You are so much more to me than hockey has ever been. More than it will ever be. And I know you're gonna be around longer than hockey is. But I also realized that loving hockey and getting to be the best I can be at it has taught me a few things I need to apply to us."

She smiles. "I'm listening."

"Hockey has taken me time. There were so many years when I wanted the championship, but I was very far from being the guy who could get his team there. I wasn't strong enough. I wasn't smart enough. I wasn't experienced enough to deal with everything that could come at me in a game or a series. So I needed to put in the work. I needed to get better. And not just physically, but also mentally. And now the work is paying off. I'm seeing what can happen with real focus and passion."

She studies my face and I can tell she's processing everything I am saying.

"While I love you with everything in me and I have no intention of going anywhere, I don't think I'm actually ready to be your husband. That's next level. Yes, I definitely want to be the best boyfriend I can be, too, but we both know that being a husband takes something more. I think I have a little more work to do before I'm the man who can really step up and be that guy. I know you love me as I am now, and vice versa, but I think we have some more training to do as a couple before we're ready for everything life's going to throw at us. I want to be your champion. I'm just not quite there."

She gives a soft laugh and squeezes my knee.

I grin too, but I shake my head. "I'm serious. I still have some growing up to do. Maturing. Things are great right now and it's going to get better. And when I'm ready to give you everything you need as a husband, I will absolutely drop down on one knee and put the biggest fucking ring you've ever seen on your finger."

I can see tears shimmering in her eyes but she laughs lightly. "You better not get a bigger ring than Nathan does."

I grin. "Oh, you know I fucking will."

She sniffs and laughs. "So are you talking maybe marriage after you retire or something?"

"Good question. Maybe. That might be the most responsible thing. When I can fully focus on you and a family. But I don't know if I can wait that long, Dani girl." I stroke her cheek.

She presses her hand to mine. "As long as you're here, still in my life, we can do this however you want to. I mean, I have no idea if I'm going to be a good wife either."

"Nathan and Michael are going to be the luckiest bastards in the world, sweet girl."

"I hope so. It is a big deal. I know what you mean. Wife definitely feels different and bigger than girlfriend."

"It should. That's the way it should be. It's a huge commitment." I lean in and cup the back of her head, bringing her forehead to mine. "You are the best thing that has ever happened to me, Dani. Hang in there with me, okay?"

"I'm not going anywhere, Crew."

Then I kiss her. And I feed her peanut butter and jelly. And we talk about the upcoming championship game. And I realize not for the first time, that I am living with, sleeping with, and someday going to marry my best friend.

And I probably don't deserve her.

But I'm never letting her go.

CHAPTER 33
Michael

THERE'S nothing as amazing as falling asleep with my fiancee in my arms, sexually satisfied and one hundred percent secure in where my relationship with her and with Nathan and Crew stands.

There's nothing as startling as waking up the next morning to the sound of someone throwing up in the bathroom.

It's Dani. I not only sense immediately she isn't in the massive bed with me and the guys, but I recognize her groans of distress between heaves. A quick glance around the room shows Nathan is gone, most likely at the gym. Crew, who can sleep through a tornado, is snoring, torso covered by the sheet, legs dangling off the side of the bed.

I slide out in the opposite direction, frowning as I try to remember what Dani ate and drank the night before. She hadn't had any alcohol at all, and I wasn't with her for dinner. Maybe she ate a bad hot dog or something at the arena?

After pulling my briefs on, I pad across the hardwood floor, appreciating how the original floors creak. Nathan hates the creaking, but I love it. It gives the house character and reminds me it's stood here for a hundred years. We're adding to its lengthy history with our own story. One that now includes planning a wedding and a future as a family.

The sight of Dani naked, bent over the toilet, pale and trembling, makes my heart squeeze. "Hey, what's going on? How long have you been in here?" I ask in concern, shifting in behind her to gather her curls and pull her hair gently out of her face. She's clammy as hell, the back of her neck damp. Red curls cling to her skin.

She gives a shudder and sits up a little, done heaving for now. "I woke up and had to pee. When I walked across the bedroom it just hit me."

"Are you dehydrated? Did you drink enough water yesterday when you were traveling?" I lean and grab a hair tie off the counter. Dani's hairbands are scattered all over our house in cute little reminders of her. I pull her hair into a loose ponytail, wrapping the band twice. Having little sisters, I grew up being pressed into service doing hair in a pinch and I know full well not to pull the roots too hard.

"I thought so." Dani is on her knees and she leans against the wall, her cheeks pink.

I check her forehead. "No fever." Grabbing a washcloth, I get it damp and wipe first her face, then her mouth. "Maybe you ate something that was off."

It's late in the year for the flu, but stomach viruses can be picked up anywhere.

I get a second cloth, letting Dani finish wiping her mouth after she spits into the toilet. I put the cool, damp fabric against the back of her neck.

She shakes her head. "I didn't eat anything that would make me sick."

That makes me frown. "I'm going to text Nathan to grab some electrolyte fluids on his way home. I think he's at the gym."

Dani gazes up at me, teeth digging into her pink bottom lip. Her green eyes reflect worry. "Michael…"

Her hesitation scares me. Instantly, my heart rate kicks into overdrive. "Yeah, baby, what's wrong?"

I don't know why she looks like this and it's freaking me the fuck out.

"I think Nathan should pick up a pregnancy test too."

I'm so stunned, it takes me a second to process. Then relief surges through me, followed by awe.

She rushes on. "I'm late for my period. At first, I thought it was just stress or just one of those things, but now it's been…way too long."

Now that she says it, I realize it *has* been way too long. If I'm counting correctly, six weeks. Definitely since before we were in Vegas. In fact, I don't think she's actually had her period since we moved into the house because Nathan always acts like a pouty asshole when she does, like nature's sole purpose is to blue ball him. I can't recall any of his period surliness lately.

I fight the urge to grin, needing to gauge her feelings on the possibility of a baby before I do a semi-naked cartwheel in the bathroom. Hell, *yeah*. A baby. A tiny little replica of Dani? I can already picture a head full of downy auburn hair. It could be mine or Crew's, I'm not really sure, but I don't care. A baby would be the perfect completion to Cookie and Co.

"Okay, sure, I'll let him know," I say, calmly, because she needs me to be calm. She looks terrified. Of having a baby, or my reaction, or both, I'm not sure. "I love you, sweetheart. Always remember that."

"I love you too. Is this, would this, be…okay?"

That doesn't even begin to cover it. I grin and run a hand over her head. "Jesus, Dani, of course it would be okay. It would be amazing. I want a family with you." I brush a kiss onto her forehead.

She nods rapidly, sniffling, swallowing hard.

Goosebumps have appeared on her flesh and I am aware she's sitting naked on a marble floor in early April. She must be freezing. "Do you think you're going to throw up again?" I ask, reaching for her plush terry cloth robe that hangs on the back of the door.

"I think I'm good. For now." When I reach out to lift her under her armpits, her voice wavers. "Michael?"

Her skin is cold so I gather her in my arms, wrapping the robe over her shoulders. I tug her close to me, so her bare flesh is snug against my warm body. I rub her back over the robe. "Yes?"

"I really think I'm pregnant."

I nod. "It's very possible. There aren't a lot of reasons for a woman your age to be that late." I've already run through any medical explanations and have dismissed most of them.

"I know. And I can *feel* it. I'm pregnant. I'm sure."

My heart is so full I feel like I'm about to cry. "I can too, Cookie. This feels right. I hope you're happy, because I'm thrilled at the idea. I want you to know that. I'm so damn happy right now. I feel like I don't deserve it. This, you, a baby, our family, is everything I've ever wanted."

She nods, her eyes shining with unshed tears. "I am happy. I'm terrified, but I'm excited."

"I'm just excited." I kiss her softly. "I'll text Nathan to go to the store."

Nathan appears in the doorway in shorts and a sweatshirt. He strips it off over his head. "Don't text Nathan. I'm home and I'm not going back out until I shower. Whatever you need, we can order it."

I raise my eyebrows at Dani and murmur in her ear. "Do you want to tell him or should I?"

Nathan's workout T-shirt is coming off over his head after the sweatshirt.

"I'll tell him." She gives my shoulders a squeeze and smiles up at me before stepping away, slipping her arms into the robe. "Nathan, I need a pregnancy test. Can you order one from DoorDash?"

His arms pause. The shirt is right over his face. Then suddenly his head pops out and his eyes are wide. "What? Are you fucking with me?"

She shakes her head. "No. I'm over two weeks late, and I just threw up."

A grin splits his face. "Baby, that's amazing news. Well, not that you got sick, but that you might be pregnant. How did I not realize you were late? It must be all this craziness with the playoffs…wow. A baby? Fuck DoorDash. We're not waiting for that. I'm going to the store now."

He pulls his shirt back on and leans over and gives Dani a hard kiss. "I love you."

"I love you, too."

The joy on Nathan's face makes me lose my cool. Knowing that he can't have his own biological kids, and wants a baby with us, is just the confirmation I need that the decisions we've made to share our lives have all been the right ones. I clear my throat and swipe at my eyes.

Nathan sees it and gives me a fist bump. His own eyes look a little watery. "Be right back."

He grabs his sweatshirt and is out of the bathroom before I can even speak. When I take Dani's hand, she's sporting her own grin at Nathan's reaction.

Crew's eyes are still closed but he's grumbling. "Why is everyone being so loud?"

"Can't talk," Nathan says. "Going to the store."

"Can you get me a breakfast sandwich?" Crew asks, yawning.

"No time," is Nathan's response. "Order one for delivery. Where the hell are my shoes?"

"No breakfast sandwich. Dani's nauseous," I protest. The smell of greasy foods is the last thing she needs.

Crew's eyes open and he's fumbling around, reaching for his phone on the nightstand. "You're sick, pretty girl?"

"No. I think I'm pregnant," Dani says quietly.

I squeeze her hand for support. We both know Crew might not be as enthusiastic about this news as the rest of us.

Crew is leaning too far over. When he jerks at her words, he falls right out of the bed. He lands on the wood floor with a hard thump. "Ow." His head pops up from the floor. "Michael did it, not me! I was out of commission for a week."

His panicked words give me pause. He's probably right. Between our time in Vegas and his being on a sex break from his injury, the timing would be right for the baby to be mine. Not that it would matter to me. I truly believe I'm capable of loving any child that Dani has as my own.

Nathan states what I'm thinking. "It doesn't matter who did it." He's shoving his feet in his sneakers. "Point is, *we're* going to do it."

"*Maybe*," Dani protests. But she's smiling now.

"Good thing I bought the house in Franklin with the barn," Nathan says. "Daddy Nathan is buying our baby a pony."

Crew's still lying on the floor looking like he's about to follow Dani's lead and throw up. Nathan is already spending money on lavish gifts in his head. Dani is laughing in pure delight.

And me?

I'm taking it all in.

The *dad* of our created family.

It's a role I'm going to enjoy every second of for the rest of our lives.

―――

Thanks for reading Seriously Pucked! Read the FREE bonus scene at https://subscribepage.io/seriouslypuckedbonus to find out what happens when Dani takes her pregnancy test.

And yes, we agree that Luna needs a book! And yes, of course it's going to be why choose! Icing It releases in March. Here's a hint: Alexsei and Cameron.

Then preorder the final book featuring Dani and her three sexy guys, Permanently Pucked! We're going to hate to let go of writing about these four because we *adore* them, but we promise to give you all the sexy swoon in their happily-ever-after!

About the Author

Emma Foxx is the super fun and sexy pen name for two long-time, bestselling romance authors who decided why have just one hero when you can have three at the same time? (they're not sure what took them so long to figure this out)! Emma writes contemporary romances that will make you laugh (yes, maybe out loud in public) and want more…books (sure, that's what we mean 😉). Find Emma on Instagram, Tik Tok, and Goodreads.

Also by Emma Foxx

Permanently Pucked

Chicago Racketeers Book Four

I don't do casual hookups. Never have. Not even with the three supposed-to-be one-night stands I had six months ago.

They all turned into the loves of my life.

But now I know *exactly* what to do with the three hot guys I met at that serendipitous hockey game.

Love them.

Forever.

At least that's the plan.

(Okay, yes, there's still a lot of headboard-banging nights--and days--happening around here too.)

Our house is truly a home, the naked-times are better than any dirty romance I've ever read…or written…and our relationship is rock solid.

At least, I'm pretty sure it is.

As long as we can take our foursome to four plus a bundle of joy without any of my guys deciding that our unconventional approach to family is just a little more than he bargained for.

Permanently Pucked is the fourth and final installment in Dani, Nathan, Michael, and Crew's romance!

ICING IT

A fun spin-off in the Racketeers world featuring Luna, Crew's sister!

Missed the first two books in the series?

Read **Puck One Night Stands** and **Four Pucking Christmases**

Milton Keynes UK
Ingram Content Group UK Ltd.
UKHW011220280324
440101UK00005B/469